GRAVESEND

ALSO BY WILLIAM BOYLE

THE LONELY WITNESS

GRAVESEND

A NOVEL

WILLIAM BOYLE

PEGASUS CRIME
NEW YORK LONDON

GRAVESEND

Pegasus Books, Ltd.
148 West 37th Street, 13th Floor
New York, NY 10018

Copyright © 2018 by William Boyle

First Pegasus Books hardcover edition September 2018

First edition from Broken River Books, September 2013

Interior design by Sabrina Plomitallo-González, Pegasus Books

ISBN: 978-1-68177-849-5

10 9 8 7 6 5 4 3 2 1

Printed in the United States of America
Distributed by W. W. Norton & Company, Inc.

For my grandparents, Joseph and Rosemary Giannini

This book wouldn't exist without the help, support, and encouragement of the following people: my wife, Katie Farrell Boyle, and our son, Eamon; my mother, Geraldine Chiappetta; J. David Osborne; Alex Andriesse; Jimmy Cajoleas; Connolly Jean Boyle; Nat Sobel and Judith Weber; Katie McGuire and Pegasus Books; No Exit Press; François Guérif; Simon Baril; and Jeanne Guyon.

When a man knows another man
Is looking for him
He doesn't hide.
—Frank Stanford, "Everybody Who is Dead"

You'll always end up in this city. Don't hope for things elsewhere:
there's no ship for you, there's no road.
Now that you've wasted your life here, in this small corner,
you've destroyed it everywhere in the world.
—C. P. Cavafy, "The City"

INTRODUCTION

On a map, Brooklyn looks like nothing so much as a crumpled napkin. Its thousand gridded streets are set at odd angles, like so many fractal variations or carnival-mirror reflections of its slim-waisted sister city to the west. Of all great towns, Brooklyn (in the words of James Agee) is the nearest to Manhattan's "mad magnetic energy," and yet it is provincial nonetheless—a patchwork of neighborhoods, as Agee puts it, "where people merely live." Perhaps this is no longer the case, at least in the northwestern quadrant of the borough, where people now flock to live, and write. No reader of contemporary American fiction can fail to notice that the recent Brooklyn real-estate boom has coincided with a surge of interest in Brooklyn-based fiction. The last fifteen years have given us too many "Brooklyn novels" and "Brooklyn writers" to count. Most of these writers aren't natives of the city. A few of them aren't even locals. And why should they be? In fiction, what matters is the quality of the words on the page, not the quality of the experience behind them.

Sometimes, though, a native writer's mingled love and hatred for his homeplace allows him to make something special of his experience, something to which non-natives may only aspire. So it is with William Boyle's first novel, which sets its sights on a Brooklyn neighborhood down toward the bottom of the city's crumpled map, not quite far enough north to count as Bensonhurst, not quite far enough south to borrow the faded glow of Coney Island: a gray stretch of avenues and chain-link streets called Gravesend.

If you search for *Gravesend* online, you'll probably find it called a crime novel or hardboiled fiction, "Brooklyn noir" or "neo-noir." And it's true that Boyle's characters tend to live outside the law, or at the very edge of it, and that his style owes something to the venerable tradition of hardboiled American writing that runs from James M. Cain to James Ellroy, from Daniel Fuchs to Daniel Woodrell. But Boyle's participation in this tradition doesn't begin to account for just how good, just how singular, just how stunning *Gravesend* turns out to be—not that I claim to take a dispassionate view of the matter. We're friends, Boyle and I. But even if I had never met him, I would admire his novel no end.

The first thing to admire about *Gravesend* is its style. Boyle has an eye for precise pictorial detail and an ear for language that cleaves close to his characters' ways of looking at the world. So, through the eyes of Conway D'Innocenzio, we see a big moon "shaded rusty"; we see pigeons congregating on the sidewalk and boots flung up on telephone wires near Augie's Deli; we see seagulls pecking at dirty sand where condom wrappers rim a "seaweed-skirted shoreline." At a dive called The Wrong Number, we see bartenders with "bad histories, greasy, balloon-chested fucks in Nautica gear with Yankee tats on their necks and white date rape caps." Through the eyes of Alessandra Biagini, we see a "bearded dude eating mangled fries" at a trendy sports bar, "washing them down with a wet-labeled Coors Light." Through the eyes of Eugene, we see a kid named Tommy Valentino—a tall, B-team basketball player—who is always "hunched over his locker . . . spooning candy from an envelope into his mouth with a wooden stick and washing it down with Gatorade."

Such images play a large part in making *Gravesend* as memorable as it is. But I wouldn't want to suggest the book is only a stylistic tour de force, because it's more than that. The style is striking, but the story is a knockout. Like Thomas Hardy and Bernard Malamud before him, Boyle shows himself to be many things at once. He is a novelist who, as Auden said a novelist must, knows how to be just among the just and filthy among the filthy. He is a wordsmith with all the devices of the nineteenth- and twentieth-century novel at his disposal. He is, in short, a damn good storyteller.

In the first pages of *Gravesend*, we learn that Ray Boy Calabrese is about to be sprung from prison sixteen years after he and a group of friends murdered a young gay man named Duncan. Duncan's brother, Conway, has never really left the old neighborhood and has no intention of letting bygones be bygones. He hates Ray Boy for what he's done, and the reader hates Ray Boy too. At the end of the first chapter, the story seems made to run along ancient lines. We're expecting a kind of *Revenger's Tragedy* for the twenty-first century, and we think we know what kinds of questions to ask. How long is it going to take Conway to track Ray Boy down? How long until Ray Boy, or Conway, or both of them, wind up dead?

As it turns out, though, blood vengeance isn't what drives *Gravesend*. What drives it are the characters and their experience of the neighborhood, more cluttered with junk and the molding stuff of life than any Old World rag-and-bone shop. This is clear to us from the second chapter, when we are introduced to Alessandra, a failing actress who has returned from a stint in Los Angeles back to her Brooklyn home, where everything smells "like dirty sponges":

> a puzzle she'd done with her mother when she was ten or eleven was on a TV tray next to the cabinet. Dust bunnies poked from between the wilting pieces like weeds. Her father came over and sat next to her. He smelled like a dirty sponge, too.

There are a number of characters in *Gravesend* you are bound to remember long after you've finished the novel. There are the high school boys Eugene and Sweat, who worship Ray Boy for the crime he's committed. There's Ray Boy himself, the murderer who thinks of nothing so much as his own death. There's Cesar, who might be straight out of Dickens, except he's a gun-dealing, rap-writing purveyor of exotic birds, working out of a thrift shop backroom on Mermaid Avenue. And there are all the mothers and fathers of Gravesend, for whom the neighborhood has become the meridian of their lives, the jigsaw puzzle they're never going to finish. But the story of Alessandra—the story of a young woman who has left the neighborhood only to find herself drawn back into it again—is the beating heart of the book.

The way Alessandra's story is told, and the way it gets tangled up with the stories of Ray Boy and Conway and Eugene, may remind some readers of the best of George Pelecanos and Dennis Lehane. It also brought to my mind Malamud's masterpiece, *The Assistant*. Both *The Assistant* and *Gravesend* are full of the poetry of Brooklyn speech (without ever condescending to or parodying that speech), and both blur the line between the urban crime novel and literary realism writ large. Alessandra, like Malamud's Helen Bober, lets us readers see into the life of the neighborhood because she herself is so painfully conscious of the world beyond the neighborhood. "I want a larger and better life," Helen Bober tells a young man hoping to court her (and keep her in Brooklyn): "I want the return of my possibilities." Alessandra would sympathize. She, too, wants the return of her possibilities. And I hope she finds them, as I hope maybe someday she'll come across a copy of *The Assistant* among the paperbacks at the Strand or East Village Books.

Throughout *Gravesend*, Boyle's great gift is to make the reader care about his characters—to make them come alive in the reader's mind. The novel is not only a display of talent; it's a rare demonstration of talent going beyond the flash of isolate phrases and sentences to enliven every page. This is a Brooklyn novel, yes, but it cuts the new ballyhoo Brooklyn back down to sorrowful human scale. This is a crime novel, without a doubt, but it has the realism of Malamud and Yates in its blood. The writer John Brandon has said of *Gravesend* that he "can't remember being more convinced by the people in a novel." I couldn't agree more. Fiction, even of the relatively realist variety, is a mystical business. It requires a summoner of souls. And Boyle has what's required.

—Alex Andriesse,
Originally published in *North Dakota Quarterly* 79.3&4 (2014)

1

It was the middle of September, and Conway had let McKenna take him out to a firing range in Bay Ridge to show him how to shoot. McKenna had been a cop for six years until he shot someone in the line of duty and they put him out with three-quarters pension.

"Can't believe Ray Boy's out," Conway said. "Free. Just walking around." He held up the gun and fired at the paper target, missing wide.

"Dude," McKenna said, taking out his earplugs, "you really should put these on." He offered a set of headphones.

"I'm gonna go what, deaf?" Conway did feel a light ringing in his ears, but it was like a far-off music.

McKenna said, "When you shoot, you gotta have confidence. You got no confidence now. The way you're letting the gun pull you around, you're gonna always miss outside."

"Ain't gonna miss I got the gun right in the guy's gut," Conway said.

"That's a situation you're probably not gonna find yourself in."

The firing range was in a warehouse next to an abandoned textile company and right across from a Russian supper club. From the outside it looked like the kind of place where snuff movies got made. But gun nuts, cops and otherwise, knew about it and came in and fired down brown-lit rows at cardboard cutouts and paper targets. On some targets there were snaps of ballplayers, Mets gone bad, slumping Yanks. Conway had an old newspaper clipping of Ray Boy, and he'd tacked it onto his target. Thing was he hadn't even hit it yet and it was big, a fold-out page from the *Daily News*. Ray Boy, all those years ago, freshly collared, on his way into the Sixty-Second Precinct. Wearing sunglasses, the fuck.

McKenna stood next to Conway now and showed him how to grip the gun. "You got fish hands, Con. Close up your fingers."

Conway tightened up his hold and pulled the trigger again. Wide right. "Maybe it's this type of gun."

"You don't know shit about guns. Trust me. Twenty-two's good for you."

"I need a sawed-off shotgun."

"That's for the movies. This is what I got you."

Conway fired a few more times, hitting the outer rim of the target once but still missing the picture of Ray Boy, and McKenna seemed to be growing frustrated.

"Maybe I'll just come with you," McKenna said.

"I'm not taking you away from Marylou," Conway said. "Things go wrong, I don't want you near me."

"And what about Pop? What happens to him?"

"Let me worry about that."

"Bunker is supposed to call you when?"

"This afternoon."

Bunker was a private investigator out of Monticello who McKenna had hooked him up with via some retired cop who'd settled in Forestburgh. McKenna had used another connection, a State Trooper who knew a guy who knew a prison guard at Sing Sing, to find out that Ray Boy had settled somewhere in the general vicinity of Monticello after getting out. Where exactly, they couldn't pin down, but Bunker claimed to be on it.

McKenna said, "You're going too quick. I understand why. But you're gonna do this, you should wait. Few days. Few months. A year. Don't go in underprepared."

"Every day he's out I've waited too long," Conway said. The truth was that he didn't want to be prepared. He wanted to be primitive about it.

"You better keep shooting." McKenna turned away.

Conway held the gun out and tried to see Ray Boy running away from him. It wouldn't happen like that, Ray Boy backing down in his crosshairs, but it was what he needed to see if he was going to show McKenna he could place a shot. He fired again. Barely clipped the outer edge of the target. It was a start.

Bunker called at three. Conway was on the bus home to Gravesend, the gun wrapped in towels in a gym bag at his feet.

"This Ray Boy's doing well," Bunker said. "Know you're not wanting to hear that."

Conway moved in his seat. Tried to picture Ray Boy living the high life. "You mean, what? He's got money? A girlfriend already?"

"He's got this house in Hawk's Nest. Been in his family for years. Does a shit ton of push-ups. Gets checks from his mother."

"Hawk's Nest?"

"About twenty minutes from Monticello."

"You can take me there?" Conway said.

Bunker said, "Whenever you want. You come up here, I'll meet you at the racetrack and show you the way."

"How long's the drive from the city?"

"Three hours, maybe. Little less."

Conway flipped the phone shut and looked around at the other people on the bus. An old lady with shopping bags. A couple of Our Lady of the Narrows kids clutching bulky knapsacks in their laps and listening to iPods. This guy, Hyun—Conway knew of him but didn't really know him—who ran numbers for Mr. Natale and was sweaty and nervous, holding onto the overhead strap with one hand and gripping a thin stack of papers with the other. And there was the peg-leg homeless lady who rode the B1 and the B64 all day, her wheelchair ornamented with shopping bags. None of them knew he had a gun. None of them knew he was going to get in his car, drive upstate, and kill Ray Boy Calabrese. Probably none of them knew Ray Boy. Or they'd forgotten his face from the papers. The kids weren't even alive then. A lot got washed away in sixteen years. Conway thought of Duncan's grave: all those paper poppies from his once-a-week visits. He'd knelt there and made a promise that none of the people on the bus knew about.

Walking back home, Conway watched pigeons on the sidewalk out in front of Johnny Tomasullo's barber shop. He looked up at a pair of boots hanging from the telephone wires. People didn't do that much anymore. He remembered throwing his school shoes up there after he was done with junior high. Then he leaned against a parking meter and thought about how he was going to deal with Pop. Kid gloves. Lies.

Pop was at the door to greet him when he came in the front gate. "You've been where?" Pop said.

"Bay Ridge with McKenna. At the gym."

"I need you to pick up my prescription."

"Not now."

"When?"

"Maybe later. We'll see. Otherwise I'll get Stephanie to run it over."

"No, no, no. That's too much trouble. I'll go get it myself. To put Stephanie out, ridiculous."

"Don't walk up there with your leg, Pop. Stephanie doesn't mind. She's my friend. It's four blocks. She doesn't mind."

"Ridiculous."

Conway went inside and got his car keys off the hook in the kitchen and a roll of duct tape out of the tool closet. He put the duct tape in the gym bag. Pop followed close behind. "I'm busy, Pop," Conway said.

"But you'll go get it?" Pop said.

"Maybe."

"I'll go."

Conway said, "Okay. I'll go up and get it."

But he had no intention of going. He left the house and went down the block and found his Civic parked by P.S. 101. He opened his phone and called Stephanie. Asked her to deliver the prescription to his old man. Told her just call first so she didn't scare him. Ring the bell a few times, he said. Sometimes Pop couldn't hear it. Stephanie was happy to do it, thrilled to get out from behind the counter. At least that was taken care of. And Pop would have company to distract him, even if only for a few minutes at the door. Stephanie was goofy, she had this frizzy hair like in cartoon strips and an accent nasty with the neighborhood, but she was kind, especially with old timers.

Driving away up Benson Avenue, headed for the Belt, Conway tried not to picture Pop in their sad living room with the dusty cross on the wall and the Sacred Heart Auto League calendars everywhere and the lampshade that was stressed to flimsy. But the picture came anyway: Pop in a ragged recliner, pillows everywhere, reaching out for the channel changer and trying to hear what they were saying on TV. Pop clawing his fingers into a go-to jar of Vicks VapoRub and massaging his neck, the Vicks blobbing up in his neck hair like a wispy chrysalis in a tree. Just waiting for Conway to get home with the scrip.

Now, beginning this very moment, Pop had nothing, had no one. Conway knew he wasn't coming back. He was at the end of something. Maybe Aunt Nunzia would come around to check on Pop, but she had her own problems. A construction worker son who gambled away her social security. Squirrels in the wall. Her husband's loans she was still paying off. Pop had squat. The house and his prescriptions. The windows he stared out. The kids around the corner he liked to call the police on. With Conway gone, he might try to stop living. Not off himself. Just give in quietly. Stop breathing with the TV on.

Plumb Beach wasn't on the way, but Conway backtracked on the Belt. You could only get there by a short lane exit off the eastbound side after Knapp Street.

A parking lot was split in half on either side of the gated entrance. Conway pulled in and parked next to a small Dumpster. It was the same spot they'd found Duncan's car parked. Conway kept a tally of his visits on the Dumpster. He used a rock or whatever sharp was around to scratch a line. He'd come at least two or three times a week for sixteen years. A whole long section was covered in his deep-etched lines. He leaned over and added one now with a snapped-off bicycle handle he found near his front tire.

He stood and went through his routine. He walked past a huddle of Rent-a-Throne port-a-potties where old Russians came to shit and then curved around the abandoned pavilion, squat and shadowy, stickered with regulations and peeling-off fish decals and a sign that said HORSESHOE CRAB HARVESTING IS NOT PERMITTED. A pair of children's sneakers hung from the broken-down beach fence in front of him. Seagulls pecked the dirty sand. Empty Corona bottles and Newport packages and condom wrappers rimmed the seaweed-skirted shoreline. He went down to the water and looked out at the Gil Hodges Memorial Bridge in one direction and Kingsborough Community College in the other. Fort Tilden and Jacob Riis were across the bay.

Ray Boy, who had tormented Duncan for being swishy since grade school, called Duncan one afternoon pretending to be a kid he met in the city, saying he wanted to meet out at Plumb Beach and hook up, and Duncan just goddamn went. He'd gotten his license a couple of months before, and he drove to Plumb Beach, parked next to the Dumpster with the lights off, and went down to the shoreline. The scene unspooled on repeat in Conway's mind: Ray Boy and his crew, Teemo and Andy Tighe, charging Duncan from out of nowhere, pounding and kicking him, Duncan getting up, making a break, realizing he'd dropped his keys somewhere, running past his car, jumping over a guardrail and onto the Belt, dodging lights and cars, knowing that someone would stop to help.

Next Conway walked from the shoreline back to the guardrail beyond his car. He stood up on the rail, balancing himself with his arms out, watching the cars rip by on the Belt. The car that didn't have the time to get out of Duncan's way had been doing seventy.

The court called it a hate crime. They also called it manslaughter. Pressure came down from the LGBT Alliance, and Ray Boy, Teemo, and Andy Tighe got sent away for as long as the judge could get away with. Conway called it cold-blooded murder, and he knew that Ray Boy had been the ringleader. Conway was twenty-nine now, working at a goddamn Rite Aid on Eighty-Sixth Street, living with his old man who had never recovered from Duncan's death and wondering what had happened to his mother who was long gone to alcohol. He wanted Ray Boy's blood. The fucker deserved to wind up dead in a trunk, buried out in some shithole spot with no fanfare, no marker, just skin and bones rotting back into the earth. He tried not to imagine his brother dead on the Belt all those years ago, a picture that always came back to him. He got down from the guardrail and went to the car.

The drive up was quick, no traffic, and Conway kept the pedal to the floor. He'd only been outside the city a few times. Long Island for his brother's grave. Jersey for a cousin's confirmation. Baltimore for a shitty wedding. Mostly, Staten Island and the Bronx were the ends of the earth. He marveled at the world on the other side of the George Washington Bridge. The Palisades Parkway. Bear Mountain. A traffic circle where he followed signs to Central Valley. Trees everywhere. Leaves turning colors. Cars with their tops down. Then he got on 17. Factory outlets. Strip malls. Exits into towns with names that sounded like what you'd call your dog. Monroe. Chester.

Conway hooked up with Bunker at a Shell across from the Monticello Raceway. He pulled up behind Bunker's Citation.

Bunker got out, lit a guinea stinker, and came over to Conway's window. He looked more like a washed-up substitute teacher than a private eye. "Conway?" he said. "You want to get a coffee?"

"Not really," Conway said.

"Ray Boy's is about fifteen, twenty miles up the road. When we pass the place, it's on a road called Parsonage, big white house on the left, I'll put my blinker on one-two-three and then keep driving."

"That's fine."

"If you get down to the train tracks and the river, you've gone too far. I'm not turning around there. I'm taking a different way back. But at the river, if you get down there by accident, you pull a U and go back up Parsonage."

"How much I owe you?"

"Your buddy took care of it."

Conway nodded and said nothing.

Bunker headed back to his car and drove away, kicking up gravel on the side of the road. Conway followed him up Route 17B. His phone buzzed in his pocket. He took it out and flipped it open.

"Where you at?" McKenna said on the other end.

Conway said, "Heading there now."

"I should've come with."

"No."

"Listen, dude, I got bad news. *The Village Voice*, I just found out they did a spread on Ray Boy getting out. Had a thing remembering Duncan. Said the case didn't get enough attention back in the day."

"So?"

"That's a lot of eyes on Ray Boy is what I'm saying. I'm gonna reemphasize I think you should wait."

"Can't wait."

"They'll send you up anyway."

"I'm not going to jail," Conway said.

McKenna said, "I'll have Marylou put out her Mary statue."

Conway closed the phone. He had this thing with McKenna where he just stopped talking. He'd always liked it, but now it was permanent, like he'd said the last thing he was ever going to say to him.

Could be he killed Ray Boy, got caught, went to jail at Sullivan Correctional. Or he got away with it, made a break for Canada. He had always wanted to see Nova Scotia. But maybe Ray Boy got him, strong-as-shit Ray Boy who could probably crush the gun out of his hand in a second flat, laughing at him for being puny while he did it. Cool-as-shit Ray Boy, grinning like he did on the way into the courtroom the first time Conway saw him after Duncan died, just grinning so no one could see, that grin saying, *I killed your fag brother, kid*.

The last stretch to Ray Boy's place was down a broken road with no shoulder. Small houses on the side of the road looked left for dead. Sawhorses blocked driveways. Shattered windows were stapled shut with plastic. Roofs were buckled and crumbling. Conway shut the heat and the radio and focused on Bunker's left blinker, waiting for the signal.

They made a quick left turn onto Parsonage. Bunker slowed down and flashed his blinker and then kept driving toward the river and the train tracks.

Conway stopped the car and looked up: a white frame house at the end of a long uphill driveway. A dump pile and a burn bin and a couple of abandoned trucks dotted the yard. The mustard-colored shades on all the windows were pulled. The white paint was ribbed with dirt. The front steps sagged. Wet wood was stacked on the porch. Other houses were scattered on the road, but they were not close.

Conway opened the gym bag and took out the duct tape and the .22. He turned the gun over in his lap and looked up at the house again. He tried to see through the walls. Imagined Ray Boy doing pull-ups on a bar tucked into a doorway. Imagined Ray Boy drinking coffee from a Styrofoam cup, legs up, watching the news. Imagined Ray Boy's new prison fierceness, a thousand times harder than before.

Paralyzed wasn't the word for how he felt, but he couldn't move. Just like when he was a kid next in line for confession. Those days he'd choke and cough, get pushed into the confessional by Sister Erin or Sister Loretta, and he'd lie to the priest: "I had bad thoughts about Alessandra Biagini. I stole a comic from Augie's. I told my mother I did my homework even though I didn't so I could watch cartoons." Now there was no nun to push him out of the car, but he wished there was.

The front door of the house opened. Ray Boy came out on the porch and turned on a swampy floodlight overhead and lit a cigarette. He wasn't wearing a shirt. Just boxers. He was muscled up and had homemade-looking tats on his chest and forearms.

Conway crossed himself and said a prayer. He knew it was wrong to pray about this kind of thing, and maybe he didn't even believe that prayer did anything. Probably he didn't. But he'd never stopped going to church, never stopped praying, even if it was only as good as rubbing some bullshit lamp and making wishes. In church, when he was a kid, he'd stare at Duncan, who had these polished brown rosary beads and was always praying decades like a fiend, and he'd be amazed that his brother even believed.

The image of Duncan praying kicked Conway in the heart, and he got out of the car. He charged up the driveway, the gun in front of him and the duct tape in his jacket pocket.

Ray Boy, his eyes all squinty, seemed to notice him, and Conway was surprised that he didn't bolt or charge, that he just leaned back against the porch rail, blowing smoke.

"Get down," Conway said, approaching the porch behind the gun.

Ray Boy went to his knees. "Hey," he said.

"You know who I am, right?"

"I've been hoping you'd show." Ray Boy tossed his cigarette over the porch rail and got all the way down, hands locked behind his head.

"Been thinking about you, too," Conway said.

Conway squatted over Ray Boy and jacked him in the back of the head with the butt of the gun to knock him out like they did in movies. It didn't work. Ray Boy didn't really even seem fazed by it. Conway told him to stay still and taped his feet and hands and mouth. Ray Boy didn't move.

Conway pressed the gun against Ray Boy's back. He still wasn't struggling. Conway wanted him begging the way that Duncan was no doubt begging that night out at Plumb Beach. That was always what Conway had hated to think about most, Duncan down on all fours like a dog, Ray Boy and his buddies spitting and saying fag-this and fag-that.

Conway peeled the tape away from Ray Boy's mouth a little and said, "Say, 'Don't.' Say, 'Please don't.'"

But Ray Boy said nothing. His lips were against the rotted, peeling porch floor.

Conway noticed one of the tats on Ray Boy's arm. Duncan's full name spelled out in shaky green print. Below that, Duncan's death date.

"Fuck's this for?" Conway said.

Still nothing.

"What'd my brother say to you that night? He begged you?" Conway jabbed the gun deeper. "Answer me. Fuck did he say?"

Ray Boy said, "He went, 'Remember third grade. We were friends. Please don't do this.'" And started crying.

2

The whole house smelled like dirty sponges. Alessandra was sitting in the living room with her suitcase at her feet. She had come in on a red-eye from Los Angeles and taken a taxi straight home from the airport. She looked up at her mother's china cabinet. It hadn't been dusted in years. A puzzle she'd done with her mother when she was ten or eleven was on a TV tray next to the cabinet. Dust bunnies poked from between the wilting pieces like weeds. Her father came over and sat next to her. He smelled like a dirty sponge, too. "I'm happy you're home," he said.

Alessandra put her face in her hands. "I've been a terrible daughter."

"You were a joy to us."

"The funeral went okay?"

"A lot of family. We celebrated her life."

"I'm so sorry I wasn't here."

"You're here now. You want something to drink? Black coffee?"

Alessandra nodded. "With Sambuca and a little lemon," she said.

Her father went into the kitchen and got the espresso started. Everything he did made him look like he'd been defeated. His clothes were rumpled. He needed a haircut. His glasses were scratched and taped between the lenses. He'd cut himself shaving in five or six different places. It wasn't working for him, not having his wife around.

Alessandra had gone out to Los Angeles when she was eighteen. She'd wanted to get far away from Brooklyn and she wanted to be an actress, so L.A. seemed like the place to go. Her parents, especially her mother, didn't understand. Why leave the neighborhood? Manhattan was right across the bridge, be an actress there. But something about the neighborhood made Alessandra anxious to get away. She was accepted into USC and her parents even fronted her the tuition, but she dropped out at the end of her first semester and tried to get by on commercials. She got work here and there, mostly stuff on the Home Shopping Network, but she started singing in a wedding band to pay the bills. She didn't have much of a voice, but the guys in the band liked her looks so they let her on board. It'd been almost a decade of scraping by out west and when her mother got sick she thought she'd just finally give up and go home. But she waited, kept doing what she was doing, and her mother got sicker and her father called her five times a day and she just couldn't face it. Now, almost two months after the cancer had spread to her bones and her mother had died, nothing the doctors at Sloan-Kettering or Columbia could do, Alessandra was back home in Gravesend and things were sadder than she could've imagined.

Her father came back out with two espresso cups on saucers. He'd rubbed the rim of hers with lemon the way she liked and left the wedge next to the spoon. She thanked him and then said she'd like to go visit her mother's grave.

"We'll go to Holy Garden whenever you want," he said.

"I'll just get unpacked and take a quick shower." Alessandra sucked on the lemon and then took a sip of espresso. She started thinking about all she needed to do now that she was back. She had shipped most of her stuff and it was supposed to arrive the next day or the day after that. "I'm gonna need to find work," she said.

"One thing at a time," her father said.

"And a place."

"You'll stay here. Plenty of room."

Alessandra got up with her espresso and walked around the room. She looked out the front window. Her father had decided to have the big oak that hung over the driveway cut down and now there was just so much space that she could see in the windows of the house next door. She stared at Jimmy's Deli on the corner across the avenue, the place where she'd bought quarter waters and ice pops as a kid, and thought of her mother walking her over there and then coming back to work on her tomato plants. "We should've buried Mom out there in the yard," Alessandra said. "Where she gardened."

Her father seemed shocked by what she'd said. "This cemetery, it's a nice place, a proper place," he said.

"We should bury people in places they love. Or scatter their ashes there. Mom loved the yard, she had to. She was out there all the time. With her plants. Or just sitting, listening to the Yankees."

"Your mother liked Holy Garden," her father said, getting fed up. "We chose it together. Rosie DeLuca and Jimmy Licardi are buried there." He paused. "We don't bury people in yards here."

"I just thought it might've been nice."

After unpacking in her old room, putting her clothes in a closet and drawers that were still full of high school prom dresses and cutoffs and New Kids on the Block T-shirts, Alessandra took a shower. The tub was small and her father had plastered vinyl curtains on all four sides, even around the shower nozzle, to fight against mildew in the grout. It was a very dark and confining space. She remembered taking showers in the morning before school and having to close her eyes because it felt like she was alone in a submerged tank. The darkening of the stall was—and always had been—the project of a man who had failed too often in life and wouldn't be defeated by mildew to boot.

Alessandra changed into a black dress, something appropriate for the cemetery, and she brushed her hair and put on makeup at her vanity table. Her room was spacious and girly, girlier than she'd remembered it, and it was very unlike the places she'd stayed in Los Angeles. Studios where the bed and refrigerator were side-by-side. Houses that she shared with other actresses and actors, all of whom were astounded by how simply she could live. And she didn't need much. Some nice clothes and shoes, good makeup in her purse, a trip to a spa every now and then, time on the beach. She'd especially miss the L.A. beaches. Here, she had Coney and Manhattan Beach not too far away, but it wasn't the same. New York beaches were too gritty for her. Coney especially. But maybe they'd changed, been cleaned up.

They drove to the cemetery with the oldies station on, Alessandra's father asking her questions every few minutes. She gave short answers. He wanted to know about her boyfriend, the one that surfed. She said that ended a long time ago. He wanted to know about the weather out there and the traffic. She said warm, everyone drove. He wanted to know about the one big picture she had worked on. She said she'd only been an extra, it wasn't anything, you couldn't even see her in the final version. He wanted to know why she hadn't auditioned for that singing show with the judges. She said she had, four times, and hadn't made the cut. Weddings were all she was good for.

After that, things got quiet. Alessandra fiddled around in her purse, wished she had a pack of American Spirits. Her father had quit years ago, she knew, but she figured he had a pack stashed somewhere in the car. Everyone who quit had a car stash. "You have any cigarettes?" she said.

He said, "You smoke?"

"Just sometimes."

"No good."

"I know. So?"

"Glove compartment."

She popped open the glove compartment and there was a package of Top rolling tobacco on a stack of old Esso maps and no-good-anymore insurance and registration cards. "I can't roll," she said.

"I rolled a few already. They're in the bag."

She opened the package and found a few rolled cigarettes with homemade cardboard filters. A tobacco-flecked matchbook from Benny's Fish & Beer was also in there. She lit a cigarette and opened the window. "You want one?"

"No," he said. "Not now. Your mother wouldn't approve."

Alessandra laughed. "Serious?"

"It's a disrespect."

"Ma smoked."

"Years ago, when you were just a kid."

Alessandra blew smoke out the window. She looked beyond passing cars at a squatting strip mall built on what a sign said used to be a landfill. Where were they anyway? She thought they were on the Belt, but it no longer looked familiar. Traffic was heavy in the middle of the day. Cars rocketed around them. Her father was a cautious, slow driver. He was doing the speed limit but it felt like they were going fifteen. All this to stand at a grave and weep. What did it even mean to cry over bones? She wasn't there when it mattered, when her mother was alive and asking for her, but she'd go through the motions, act like a grieving daughter who had been too busy to make it home for her mother's last days or even for the funeral.

The cemetery was worse than Alessandra had imagined. Her mother, she knew, wanted to be buried at St. John's in Queens—that's where her whole family was—but her father had no doubt talked her into going cheap. As far as cemeteries went, St. John's was beautiful. This place, Holy Garden, was a catastrophe of bleakness. Gray prison walls surrounded plots that looked like they'd been hammered out of the earth. Headstones were tacky. Only paper flowers were allowed.

"Nice place, no?" her father said. "Peaceful."

"Jesus, Daddy. Why didn't you guys just get plots at St. John's?"

"What?"

"It's awful," Alessandra said. She went back to the car, got another cigarette out of the glove compartment, lit it, came back to her mother's grave,
and kneeled over it. She picked some pebbles from the dirt and arranged
them in a circle on top of her mother's tombstone.

"That's supposed to be what?" her father said.

"An offering."

"Jesus, Mary, and Saint Joseph." He paused. "Your mother liked it here.
She did."

"Her whole family's at St. John's."

"Yeah, well, St. John's costs an arm and a leg. There's only one spot left
in the family plot and her sister Jenny had seniority. So we came out here.
Mikey the Goose's mother and father are buried out here. Rosie and Jimmy.
Frankie's kid, got killed."

"Frankie D'Innocenzio's kid's here? Duncan?"

"Poor kid. I don't remember you knew him."

"Of course I did." Alessandra stubbed out her cigarette and put the butt
in her pocket. "I want to visit his grave. You know where it is?"

"Say goodbye to your mother."

Alessandra touched the headstone and pretended like she was praying
over it. Her father turned his back. "We should've got flowers," he said.

"Those paper flowers?"

"They sell them up in the main office."

Alessandra ignored him. "Where's Duncan?" she said.

He showed her the way, down a broken brick bath, to a stretch of flat
in-the-ground headstones under a collapsing sycamore with roots that were
pulling the dirt up around Duncan's grave. Paper flowers littered the patches
of dead grass around the headstone, the kind old VFW guys sold outside of
supermarkets on Saturday mornings. The stone said Duncan's name and the

date he died. Below that: BELOVED SON, BELOVED BROTHER. "Sixteen years," Alessandra said. "Christ."

"Shame," her father said. "I mean, I don't understand the gay thing, but he didn't deserve this."

"That's a stupid thing to say, Daddy."

He turned his back again and started to walk back the way they'd come.

Alessandra stared at Duncan's grave. She remembered not believing it when she heard that he'd died. How it happened was the worst. It'd been a year since she'd been in school with his brother Conway at Most Precious Blood and she just remembered feeling sorry for him. Conway always sat behind her in homeroom because his name came after hers. And she knew Ray Boy, too. He was four years older, and she used to see him around the neighborhood. He had these glassy blue eyes and wore a gray mechanic's jacket with red stitching and she crushed out on him like the kid she was. Those eyes. She knew he'd picked on Duncan for a long time, a lot of guys did, but he was the worst and back then it didn't bother her. You were a fruit, you got picked on, that was just the way of it. Now she knew somebody should've stepped in. Poor Duncan, always having to avoid guys, making it to senior year and thinking he was in the clear. But Ray Boy wasn't grown up enough to let it be. He had to get Duncan one last time. She bet Ray Boy grew up pretty fast in jail.

She walked away from the grave and back to the car. Her father was sitting behind the wheel, smoking a cigarette. He had the radio on WABC and was listening to the news. "I'm sorry," he said.

"You don't need to be sorry," she said.

"I am," he said.

"Don't worry, Daddy," she said, and she bummed one last cigarette.

Back at the house now, Alessandra and her father ate dinner. Pasta with gravy he'd defrosted that afternoon and *braciole* from her Aunt Cecilia. She'd forgotten how good it was to eat like this. In L.A. it had been all hummus

and avocados and smoothies, quick and healthy stuff on the run, and she
didn't miss it. This gravy tasted silky and sweet with a garlicky bite and the
parmesan from Pastosa was unlike anything she could get out west. They
shared a bottle of red wine, something dark and bitter and unlabeled from a
neighbor's basement, and she could barely drink it, the taste was so off, but
she forced herself because she wanted to be drunk.

After dinner, her father sat down in his recliner and watched the Yankees.
She went upstairs and changed clothes and redid her makeup and decided
she was going to go out and see who was still around. She thought about Bay
Ridge but didn't want to deal with car service. There weren't many bars in the
neighborhood, not that she could remember. A dive called The Wrong Number
with graffiti on the sign. And Ralphie's, a clammy sports bar full of fat cops and
smooth Italian boys stinking of cologne. Those were the options back when.
She went downstairs, dolled to the nines, and asked her father if any new places
had opened up. He understood her needing a drink out and he said yeah those
places were still there and there were a couple of new joints too, a Russian
supper club and another sports bar called Murphy's Irish. Alessandra thought
that Russian supper clubs must have been all sweat and vodka and getting
hoisted up on men's shoulders, and she wanted to steer clear of sports bars, so
she decided to slum it at The Wrong Number. She wished she had girlfriends
from the neighborhood she was still in contact with, someone she could call
and coax into hanging out, but part of what had been appealing about going
to L.A. was leaving behind the kids she had grown up with. Anyhow, she was
never that close with any of them. She'd had some laughs with the two Melissas,
out in Bay Ridge or Canarsie, and she spent a lot of time with Joanne Galbo
and Mary DiMaggio in the Kearney days, but that was it. Stephanie Dirello,
who used to live right up the block with her family and maybe still did, was the
one girl she'd gone to school with for twelve years, at Most Precious Blood and
at Kearney, and she used to see her in church every Saturday night, and sometimes they'd do homework together after school on the bus, but they'd never
really been close friends, just two girls who lived a few houses apart. But she

was nice, Stephanie. Always wore a too-big Mark Messier jersey. Maybe she'd go knock on Stephanie's door, see if she was still in the neighborhood.

Alessandra took a front door key and kissed her father on the head and walked up the block to what she hoped was where Stephanie still lived. Chances were she'd moved out years ago, but you never knew around here. People lived with their parents forever. Scary thought. Alessandra had only been back for a few hours and she was already itching to find her own place.

Alessandra walked into the yard and knocked on the front door. The mailbox still said Dirello.

"You're who?" Stephanie's mother said, opening up, right on top of it, as if she'd been waiting for a knock.

Alessandra said, "Hey, Mrs. Dirello, I'm Alessandra Biagini. You remember me? From up the block? I went to school with Stephanie."

"It's late."

"I'm sorry. It's just eight. I got home today and I thought I'd see if Stephanie still lived here."

"Of course she lives here. She's gonna go where?"

"I'm sorry, Mrs. Dirello. Can I talk to her?"

Mrs. Dirello looked at her through slitty eyes. She was wearing a housecoat, and Alessandra noticed liver spots on her arms and all of these little brown moles that drooped from her skin like withered worms and networks of varicose veins that tattooed her calves. "You're who?"

"Alessandra from the block. You don't remember me?"

"Stephanie!" Mrs. Dirello said over her shoulder. Then to Alessandra: "You stay out there."

"Okay," Alessandra said. "Thanks so much."

"You trying to sell us something? I don't need those chocolate bars. I buy chocolate from Chinese Mary's son."

"I'm not selling chocolate."

Stephanie appeared behind her mother. She was wearing an over-sized sweatshirt and jean shorts. She looked pretty much the same except she didn't have braces. Her hair was frizzed out and she wore cheapo glasses probably from the Eyeglass Factory on West Twelfth. She still had a thin mustache too, had never taken the time to wax it or pluck it. Maybe Alessandra could help her out, give her a makeover. The possibilities. "Hi, Steph," Alessandra said. "Been a long time."

"Alessandra?" Stephanie said. "Wow. What're you doing here?"

"Trying to sell us something, I think," Mrs. Dirello said.

Stephanie pushed past her mother. "Give us a second here, Ma," she said. Mrs. Dirello huffed back into the house, and Stephanie opened the door. "You look great, Alessandra. Wow. You really look like an actress."

"Thanks. You look great, too. Haven't changed."

Stephanie rolled her eyes. "Guys are knocking down the door, trying to get under my big sweatshirt."

Alessandra laughed. She'd forgotten Stephanie could be really funny. And that accent. Man, Alessandra was happy she'd lost hers. Stephanie's was thick, cruddy. "I just got home today. Haven't been here in a long time."

"Your mother," Stephanie said. "I'm so sorry."

"Thank you."

"She used to talk about you all the time. I'd see her where I work, she'd be picking up your dad's blood pressure pills, and she'd talk about you. 'Alessandra's starring in this movie, she's doing this commercial.' She was really proud of you. And she was such a character. She'd go around with her shopping cart, just pushing people out of the way."

"I miss her, yeah. I didn't get home, but we talked a lot."

Stephanie lowered her voice. "My mother's half-a-psycho. She doesn't leave the house. It's making her crazy."

Alessandra shrugged. "You want to come out, get a drink?"

"I don't really drink."

"Just for the company then. I need a drink out, I want to catch up."

"Where?"

"Not many options. Wrong Number?"

Stephanie said, "Heck. Let me go up, change clothes. Come in and sit down."

"I'll wait out here," Alessandra said.

Stephanie disappeared up a back staircase and Mrs. Dirello followed fast on her heels. Alessandra could hear her, saying she better not think she was going out, what did she think she was doing, this girl out front was all whored up and looking for trouble.

Girl was twenty-nine. Imagine. Living like she was still fourteen. Alessandra couldn't get over it.

Stephanie came out a few minutes later, wearing jeans that rode high above her waist and a pink blouse with ruffled shoulders. She'd put some rouge on her cheeks, with a spray gun it looked like, and her lipstick squiggled out at the corners. "I'm ready," she said. "*Voila*. Watch them line up." She curtsied.

Alessandra laughed again.

"Never could figure out how to make myself look nice," Stephanie said.

"You do look nice," Alessandra said.

"So acting and lying are pretty much the same thing, right?"

The Wrong Number wasn't as much of a dive as she remembered. Or maybe they'd cleaned it up. It wasn't a big glossy sports bar by any stretch, but it also wasn't an end-of-the-world shithole. Alessandra ordered a gin-and-tonic from the bartender with the aped-out chest and waxy chin and Stephanie got a ginger ale with a lime wedge. They sat at a booth in the back by a jukebox and talked over a Budweiser bottle corked with a low-burning pumpkin-scented candle. "It's just crazy to be back," Alessandra said. "So crazy."

"I can't imagine," Stephanie said.

"So, you're what? A pharmacist?"

"At Rite Aid over on Twenty-Fifth Avenue. Conway D'Innocenzio works there. You remember him?"

"Sat behind me in homeroom for nine years."

"He's a stock boy. Works the register sometimes."

"We were out at the cemetery today, visiting my mother, and we saw Duncan's grave. Made me remember the whole thing. Hadn't thought of it in years."

Stephanie said, "Family never got over that. Conway lived in the Bronx for a few years but he got into drugs pretty bad and wound up coming home. Frankie's just a shell. Mother's gone, just whoosh, disappeared one day." She looked over at the bartender and nodded in his direction. He was pulling a draft for a hook-nosed old timer in a Yankees cap with a flat brim. "You know who that is?"

"The bartender?" Alessandra said.

"Teemo. Ran with Ray Boy Calabrese. He got out years ago. You remember the trial and everything?"

"I could forget?" Alessandra paused. "You got any cigarettes?"

"I don't," Stephanie said.

"Christ, it's weird to be home."

Teemo came over to the table with a dishrag over his shoulder. "You ladies okay?" he said, only looking at Alessandra.

"Fine," Stephanie said.

He smelled like ten different kinds of shitty cologne and wore designer jeans with pre-ripped holes and a frayed waistband and had a fake tan that had left orange run marks on his neck and arms. His white sneakers were spotless. "Just checking in," he said, getting closer to Alessandra. "Don't want you ladies to be thirsty."

Alessandra said nothing, ignored him.

"I know you?" he said to her.

"No," Alessandra said, though they'd been at the same parties hanging out a dozen times in high school. She didn't really know him, hadn't hooked up with him or anything, because he was a few years older, but they'd been around each other a lot. She was glad he didn't totally recognize her, didn't remember her name.

"You look real familiar."

"I don't know you," she said. "Let it go."

"End of the night, you'll be begging for my number," Teemo said, shrugging. He walked back to the bar slowly, showing Alessandra his ass in the tight jeans and laughing. "Begging!"

Alessandra lifted her drink. "This guy," she said to Stephanie. "You believe him?"

Stephanie said, "He's always been awful."

They finished their drinks and left, reluctant to order another round from Teemo. They walked around the neighborhood instead, and Stephanie told Alessandra what had become of everyone. Joanne Galbo was living in Bay Ridge, teaching Biology at Our Lady of the Narrows. Mary DiMaggio worked for a urologist in Dyker Heights. Melissa Sanchez was a cop, you believe that? And Melissa Murphy died on 9/11, worked at Cantor Fitz- gerald on the 101st floor of Tower One. Adrienne Marra and Vinny Sor- rento were married and had boinked six snot-nosed kids into existence. Andy Pascione worked construction, hurt his back on a site, and was hooked on pain meds—his wife and daughter had left him and moved to Florida and he just rented pornos from the last video store in the neighborhood and stayed inside with a box of tissues and the shades drawn.

Alessandra felt exhausted.

Back by Stephanie's house now, they stopped outside the front gate and Alessandra could see Mrs. Dirello framed in an upstairs window, watching them.

"I'm glad you came by to see me," Stephanie said. "I'm happy you're back."

"Your mom's watching us," Alessandra said.

"She's got nothing better to do. Forget it."

"It's creepy."

"Sorry," Stephanie said, and she reached out to hug Alessandra.

Alessandra took the hug, patting Stephanie on the back. "Okay, sweetie," she said.

Stephanie ran inside, opening and closing the door gently, and Mrs. Dirello disappeared from the upstairs window. Alessandra walked home, wishing she had her father's smokes, wishing she'd been born in another place.

3

Conway was on 17B headed back toward Monticello. There was no noise coming from the trunk. Ray Boy seemed peaceful. Conway held the wheel with his hands at ten and two, going just under the speed limit. He knew the only ones who drove this way were eighty year olds and people who had something to hide. He got pulled over, maybe he could explain it to the cop: *This guy's responsible for my brother being dead. Let it slide this time.*

None of it made sense. He should've just brought Ray Boy into the house. But the tattoo and the crying jag had thrown him off and he'd gotten the idea that he should take Ray Boy back to Brooklyn, to Plumb Beach, and that nothing could stand in his way there, not in the place that Duncan had been killed, and that it would mean more there anyway.

Seemed like the guy wanted to be put out of his misery. It almost made things harder. Conway had always envisioned a fight.

But it was going to have to be an execution.

The movie of the next couple hours played out in Conway's mind: Ray Boy on his knees at Plumb Beach, eyes closed, the headlights of cars from the Belt flickering over them, Conway pressing the gun up to Ray Boy's head, pulling the trigger, the fucker's brains going splash in the dark. Roll credits.

Guts up, Conway thought. *It's all been leading to this. Probably this is the way it's supposed to happen.*

He passed an abandoned Hasidic children's camp and then a strip club called Searchlights that was just a rundown house with a trailer attached to it. He considered, honestly, stopping to get a lap dance. Why not? Ray Boy resting in the trunk, not going anywhere, Conway just letting off a little steam. He thought better of it, though. He was also scared shitless of what he'd find in a trailer trash strip club on a dark-as-hell road between Monticello and Hawk's Nest. Toothless amputees probably. Obscenely fat women who had to be brought on stage in wheelbarrows and emptied onto the pole. Imagine.

Once he was back on 17, signs called it the Quickway, not a back road anymore but the four-lane that would bring him back to some kind of civilization, he felt better. Lights. Other cars. Town names he remembered from the way up. Wurtsboro. Middletown. Middletown—Fuck kind of name was that? Middle of where?

Conway put the radio on because he wanted to hear something. The Yankees were coming in fuzzy and distant, but he listened anyway. The bad reception was full of sizzles and pops. The clawing sound filled the car. He hoped it was loudest in the trunk. Quiet, forgive-me-please Ray Boy getting his ears blown out.

The world outside shot by like a flip book in reverse. Dog name towns. Getting back on 6 over the mountain. That traffic circle like it was Grand Army Plaza or some shit. The narrow Palisades hugged the Civic in the dark. No shoulder. People did seventy-five in a fifty. Deer eyes glowed in the trees. Conway was paranoid of stupid deer and stupid Troopers. At the

George Washington, the sign of almost being home, he thanked Christ he had an EZ Pass. All the while, Ray Boy didn't move. The radio was on loud, getting clearer as they got closer to the city and then all the way clear and booming, the Yankees getting routed by the Blue Jays, Cano hitting two homers and it not being enough, the pitching just not there.

On the West Side Highway, he finally got to jerk the car around a little, no chance of getting pulled over unless he broke a hundred or blasted through a light. He moved from lane to lane, took bumps without braking, and he could hear Ray Boy finally, rattling around, groaning through the tape over his mouth, being lifted into the trunk hatch and then plopped back down.

He took the Battery to the Gowanus and then cut left onto the Belt, the gas light on now, no time for detours to gas up in Dyker Heights, no stopping until Plumb Beach. The Belt was electric, thrumming with zipfast cars, and Conway rolled the window down to let the cold in. He saw his breath in front of him on the windshield.

At Plumb Beach, out of the car and stretching, Conway looked around. No action. He went to the Dumpster, squatted, and scratched a line with a jagged twist of wire he found in a groove of cracked pavement. Then he put an X through his entire tally of visits. This would be his last time coming out here.

He went back to the Civic and got the .22 from the glovebox. He held it at his side. He went around to the trunk and beat on it with his fist. He said, "I'm opening up. You do anything, I'll just start firing into the trunk."

Nothing.

He wondered, for a second, if maybe Ray Boy had suffocated.

He opened the trunk, poking the gun in first. Ray Boy was just curled up there with his eyes open, shivering.

"You heard me?" Conway said.

Ray Boy nodded.

"Can you get out?"

Another nod. Ray Boy threw his taped-together legs out of the trunk and stood up in front of Conway. It seemed impossible, twisting his upper body out the way he did. Ray Boy could probably do whatever he wanted to. Break free. Run. Beat Conway down. But he was resigned to his fate. Conway didn't even need the gun. But he stuck it in Ray Boy's side anyway and told him to move.

Ray Boy shook his head. He couldn't walk with the tape around his legs, but Conway wanted to see him try and fall. If the guy was just going to go down like a dog, Conway wanted to humiliate him at least. He pushed him forward with the gun and Ray Boy toppled, face-planting into the glittery blacktop of the lot. He lifted his head up and showed scrapes on his cheeks and chin.

"Can't walk," Conway said. "Maybe I should make you wriggle out into traffic." He paused. Then: "Too good for you. Get up."

Ray Boy turned over and tried to kick himself into a stand. He couldn't quite do it and stayed on the ground, looking up at the sky.

Conway wondered if people could see them from the Belt. Probably not, driving by as fast as they were. He took the car key out of his pocket, straddled Ray Boy and cut the tape from his legs. Guy wasn't going to run, and he needed to get him out to the shoreline.

Ray Boy stood up, his hands still taped behind his back, his mouth taped shut, his upper arms taped to his sides. Tape covered his legs, but there was an open seam that ran from his boxers to his ankles, allowing movement. Ray Boy was shivering harder, his skin red now, and Conway stared at the Duncan tattoo.

Shuffling forward, silent, goose-skinned, Ray Boy had his head down and was walking like a condemned man in shackles.

"I hope you see Duncan out here," Conway said, behind Ray Boy, the gun fixed on him. "Everywhere you look." Pause. "You see him?"

Slow nod.

"He's gonna get some peace tonight. Finally."

They were out at the shoreline now, the dark beach littered with ocean-soft glass that caught sparks under the moon.

Conway pushed Ray Boy down in the pebbly sand, and he turned over, his eyes open. "You get a tattoo, you think what? All's forgiven?"

Ray Boy just looked at him.

Enough with the silence. Conway wanted to hear some begging. He stripped the tape from Ray Boy's mouth.

"You think I should forgive you?" Conway said. "That's really what you think? 'Sorry, man. I was a different person then. I made mistakes.'"

Head shake.

"Say something," Conway said. "Say, 'No.'"

Ray Boy said, "No. I don't think that."

"Good." Conway got over Ray Boy, just stood over him, and aimed the gun down at his face. He held his other hand out as if he'd block the blowback, the brain splatter, something he'd seen in a movie. "You feel Duncan out here? His spirit?"

"I do," Ray Boy said.

"He's happy, I bet." Conway's finger was on the trigger, trying to pull it in, trying to screw a bullet into Ray Boy's eye. If he got the one in, then maybe he could annihilate Ray Boy's whole face, empty the gun into his mouth and forehead and cheeks, so all that was left when he was done would be a stumpy blob of throat and hair. To have Faceless Ray Boy on the shoreline, washed over in the dark with the tide, that'd be a thing to carry him.

But he couldn't make his finger do the work.

Ray Boy just waited. He seemed willing to let him figure it out. Ray Boy said, "I deserve it."

"Shut the fuck up," Conway said. "You wanna die so bad, why didn't you just kill yourself?"

No answer.

"Huh?" Conway said.

"Has to be you," Ray Boy said.

Conway was a pussy. He'd always been a pussy. He was shaking. He was picturing Duncan dead on the Belt, head run over, body mangled and tire-tracked. And here was the guy that did it. Not begging for mercy. Begging for justice, saying Conway had an obligation to execute him. Conway couldn't. No guts to fire. No strength in the hand that he needed to make it happen, his trigger finger gone fishy, his bones melted under his skin. A coward, that's all he was. He stepped back from Ray Boy and put the gun in his waistband.

Ray Boy said, "No."

"I'll leave you out here," Conway said. "Maybe you'll freeze. Or starve."

Again: "No."

Conway turned and rushed back to the car, leaving Ray Boy there in the sand. He got in and drove away in the dark. He panted onto the steering wheel, the windows fogging up. Someone flashed him as he merged back onto the Belt, and he snapped the lights on.

"You gotta be fucking kidding me," McKenna said. "I should've been there."

"I don't know what happened," Conway said.

They were sitting in a booth at Murphy's Irish, the only joint they went to since Teemo started tending bar at The Wrong Number. The place was awful and bright with five TVs showing ESPN and bartenders that could've been Teemo, probably had their own bad histories, greasy, balloon-chested fucks in Nautica gear with Yankee tats on their necks and white date rape caps. But Conway and McKenna didn't know anything about them and could pretend. McKenna had gotten there before Conway and lined up a few shots of Jack and two pitchers of Bud. Conway was feeling the booze, his clothes sweaty even though he was cold. "I just couldn't do it. My hand wouldn't let me." He pounded his shooting hand on the table and then brought down his other fist on top of it. "As good as broken."

"Take it easy," McKenna said. "So you just left him out there?"

"I'm gonna do what else? Give him a ride home?"

"Guy comes after you, what then?"

"He won't." Conway shook his hands out.

"That's for sure?"

"You didn't see him."

"This is fucked." McKenna chugged a cup of beer. "Royally. Now what?"

"Don't know."

"You go back to stocking shelves and Ray Boy gets on the first bus back upstate?" McKenna stopped, scratched his chin. "He stays in the neighborhood, what happens? Christ. Ray Boy back around. Scary thought."

Conway couldn't even consider it.

McKenna said, "I say we go out there now. Few drinks calmed you down. I'm there, I'll do it if you can't."

"He's still out there, you think?"

"He's gonna go where? On the Belt and put out his thumb? Way you tell it, the guy's just waiting to die."

"He is," Conway said, and he stood up, knocking the underside of the table with his knees, sending plastic cups toppling onto the floor.

They were both drunk and McKenna was driving. He got pulled over, he knew what to do. No cop was going to take him in or even give him a ticket. Conway was sweating, the gun clammy against his waist. The defroster in McKenna's car was throwing off steam, slicking the windows over and making the brake lights ahead of them hazy. Another run, another chance to fail.

"I should just use it on myself," Conway said. "I'm the one needs to be put out of my misery."

McKenna said, "Fuck that. What'd this guy do to you? Play some mind game?"

"I off myself, it's all done. That's it."

"You're talking shit now, Con." McKenna wiped the windshield with the back of his sleeve, swiping out a clean view. "I ain't gonna pity you, that's what you want. Get your shit together. You do this or you don't, that's it."

Conway looked down at his lap. He couldn't believe it. A chance, finally, and he turned out to be a full-on chump. All those years of lying to himself.

"You were ready when we left Murph's," McKenna said.

Conway shook his head, tried to will himself to have strength, tried only to think of Duncan, seventeen forever, his blood scabbed over by grit on the Belt.

Back at Plumb Beach, Conway marked the Dumpster again, on his knees, booze-shaky. McKenna looked at him like he was a total fucking whackjob. Conway etched a little claw onto the right foot of his squat, slashy X. Then they walked to the shoreline, Conway leading, gun drawn, McKenna close behind. Marks in the sand where Ray Boy had been but no Ray Boy. Signs of rolling around. Footsteps. Tape he'd shed.

"Fuck me," Conway said.

"Free and roaming," McKenna said. "He played you."

"That's not how it went. I just pussied out." Conway wound up to throw the gun.

"Fuck you doing?" McKenna said, trying to stop him mid-toss with a forearm shiver, but it was too late. Conway let go as McKenna made contact and the .22 went arcing out, landing in the water with a chirp. "You gotta be kidding." McKenna put his arms up over his head.

Conway said, "It's over, dude."

McKenna pushed him. Conway fell backward, landing in Ray Boy's tracks. McKenna huffed, fed up, disappointed.

"I'm sorry," Conway said.

"You're sorry?"

"Sorry I threw the gun away."

McKenna shook his head, walked back to the car.

Conway sat there, propped on his elbows, looked up at the dirty, starless sky. Just a quick cut of moon behind some cashew-shaped clouds. Conway remembered how Duncan would always tilt his head back on nights they sat out on the front stoop and say, "Look at the moon, man, it's beautiful."

Getting up, dusting himself off, Conway walked with no purpose back to the car. McKenna had the radio on loud, didn't want to talk, made throat-cutting signals when Conway offered to drive. McKenna took off with spinning wheels, back into the tragic flow, away from Plumb Beach, the moon staying framed in the back window.

Pop was waiting up, standing at the door, looking out from behind the musty curtain over the glass. Conway could see him from the car. McKenna still had the radio on loud, the engine running, just waiting for Conway to leave. Conway wanted to apologize again, say something, anything, but he just got out of the car and watched McKenna drive away up the block, red lights fizzing out in the distance.

Pop turned off the alarm and came outside. "Been worried sick," he said. His pajama bottoms hung low and he wore a heavy North Face coat, making sure Conway knew it was a lot for him to be outside this time of night.

"Sorry, Pop," Conway said.

"Where you been?"

"Just taking care of some stuff."

"You said you'd get my prescription." Pause. "Stephanie brought it. I should've gone myself."

"Pop, I'm sorry," Conway said, feeling suddenly sore all over, hungover already maybe, or on the sour end of a cheap beer drunk.

"You stink like booze." Pop put a hand on his shoulder and scrunched his nose up.

"I had a few. Let me be, huh?"

"Let you be. I got one son left, I gotta worry."

The guilt trip. Conway couldn't take it. He walked past his old man and went inside. Didn't brush his teeth. Didn't drink water. Just went to his room and flopped on the bed, feeling the headache settle.

It took Pop a few minutes to reset the alarm and close up the house, but then he was hovering over Conway in the bed, saying, "Where you been? Stephanie said she was worried. Said you sounded upset."

"It's nothing, Pop."

Pop paced next to the bed, frantic, spry when he wanted to be. "I'm alone here, what can I do?"

Conway, eyes closed, tried to ignore it. He wanted to dream about something good. But what? Girls? He hardly knew any. He wasn't going to dream about getting a blowjob from Stephanie, that was for sure. Actresses maybe. That cute redhead from the zombie movie he'd just watched. Her legs in those cutoffs. Conway tried to keep the picture of her up in his mind, saw it like a flickering image on an old drive-in movie screen, no sound. Pop's voice killed it, droning on, the old man half-complaining, half-begging. Conway wanted, for once, to say, *Please please please shut the fuck up*, but he didn't have the balls. He never had the balls.

Pop kept going strong: "I'm worried sick over here. I don't know who to call. I'm thinking maybe an accident. I'm looking up numbers to hospitals. Victory's closed. Where they gonna take him, I'm saying. Methodist? Maimonides? I'm sick."

Conway's eyes shot open, the ceiling fluttering. He said, "Please, Pop."

"And you got a big head." Pop sat on the edge of the bed. "That's all. Out drinking. I'm here worried, you're at a watering hole, no worries, no thought for your old man."

"Please."

"Sleep it off. Mass is at 7:30 tomorrow. Or you gonna give up on that?"

"I'll be up," Conway said.

Pop got up, paced some more, and then left the room. "Sleep it off," he said on his way out.

"Night, Pop," Conway said, closing his eyes again, trying to get the picture of the actress back, anything but Ray Boy.

Next morning, at Mass with Pop, Conway felt hammered flat as elephant shit. He hadn't showered or brushed his teeth. He'd peeled himself from the bed and walked to Murphy's Irish to retrieve his car and then went back home to pick up Pop, making them almost ten minutes late for church, walking in on the second reading. He'd taken three aspirins for breakfast, washed them down with Tabasco-spiked tomato juice, and tried to eat a piece of toast but found he couldn't. His stomach was all knotted up. He had a tightness in his chest, too, like what asthma probably felt like. And he kept seeing Ray Boy everywhere he looked. Ray Boy just out walking. Ray Boy in passing cars. On the bus. Leaving a deli with the *Post* folded under his arm, blowing on a steaming cup of coffee. Ray Boy, alive in everything.

Eyes going squiggly, temples pounding, Conway looked around the church, trying to zone out on something. Only about fifteen other people were there. Mostly old timers. No one to mistake for Ray Boy. One woman, his age maybe, wore sunglasses and a scarf in her black hair and didn't belong to the scene. She looked familiar. He wanted to nudge Pop, *who's that*, but held off, going through an internal Rolodex of jerk-off material from the past. Had he gone to school with her?

When Mass was over, Father Villani greeting people on their way out, Conway's eyes followed Scarf and Sunglasses, trying to place her. She put her small hand in Villani's and spoke to him for a moment.

Outside, Pop was itching to get in the car. He'd walked right past Villani, never liking to shake hands with the priest on the way out, and Conway had followed him. Lapdog.

He looked back over his shoulder at Scarf and Sunglasses, her neck arched now, buttoning up her soft coat, no wrinkles on it, straight and clean like in the store.

"Hold up a sec, Pop," Conway said.

Pop wasn't happy about it but he went over to the car and waited, arms crossed, sitting on the hood.

Conway made a move toward the woman, not wanting to be a coward, wanting to say, *Where do I know you from?* Smooth, like that. But he stood in front of her, gawking. She was even prettier up close. "Hey," he said.

"Sorry, man," she said, trying to walk away.

"What's your name?"

"Listen." She took off her sunglasses and eyed him with suspicion. "It's too early for this."

He said, "I'm Conway."

"D'Innocenzio?"

"I do know you?"

"Alessandra. From Most Precious Blood."

"Holy shit."

"I was just," she said, putting her glasses back on, "I was just out visiting my mother's grave and I saw . . . I mean, I was just thinking . . ." She trailed off with what she was saying.

"It's been forever."

"Last night I hung out with Stephanie Dirello."

"I work with Steph."

"What she said."

"I heard you were out west. Where's your dad? You were with your dad, I would've known it was you right away."

"He doesn't come to church anymore. Wanted me to go, though. Figured it was the least I could do, go to church for him. I haven't been to church since high school. It's weirder than I remember."

Conway tried to play it cool. He said, "I come for my old man. Least I could do, too." It all came back to him then. Grade school. Sitting behind Alessandra for years. Her in her uniform. Olive skin. Black hair. Little feet. Root beer eyes. Always turning around to say something to him, to laugh, him doing the latest *Saturday Night Live* bit, her loving it, saying he was so funny. All those years, him going home, writing in marble notebooks over and over and over again, *C hearts A, C hearts A, C hearts A*. His biggest crush from grade school. His only crush really, not counting Dana Zimmardi in first grade. Alessandra, shit, right here in front of him now, not knowing what a coward he was, but knowing he worked at a fucking Rite Aid, and her an actress. He had no shot, none at all. *Just tuck your dick between your legs and drive your daddy home, chump.*

"I got home yesterday," Alessandra said.

"Crazy. For how long?"

"I don't know. A bit."

"I'm sorry, I'm . . . I heard about your mother."

"Thanks, yeah. I was just saying, I was . . . I was out there visiting her at Holy Garden."

"Holy Garden?"

"I saw Duncan's . . . I mean, I paid my respects to Duncan. I didn't remember he was out there."

Conway ignored it, not wanting to think about Duncan or Ray Boy right now, just wanting to think about Alessandra's killer body. "Crazy, crazy, crazy."

"Well, I'm happy I ran into you."

"You want to, maybe, go get a slice one day? Catch up?"

"Maybe," she said. "Let me see. I'm kind of unsettled, but yeah, probably I could do that."

Conway nodded, her being nice, he could tell, not really wanting to catch up beyond this. "You know where I work. Steph's got my number."

She smiled, white teeth like a commercial, and said, "Bye now."

Conway walked back to the car, his old man about to explode, sick of waiting, tired of breaking routine.

"They're gonna be out of papers," Pop said, as if Augie's would sell out of the *Daily News* in five minutes.

"Sorry, Pop," Conway said. "That was Alessandra Biagini. From MPB. You remember her?"

"I don't remember her. Who wears sunglasses in church?"

"Yeah, I don't know," Conway said, wanting to follow Alessandra as she walked the few blocks to her house, knowing maybe he would've if Pop wasn't around, just wanting one more look.

"Pretty girl, though," Pop said, softening.

Conway, casting Alessandra in his mind's newest movie, something about her and him locked in a thrashing fuck session in the confessional box, said, "No joke."

4

Eugene was in Augie's Deli. He tried to look like he was shopping for Ring Dings and Doritos and Gatorade, but Augie—with his big hairy hands and drooping chin—was on heavy-duty lookout, knowing Eugene would swipe whatever he could get his hands on. Spaldeens, Bazooka, porn mags. It was hard for Eugene to be any kind of graceful with his limp. Hard not to creak and claw through the aisles. Not to mention his headphones thudding. Eugene bopped his head to Scarface's "Guess Who's Back," a joint from back when he was in second grade, and Augie tracked him by the sound even when he disappeared behind the tallest racks. The only shot Eugene had at getting away with anything was if Augie got distracted with another customer, some Chinese girl buying Now and Laters or an old man like Tommy DeLuca from the corner coming in and ordering a deli sandwich. Right now it was just him and Augie.

Augie said, "You getting anything today?"

Eugene sniffed, wiped his nose with the back of his sleeve. He pulled his headphones down around his neck. "What's up?"

"You buying anything?"

"Maybe."

"Buy something or get out," Augie said, stomping out from behind the counter.

Eugene grabbed his nuts and yanked. "Suck my dick."

"Get out," Augie said.

"Make me."

Augie got red in the face. He looked like he was about to have a heart attack. He reached around on the counter for something to wield as a weapon. He picked up a box cutter and showed it to Eugene.

Eugene said, "You gonna cut me?"

"Get out." Augie moved closer. "I'll call the police."

Eugene laughed. "Six-Two ain't shit."

"Why don't you act how you're supposed to act? Your pants all low. That rap. From the projects, that's what you think?"

Eugene pushed his pants down even further, showing the full fly on his boxers.

"I know your mother. She's proud of what you are?"

"You don't know my moms."

"Get out, you little thug. How old are you? Fifteen? Fifteen and already a thug. You make me sick." Augie put down the box cutter and went back behind the counter. He picked up his cell. "Just like your uncle. Look what happened to him. Same's in store for you. Prison. You're on the road. You ready for that?" He was dialing. "Few years, you'll be in jail, guaranteed."

Eugene threw his fists out and toppled a display. Packaged butter crunch cookies went everywhere, spinning across the sawdusty floors like pucks.

Augie said, "Little prick." Paused. He was on the phone with a dispatcher from the precinct now. "I've got a kid here, little thug, over here at Augie's, you know the place? Little thug's shoplifting, getting ready to, threatening me, knocking stuff over."

"Threatening you?" Eugene said, laughing. He limped out of the store, letting the door clang shut behind him. Outside, he kicked over a rack of newspapers with his good leg and said, "Fuck you," loud enough so Augie could hear him through the front glass, loud enough so people sitting outside Giove's Pizza across the street looked up and shook their heads. Little thug, yeah, the whole neighborhood seeming to nod. "Pull a box cutter on me," Eugene said. "That's some bullshit right there."

Sirens tore up Bath Avenue. The Six-Two was taking Augie's call seriously. Eugene tried to book it up the block, but his leg hitched him up, and he disappeared into an alley next to Mikey Elizondo's house on Bay Thirty-Eighth. He hunched over behind a garbage can and took out his cell. He dialed Sweat Scagnetti, who was probably playing *Call of Duty* in his living room with a gallon of Pepsi and a Nutella sandwich.

Sweat answered with a huff. "What?"

"Pick me up."

"Where you at?"

"Alley next to Mikey Elizondo's. Augie called the cops on me."

"Stupid motherfucker."

"Come get me."

"Chill, I'll be there."

Sweat pulled up in his Mazda ten minutes later, wearing a powder blue XXL cardigan, J. Crew pants, and loafers. His speakers were thumping last year's Jay-Z. He had a Bluetooth in his ear and a stick of pepperoni in butcher's paper in his lap. His father owned a pork store in Long Island City and they lived in Dyker Heights. Ten grand for tuition at Our Lady of the Narrows, where Eugene and Sweat went, was a drop in the bucket for the Scagnettis.

For Eugene, fatherless, living with his mother and aunt, that tuition was a big deal. He heard about it every day, especially when he got in trouble. Less than a month into being a sophomore at OLN, Eugene was sick of the place. The uniform, the preppies, the brothers with their curly hair and big crosses and blue-and-gold sweaters. But he'd lucked into being buddies with Sweat, who was driving at fifteen with no license. His mother and father had given him the okay. No biggie, they said. Rich bastards. Sweat gave Eugene hand-me-down iPods and phones and video game systems, getting the newest stuff as it came out.

Eugene got in the car, head down, slumping in the seat. He slapped hands with Sweat, whose squat fingers glistened with pepperoni grease.

"Where we going?" Sweat said.

Eugene said, "Wherever. Coney?"

Sweat swung the car away from the curb, not even checking to see if anyone was coming, and then made a left onto Cropsey.

"You see cops back by Augie's?" Eugene said.

"One car. Just a guy talking to Augie. Didn't look like they were gonna send out the dogs. What'd you do?"

"Nothing. Bullshit. Dude pulled a fucking box cutter on me. We should go back there, fuck the store up, Molotov cocktail right through the window."

"They'll know it's you."

"I give a shit?"

Sweat parked over by Gargiulo's, his wheels up on the curb, and they got out and headed for the Boardwalk. It was pretty cold, low fifties, and the streets were mostly empty. A couple of guys were hustling at an empty pay phone bank. Old Russians were scattered on benches by the ramps up to the Boardwalk, shopping carts scissored at their feet, this weather beautiful to them. The sky was gray, mangled-looking.

Eugene was always embarrassed walking with Sweat because of the way he dressed and that Bluetooth. But the benefits outweighed the bullshit. Sweat was always quick to pay Eugene's way for hot dogs, freak shows, arcades.

Eugene knew Sweat felt the same way about him. With his bad limp, he looked like he'd been shot. He was almost a bad enough crip that people stopped and stared. The limp was something he developed as a kid, something about his hip actually, the bones not developing correctly on his left side. His whole life he'd heard about it. They called him Limp or Gimp in grade school, Crip, Frankenstein, Fuck Leg, Drag. He always lied about it now that he was in high school. Told people he *did* get shot as a kid. Drive-by attempt on him and his mother outside Martin's Paints. Kids started to buy it, saying wow and holy shit. So Eugene developed the story further. The Russian mob was after his mother for a loan she took out. He was unfortunate enough to catch a bullet meant for her. The docs said it was a miracle he lived, the bullet missed an artery by *this much*. It got so he enjoyed telling the story. He was even starting to believe it himself.

"Fuck we gonna do?" Sweat said.

"Talk to Lutz lately?" Eugene said.

"You can only hit that so many times."

"Yeah, but."

"True."

"Call her, tell her get one of her friends over, we'll have a party, whatever."

Eugene had lost his cherry at eleven to a girl with a lazy eye named Cindy, a seventeen year old who hung out in the Cavallaro schoolyard and smoked cigarettes on the swings. Then there'd been Denise and Dyana, twin sisters who liked to tag-team Eugene. Sweat had introduced him to Lutz a couple of weeks after starting at OLN and she had an endless supply of friends. Eugene was learning to last. He was taking five, maybe ten minutes to shoot out in his rubber.

Sweat was on the phone with Lutz in a second, saying, "It's Sweat. Me and Eugene. Little while. Your friend there?"

"Ask her to get the one with freckles," Eugene said.

"The one with freckles," Sweat said. "Quincy? Yeah, okay." He shrugged. "In a few then." Hung up.

"It her?"

"I don't know. Whatever."

They walked the few blocks to Lutz's apartment building, part of the Monsignor Burke complex across from the aquarium. She buzzed them in.

When they got upstairs, Lutz opened the door. Her hair was piled on her head in curls, her makeup fresh. Eugene could see Quincy behind her, sitting at the kitchen table, not the one he wanted, but not bad. He could feel a great swath of warmth coming from the apartment, the heater going full blast in there.

"Hey guys," Lutz said. "Come in."

Sweat and Eugene walked in, getting swallowed up by the warmth.

About an hour later, back in Sweat's car, Eugene was looking at himself in the mirror on the passenger visor. His cheeks were red and splotchy. "Feel like I been attacked by a lion," he said.

"Where you wanna go?" Sweat said.

Eugene shrugged.

"Home then." Sweat hunched over the wheel. "I got dinner soon."

"Whatever, yo."

They rode in silence back to Eugene's house. Sweat turned up the music with a button on his steering wheel. The speakers went buzzy. The windows down, they moved their heads to some Raekwon.

Sweat pulled up on the curb behind Eugene's mother's '95 Ford Explorer with its faded *Rudy for President* bumper sticker. Blue plastic was taped over the broken back window.

Eugene and Sweat slapped hands, and Eugene said, "Peace."

Sweat turned the music up even louder and nodded.

Eugene got out and walked down the alley next to his house, kicking a coiled hose out of the way, and he went in the back door on the deck. It was the only way he ever went in. His mother and aunt liked to keep the front door permanently locked. On the deck, tomato plants were growing in an old wrought-iron, clawfoot tub and dusty, rain-damaged deck chairs sat overturned. Eugene could hear something going on in the house. He wasn't sure what. People were talking. He heard a guy's voice that he didn't recognize, and then he heard his grandmother and grandfather.

He walked in. His Uncle Ray Boy was sitting at the kitchen table, drinking coffee and eating a grilled cheese. Eugene stopped and took it in. His grandparents sat on either side of Uncle Ray Boy, and his mother and Aunt Elaine were standing by the sink, lit up, so happy.

"Yo," Eugene said.

"You okay?" his mother said. "You look flushed."

"I'm fine."

"You remember Uncle Ray Boy, right?"

"Course." Eugene hadn't been born when Uncle Ray Boy went to jail, but he'd been with his mother to visit him in jail a couple of times. His mother didn't like the idea of taking him there, but she'd had to once when he was six because she couldn't find someone to watch him. The other time, when he was ten, she just got into her head that he needed to get to know his uncle. He was also already getting into trouble in school at that point so she wanted him to know what could happen to him.

Truth was his Uncle Ray Boy had become a hero to him. There was a lot of mythology surrounding him in the neighborhood. Stories of how wild he was. Some people thought he got a raw deal—he didn't really kill the kid after all—and that he should've been out, back up to his old tricks, way sooner. Sixteen years. Fuck. Eugene was a year away from being sixteen. That was a lifetime. Once, Eugene had found pictures in his mother's closet of Uncle Ray Boy looking like a badass in a wife-beater with girls in leather jackets on his arms, hair slicked back, smoking unfiltered Marlboro Reds. The pictures came from a time that didn't even seem real. The early Nineties. There were more snaps of Uncle Ray Boy at Yankee games, sitting on the hoods of long, solid cars, playing stickball in the P.S. 101 schoolyard.

"Hey Eugene," Uncle Ray Boy said. "You're big." He was wearing funny clothes, a loose T-shirt and too-big sweatpants. He wasn't dressed tough at all. But he was cut, Eugene could tell, and tatted up and his face was scraped like he'd been in a fight.

"You're back?" Eugene said.

"For a little while."

"Hell yeah." Eugene sat across from his uncle at the table. He said hey to his grandparents. They looked like they'd been put back together, their three kids and one grandkid all in the same room. A family.

"So, how's things?" Uncle Ray Boy said.

"Solid," Eugene said. "What happened to your face?"

"Nothing."

"He won't say," Eugene's mother said.

Eugene said, "How was the joint?"

Uncle Ray Boy laughed. "The joint?" Paused. "Joint sucked, man." Moving away from it. "How's the leg? I remember you had something wrong with it."

Eugene thought, *This guy busting my balls right now?*

"It's okay," Eugene's mother said. "It's been a lot of trouble. Eugene doesn't like to talk about it."

Eugene said, "Just a little limp. I get by."

"How's school?" Uncle Ray Boy said. "What grade you in?"

"Sophomore."

"OLN?"

"We wanted him to go to Catholic school," Eugene's mother said. "Lafayette's a mess. Metal detectors. Across the street's the projects. It's even worse than it was. But OLN's very expensive now."

"OLN sucks ass," Eugene said.

Grandma Jean reached across the table and slapped the back of his hand. "Gene, language," she said.

"It's a very nice school," his mother said. "All the money we spend on it, you need to take advantage, Eugene."

Eugene shrugged. "No girls," he said.

Uncle Ray Boy said, "I went to OLN. I liked it okay."

"Maybe if you went to Lafayette," Eugene said, "maybe you wouldn't have," and then he stopped talking, realizing what he was saying, what he was bringing up.

Uncle Ray Boy said nothing, just sat there playing with the crust of his grilled cheese.

Eugene's mother tried to reel things back in. "You're gonna stay here, right?" she said to Uncle Ray Boy. "Or you gonna stay with Mommy and Daddy?"

"He'll stay with us," Grandma Jean said. "Of course he will."

"Just for a couple days," Uncle Ray Boy said.

"How was the house upstate?" Grandma Jean said. "I had this guy from Monticello do some work on it, but you know these cheapskates. Middle Eastern guy."

"House was fine. Is fine. Nice up there. I'd forgotten."

"You never wanted to go up there, not since you were eight or nine."

Uncle Ray Boy was quiet again, looked depressed, defeated, not at all like Eugene imagined he'd be. He'd always pictured his uncle coming back to the neighborhood with sunglasses on, head shaved, pissed for being sent to jail, ready to throw down with the world.

"You gonna tell us how you wound up down here?" Grandpa Tony said, over being happy about his son's presence, now wanting to know what his ulterior motive was.

"I don't want to talk about it."

Aunt Elaine, throwing her arms up behind her head, said, "I picked him up off the Belt in his boxers. He called me from the last pay phone on earth. Collect."

"What is this about?" Grandma Jean said.

"Nothing," Uncle Ray Boy said. He got up, turned to Eugene's mother. "There somewhere I can lie down for a little while, Doreen?"

"Sure, yeah, of course," Eugene's mother said. "My room. Upstairs. First door on the right. Rest. We'll catch up later."

"Thanks for the coffee and the sandwich." Uncle Ray Boy went upstairs, and Eugene heard his mother's door close.

"He's exhausted," Grandma Jean said.

"Is it drugs?" Grandpa Tony said.

"Who knows?" Aunt Elaine said. "What that does to you, who knows? Sixteen years. Might take him a long time to reacclimate."

"It's good he's here," Eugene's mother said. "We need to convince him to stay, not go back upstate. It's better for him to be around his family."

"There's going to be press. That thing just ran in that paper about him."

"He needs his family."

Eugene got up from the table and went down to the basement. He had a room upstairs but he preferred to hang out in the basement. He had a sweet set-up down there. An old school boombox with some discs he'd bought at a Salvation Army—N.W.A. and Ice Cube and Dr. Dre and Snoop Dogg—and he had some weights and some porno mags stashed under an old dresser in the corner of the room next to the washing machine. He went over and turned on the stereo, "Lil' Ghetto Boy" coming on mid-song, and sat down on his weight bench and started to do curls with his fifteen pounders. He might've had a limp but he was planning on being built by junior year. He always felt soft in the locker room, wore his gym clothes under his uniform so he didn't have to be naked for even a second, and he'd had these big dreams to get a six-pack for a long time. Now was time to act on it. He'd been taking Creatine in the mornings and pumping weights for two hours every afternoon. He wanted to talk to Uncle Ray Boy about it, see what he'd done to get the way he was. In prison there was probably nothing to do but lift weights. And get buttfucked by gangbangers. Eugene wondered if that had happened to his uncle, if maybe that was why he looked like he'd been crushed by the world, his asshole just torn to shreds.

No way.

Eugene had seen movies. He knew you did what you had to do to avoid that kind of shit. Took up with skinheads. Whatever. He knew if you were strong enough you could steer clear of trouble.

It had to be something else.

He lifted the weights and then threw them down, not getting the bounce he'd hoped for. They sparked against the cement, seeming almost like they'd bust through to dirt. He was happy his Uncle Ray Boy was home.

5

Alessandra was buzzing, anxious to do something, anything, that didn't involve just sitting in the living room with her old man. They were smoking together. The barrier down now. Just smoking out the house with nothing else to do, the walls already getting that yellowy look. Alessandra was stressed, really feeling the smallness of the neighborhood after running into Conway at church, almost feeling like she conjured him with the visit to Duncan's grave.

"What're your plans for the day?" her father said, picking a piece of tobacco from the corner of his mouth.

"I don't know," she said. "Tomorrow I'm for sure going to the city." Thought about it. "I always hated Sundays. That Sunday feeling, you know."

"Hated Sundays?"

"Just bleak or something."

"The Lord's Day."

Alessandra didn't want to talk to her father about God. She didn't want to tell him what she really believed about the whole magic show, so she changed the subject. "Aunt Cecilia coming over?"

"Maybe," her father said. "She's got a confirmation."

Alessandra wasn't sure where to go next with the conversation, what else to talk about with her old man. The tank was empty. Weather, stories from the *Daily News*, the Yanks—the reserves used up.

They sat in silence for about twenty minutes, Alessandra clicking her nails against the can she was ashing in.

"Time is it?" she finally said, wondering if it was too early to go to the bar.

Her old man looked at his watch. It was like he was trying to make sense of the hands and numbers. Like he'd never looked at the thing before. Never been asked the time.

Alessandra thought, *Fuck it, I'm going to the bar.*

She stood up, putting her cigarette out in the can on the coffee table, ashes sloshing around in flat soda, letting off a sharp, sour stink.

"It's a little after three," her father said.

"Thanks, Daddy, I'm going out for a little while. Couple of hours at the most." Dreaming of a Tom Collins, an Old-Fashioned, a gimlet. Remembering all the great cocktail bars in L.A. and what she'd get there. Best she could hope for at The Wrong Number was a Bloody Mary with well vodka, probably made with some shitballs mix.

Back at the vanity upstairs, she went into doll-up mode. She was hoping to make an impression. She wanted to hear, *Alessandra Biagini, the actress?*

She rang up dorky Stephanie, who was as good as it got. The girl was a sweetheart anyway. She was excited to go out again. Alessandra said she'd meet her on the corner. She didn't want to deal with Mrs. Dirello in her kill-me-please housecoat and slippers again.

After hanging up, she just stared at herself, feeling like she'd run her life far off the rails and wondering if she should just wallow in the mess at the bottom of things. Drink every day at The Wrong Number. Say to hell with work. Become one of these neighborhood ghosts, old alkies in wrinkled black clothes that just skeleton around on feet like broken shopping cart wheels. When it got real bad, she could just dig in trash bins for bottles like the old Chinese, haul them down to Waldbaum's for drinking money, live in this house until her father died and they took it away from her and then she could go to a home, the one over on Cropsey, where she'd wear Salvation Army clothes and lose her hair and teeth in the sink. An actress? Forget it. Once maybe, in another city, another time. Just wispy bones and yellowing skin now. The old boozer that kids throw rocks at for kicks.

Stephanie was waiting on the corner, an embarrassing rainbow shoulder bag—probably got it up on Eighty-Sixth Street at Deal$—slung over her back. Lipstick on her teeth. "It's early for a drink, huh?" she said.

"Sunday," Alessandra said. "Standard rules don't apply."

"Well, it's good to see you again." Stephanie went in for an awkward hug.

Alessandra pulled away and patted her on the back. "Okay, sweetie."

"Maybe we can go to a movie one day?"

"Maybe, sure."

They walked to The Wrong Number, the weather cold but not brutal for September, and Stephanie stayed close to Alessandra, almost tripping her up once.

Teemo was tending bar again. Disgusting. Greased up. Shiny little diamond earrings punched into both lobes. Wearing a skintight Nautica T-shirt, a gold medal on a thick gold chain hanging out across his chest.

Alessandra stood at the bar and ordered a Bloody Mary.

Teemo flexed his pecs under his shirt, made them dance a little. "Bloody Mary, what's that?" he said.

"You don't know what a Bloody Mary is?" Alessandra said.

"Maybe you know too much, hon."

Hon. She shook her head. "You've been tending bar how long?"

"What do you want?"

"Give me a gin-and-tonic." She turned to Stephanie. "Ginger ale?"

"I'll get the same as you," Stephanie said. "Live dangerously."

Alessandra smiled. "Two," she said, and she watched Teemo make the drinks. He poured the gin with a weak hand and went too heavy on the tonic. He forgot to put limes in.

He set them on coasters in front of Alessandra and took way too long to calculate a total. "Six bucks," he said.

Alessandra paid for it with a ten. Didn't tip when she got the change. "Could we please please get some limes?" she said.

He pawed out a couple of lime wedges from the tray over the sink and handed them to Alessandra on a cocktail napkin. "Anything else, princess?"

Alessandra took the limes and drinks and ignored Teemo. She led Stephanie to the same table they'd been at the night before. Sitting down, she said, "Can't believe they let him serve here. Doesn't know what the hell he's doing."

"I know," Stephanie said, leaning close.

"We've got to find another bar."

"Exactly." She paused and looked around. "So, how was day two?"

"Dull. I don't know. It's hard. I feel sorry for my father, but it's really hard." Stephanie nodded.

"Your mom knows you're out?" Alessandra said.

A laugh caught in Stephanie's throat. She lifted the gin-and-tonic and took a baby sip. "Kind of," she said. "I lied. She didn't want me to go out with you."

"How old are you?"

"No, I know. It's embarrassing. But it's the way it is."

"You need to get out from under that, Steph. You can't live your whole life that way."

Something about Alessandra calling Stephanie "Steph" made her face light up. "No, I know, it's crazy, *fucking* crazy," like she'd never said the word, "but it's so good to have you here, you know. I've never really had to think about this stuff. Life's pretty quiet. I go to work, I go home, my mother doesn't say boo."

"I'm just saying. Don't let it get out of hand. Her controlling you. Trying. That's bad shit."

"I know. It's over. Maybe I'll get my own place." She stopped. "Hey, maybe we can—"

Alessandra realized what light bulb had just gone off in Stephanie's mind and wanted to put a kibosh on it fast. "No, well, I . . . I don't think, I'm just not sure."

"I'm saying maybe we can be roomies. Find our own place. In the neighborhood. Wherever. We could get cable, a futon, have little dinner parties."

Alessandra said, "Maybe. We'll see."

"It'd be so fun. I'm gonna start looking."

"I'm not sure, Steph. I was thinking Manhattan. A studio."

"Manhattan's so expensive. Maybe Williamsburg? Everyone lives in Williamsburg now. It'll be fun. We'll live near a market. I'll make dinner every night. Broccoli rabe and chicken cutlets. Pasta with my mom's gravy. I'm a good cook, you'll see." Stephanie put out her drink to cheers Alessandra.

Alessandra realized what she was hooking herself into but said fuck it. The gin was taking hold a little and Stephanie was sweet. She was Alessandra's only friend at home. Whatever. She tapped her glass against Stephanie's. Anything was better than being cooped up with her old man.

Alessandra, Steph, Teemo, and a couple of old barflies back by the pinball machine were the only people in the bar, so when the door got pushed open they all looked up. Five guys came in. Four of them were dressed like Teemo. The other one looked ragged in old jeans and a torn hoodie.

Teemo came out from behind the bar and just stood in front of the guy who wasn't dressed like him. "Holy shit," Teemo said.

Stephanie leaned across the table and said, "You know who that is, right?"

Alessandra looked again. She saw something in his face she remembered, but the guy was muscled up and looked half-homeless in those ratty clothes. "Can't be," she said.

The guy wasn't smiling. Just standing there in front of Teemo.

"Ray Boy Calabrese," Stephanie said. "In the flesh. The guy next to him, with the goatee, that's Andy Tighe." Stephanie wagged her finger on the sly. "And that's Bruno Amonte, Iggy Lavignani, and Ernie DiPaola."

Teemo looked like he was about to melt down. He bear hugged Ray Boy. "Fucking dude," he said. "It's good to see you."

Ray Boy wasn't hugging back.

The guy Stephanie had pointed out as Andy Tighe stepped into a three-way hug with Ray Boy and Teemo. Alessandra remembered Andy now. How could she forget with those thin sideburns and that sculpted goatee. Fatter now. Puckery nipples visible through his pink Nike shirt. Love handles that pressed against the tightness of the shirt. But he still had those watery blue eyes and that tiny mouth.

"This fuck didn't want to come out," Andy Tighe said to Teemo. "I hear from his aunt he's home, I'm like what the fuck, you kidding me? This guy's home, *home*, back in the neighborhood, and we ain't his first call? I went over there and dragged him out." He put a hand on Ray Boy's shoulder and Ray Boy seemed to shrink at his touch.

"I'm not back for good," Ray Boy said. "Just a few days."

"Still," Andy Tighe said.

Teemo let go and Ray Boy backed out of the hug. "It's good to see you, man," Teemo said. "It's really good."

Ray Boy nodded.

"What do you want to drink?"

"Nothing, thanks."

"Off the sauce, huh?"

"Long time without it."

"Then take a seat."

Ray Boy sat at the bar. Every move he made said he didn't want to be

there. Andy, Bruno, Iggy, and Ernie pulled up on stools next to him. Teemo
went back behind the bar and started pouring screwdrivers. These guys, this
crew, drinking screwdrivers like a bunch of old bags at brunch. Not proper
cocktails, not even beer. Alessandra was floored.

Alessandra and Stephanie just kept staring. The Ray Boy Alessandra
remembered was in there somewhere. But he was hardened. Older. He was
dressed like a bum but his body hadn't gone to shit like the other guys.
No Sunday dinners in jail, she figured. Probably nothing to do but pump
weights and play hoops, dream of fresh mozzarella and warm semolina
bread.

She remembered one time, in high school, just staring at him as he sat on
the hood of his car outside Kearney in his mechanic's jacket, talking to Mary
Parente and Jenny Hughes. He was playing with them. Grabbing at them
and untucking their blouses. She wanted to be somebody he wanted the
way he wanted Mary and Jenny and the rest of the hot juniors and seniors.
What she remembered most about Ray Boy was his confidence, the way he
sat on the hood of his car like nothing could take him down. He was one
of those guys that just exuded don't-fuck-with-me charm. The world bowed
down to him. Mothers cooked for him. Girls spread their legs. His car never
broke down. He always had a perfect haircut, smokes, guido cologne that
somehow wasn't too overpowering. Looked something like a young Ray
Liotta with a dash of DeNiro mixed in.

Teemo, Andy Tighe, and the other guys huddled around Ray Boy and
caught up. They were talking loud, about jail mostly. Ray Boy wasn't doing
any of the talking. Teemo said if that little fag hadn't run out into traffic they
would have had their twenties to go wild. Ray Boy seemed to tense up. He
said, "Shut up about that."

"You're gonna say that homo didn't ruin our lives?" Teemo said.

Ray Boy stood up and walked out of the bar.

Alessandra sucked down the rest of her drink. "Let's go," she said. "Now."
She tugged Stephanie out of the booth and they headed for the door.

Alessandra heard Teemo grumbling under his breath about Ray Boy but didn't really understand what he was saying.

Outside, she looked around for Ray Boy and saw him walking away up the block, his hoodie pulled over his head.

"What're we doing?" Stephanie said.

"I don't know," Alessandra said. She took out a cigarette her father had rolled for her and lit it. What was that they'd witnessed? Regret? He was so different than his old crew. "Shit, I don't know."

Back home, after dropping off Stephanie at the corner by her house, Alessandra was in bed in the dark. She thought about Ray Boy in high school, just the way he looked, and slipped her hand into the waistband of her underwear. But then the thought creeped her out. Duncan's face popped up. Then the phrase *hate crime*. That killed the buzz between her legs.

She got up and went downstairs. It wasn't even six yet.

She turned on the TV. News. Nothing.

Her old man was in the kitchen. He was smoking and playing solitaire. Nipping at the wine that was left. "I'm going for a walk," Alessandra said. "Mind if I bum some smokes?"

He withdrew four already-rolled cigarettes from his pouch and handed them to her. "Be careful," he said. "Lot of crazies out there."

She patted him on the shoulder.

She took a scarf out of the cubby by the front door, one that must've belonged to her mother, and put on her warmer coat, vintage taupe with brown piping and great seaming detail. She'd gotten it on Etsy from some seller in Pasadena before heading home. This was perfect weather to wear it.

The house where Ray Boy grew up was only a few blocks away. Alessandra thought there was no harm in passing by.

She walked under the El to get there and then cut across the street as she got closer, recognizing the green two-family frame house. Pine tree in the yard. Rotting front porch. Hadn't changed all that much. No sign of Ray

Boy. She half-hoped to see him sitting out on the front porch, smoking. The porch was empty, full of overturned chairs and dead plants.

Figuring she'd check out his sister's house next, just a block over, Alessandra turned the corner. The Laundromat she remembered being there was closed down, turned into some kind of sketchy-looking bargain bakery.

Ray Boy's sister's house was an ugly place with a big concrete lion at the foot of the driveway and a tacky fountain in the front yard next to a Mary statue with a chipped-off nose. Alessandra scanned the windows for some sign of him.

Maybe he was just out walking like her.

It was dark out, and Alessandra wasn't used to just walking around anymore. She never did shit like that in L.A.

She took a right on Bath Avenue, thinking she'd go down to the water. She used to watch her old man fish down there, casting out into the bay with a bucket of bait at his side, drinking cans of Schlitz. On the promenade that ran from Ceasar's Bay Bazaar to the Sixty-Ninth Street Pier under the Verrazano they'd stake out different spots and she'd sit on graffitied benches and watch him. She'd also count rats. Sometimes she'd look over the railing at the rocks and see dead rats. She wouldn't count those but she'd be fascinated by their guts and their squashed eyes. She'd watch boats pass under the Verrazano, afraid they wouldn't fit.

She passed the tennis courts where she took lessons as a girl. Not really lessons. It was a summer tennis camp, and she never really learned how to play. Wound up drinking forties and smoking cigarettes with the instructors instead. She hooked up with a boy, Dominic D'Amato, at that camp. And she came to the conclusion that tennis was for Southerners and Europeans.

Walking in the dark didn't seem safe. She passed a Wendy's with some kids huddled outside and thought this was the scene in the movie where the stupid lonely girl gets jumped, knifed across the throat. God forbid. What was she trying to catch up with Ray Boy for anyway? Guy made her sick on so many levels. But he still had those sharp good looks despite the sorry clothes and she kept thinking there was something about the way he was back there at The Wrong Number. She ran into him, what was she going to say? *You rehabilitated? Wanna come back to my place?*

All that was really going on here was she needed to get laid. It'd been too long. Three months since Mindy. Four since Minor. If she could just let loose, maybe she could settle down for a few days. But Ray Boy Calabrese?

When she saw Ray Boy sitting on a bench at the far end of the tennis courts, smoking, she couldn't believe it. Just her luck to actually find him. Now she had to decide whether or not she was really going to talk to this ex-con, this murderer, this homophobe.

She passed in front of Ray Boy and looked at him, huddled, hood still up, drawing in deep on his cigarette. He noticed her. Didn't say anything.

"You're Ray Boy?" she said.

Still didn't say anything. Just sat there, smoking his cigarette down to the filter and then tossing it off in the direction of the courts. Tired. Broken.

"I'm Alessandra," she said. She was nervous like she was back in the Kearney days, trying to say something to too-cool-for-her Ray Boy, back before she had a body, anything, back when she sweated Mary Parente. The way Mary wore her tights, her skirts, buttons open on her blouse, the way she talked, chewed gum, smoked cigs, hummed against Ray Boy's neck with her tongue—Alessandra wanted to be her. Feeling like that kid again, even for a second, made her want to puke. "Forget it, I'm sorry."

Still nothing from Zombie Ray Boy. Prison quiet.

She started to walk away and then stopped. "What happened back there?" she said. "You seemed upset by what your buddies were saying."

"They're not my buddies," Ray Boy said, looking up.

"They're not?"

"Listen, what do you want?"

"I don't want anything."

"Then leave me alone." He lit another cigarette.

"Sorry," Alessandra said. She bowed her head, embarrassed. She headed back the way she came and wondered if he'd call her back over to apologize. But he said nothing. She looked over her shoulder at him. He wasn't the same as everyone else. He was ruined past the point of repair.

Ray Boy got up and started walking in the other direction, toward the Verrazano.

Alessandra lost him in the darkness and walked away from the water slowly, her head down.

Alessandra wandered up and down blocks she hadn't walked since high school on the way home and found another bar. Murphy's Irish. It looked like some nightmare sports bar. Techno blared and ESPN was up on all the screens. She went in anyway. The one gin-and-tonic hadn't done enough for her. And now, fresh from being turned away by Ray Boy, she wanted to pick someone up. But what were her options? Where did you go after being ignored by Ray Boy Calabrese? Running to the arms of some chubby plumber, all ass crack and double chins? Or to some manic depressive electrician with back hair? Weren't many rungs on the ladder lower than the hate crime-perpetrating, hangdog ex-con. She was open to women, but here they were scarier than the men: balding, scraggly, leathery from tanning beds.

She sat on a duct-taped stool at the bar and ordered a gimlet from the bartender. He had too much gel in his hair. He didn't know what a gimlet was. Even if he did or even if she told him how to make it, it would be terrible. The guy wouldn't have the ambition to use real limes instead of Rose's. She was desperately missing her L.A. bartenders again. She figured she'd have to go Downtown Brooklyn or to Manhattan. Here it was just dough-eyed guidos that couldn't even yank a beer the right way. She thought twice, running through a list of what this guy could maybe pull off. Martini? Probably not. Manhattan? Doubtful. She just ordered a double Beefeater on the rocks, going all in, figuring she'd try to make herself blurry drunk to dull the shittiness of everything around her.

"What kind of music you into?" the bartender said.

She worked on her double Beefeater and didn't answer him.

The guy shrugged and went back to other end of the bar, pouring a drink for a guido who could've been his twin.

There wasn't anyone in the bar she could find any hope in. Couple of tight T-shirt jokers on the Megatouch. A bearded dude eating mangled fries at the bar and washing them down with a wet-labeled Coors Light. A table of Russians acting way too Russian. Clammy waitresses who looked prego or drugged out.

Better to go home and dream of Ray Boy as he was in high school. Just focus on his face, his eyes, the mechanic's jacket. Block everything—even poor Duncan—out.

She downed the double gin and ordered another. She tipped the bartender for keeping quiet. Then she got up and walked home. A little gin stagger in her step now. The El overhead didn't seem real.

6

Conway had gotten off his shift at Rite Aid, the whole day passing in a hangover blur, and he was driving around in his Civic with a paper cup of coffee that was burning his hand, when he saw Ray Boy trudging along. It took him a second because Ray Boy had his hoodie up. Conway followed him down to the water. He parked near Best Buy and hoofed it. He kept at a safe distance and ducked behind a fence on the other side of the tennis courts. Ray Boy sat on a bench and lit a cigarette. Conway couldn't believe it, couldn't fucking believe it, when he saw Alessandra Biagini walk up to Ray Boy, somber and respectful, like she was presenting the gifts to the monsignor during Mass. He couldn't see what they were saying to each other, but his blood was rattling, and he wanted to charge them. He wanted to throw Ray Boy down. Maybe even throw Alessandra down.

When Alessandra left, he thought about following her, but he didn't. He wanted to keep tabs on Ray Boy, who was walking in the dark to the bridge.

Conway walked parallel to Ray Boy, staying behind the tennis courts and little league fields as long as he could. Then there was no cover, so he hung back and walked in place until Ray Boy was about a hundred paces ahead.

Conway had come down here the night Duncan was killed. He'd walked the whole length of the promenade back and forth until the sun came up, proving that the world wasn't going to be dark for the rest of time.

He and Duncan had come down to the water often as kids, riding their bikes to and from the Sixty-Ninth Street Pier, weaving in and out of the bike lane, sweeping by pedestrians, tossing rocks out into the water from their bikes, trying not to lose balance, swerving to avoid smashed rats. Duncan loved to stop once they got under the Verrazano and look out at the Narrows, small boats and big boats dotting the water, and tell Conway stories about killer whirlpools that would suck you down if you ever fell into the water. Conway always asked how deep it was and Duncan always had different answers. A hundred feet. A thousand feet. Neverendingly deep. Duncan said the water got blacker and blacker the deeper you went and that there were whole races of albino fish that lived down there, white-skinned with beady yellow eyes. If they stood there long enough, Duncan would start to talk about all the people who jumped off the bridge. He'd imagine out loud what it'd be like to hit the water, probably like hitting cement leaping from that height, what it'd do to your insides. Conway never got tired of listening to his brother talk.

His father used to come down here, too. Just about every day after Duncan died and before his mom ran off. Conway would follow him, the way he was following Ray Boy now, until his father collapsed on a bench, no walk left in him. He'd feed the pigeons, sprinkling stale Italian bread at his feet, wanting the pigeons close to him. Sometimes they'd land on him. It was like pictures Conway had seen of Venice, tourists posing with pigeons on their shoulders and heads. But for Conway's father it was more about being in hell. That only lasted two or three weeks. Eventually, the old man made a sad fort of the house, hardly ever left.

Before Conway knew what was happening, Ray Boy was doubling back toward him. Conway tried to find cover, but there wasn't any. Ray Boy was in his face almost before he could blink. "You need a manual?" Ray Boy said.

"Huh?" Conway said.

"We can go somewhere. I'll draw you a map. Whatever you need."

"Why don't you just kill yourself?"

"I need you to do it."

"Why?"

Nothing.

"Why?" Conway said again.

"It's what you want, isn't it?"

Conway nodded.

Ray Boy said, "So I need you to do it. It's pretty simple why, I think. However I can accommodate you, let me know. You can't do it, you feel like you can't do it, I understand that. You're not cut out for it. Fine. Pretend you are. Just for a minute. Thirty seconds. Less. That's all it takes. Pretend you got it in you."

Conway said nothing.

"You want, we'll go back upstate. Hawk's Nest. Put me in the trunk, and we'll go back up. You're afraid of getting in trouble maybe? You won't. We'll put plastic down in the cellar. I'll show you what to do. How to silence the shot. I'll show you where to bury me. There's two hundred acres up the hill behind that house. Trees. Cold ground. Animals. That's it. I'll show you the spot to put me in the ground. I'll help you dig the hole before, you want. Then we go back to the house, do it, bring me back to the hole in a wheelbarrow, dump me in. The hole will be deep. I can't help you fill it back in. That'll take some time. Or we just do it out there in the woods to begin with."

"Your family?"

"My family what?"

"They'll look for you. Figure it's me maybe."

"I'll write them a note, say I'm gone forever. To wherever. They won't question it."

"You know for sure?"

"I'll make it so they don't."

Conway said, "What did Alessandra Biagini want with you?"

"Who?"

"Girl came up to you on the bench. Alessandra."

"I don't know. I don't know her. Nothing. This a plan?"

"She didn't say anything?"

"She wanted a cigarette."

Conway was hung up on the image of Alessandra talking to Ray Boy. But maybe it was just him putting a spin on it that wasn't there. Could've been a coincidence. Long shot, though.

"It's a plan," Conway said, and he turned and started to walk away.

"Let's go now," Ray Boy said. "I want you to do it now."

"No, I'll let you know when," Conway said. "I'll be in touch."

He drove around the neighborhood, looking for Alessandra. Alessandra Biagini. It was crazy that she sat in front of him all those years in grade school. Pure luck. There was nobody in their homeroom that had a last name starting with C. So there was Alessandra with her small back and dark hair just a foot from him. Sometimes he'd wanted to reach out and touch her hair with its melon shampoo smell. Other times he'd just get lost looking at her neck if she had her hair up, her olive skin, never any pimples like the other girls had. She'd turn around and smile at him, ask him for homework or something, and she had these teeth, shiny white, and these lips that looked freshly-glossed all the time. She chewed gum outside of class, peppermint, and she always had Binaca in class, spraying it on her tongue and then letting out a little sigh. Conway would try to sneak looks between the buttons of her white blouse, catching flashes of flowered pink training bras in fifth and sixth grade and regular-seeming bras, white and black, in seventh and eighth. The way she wore her uniform, the checkered plaid skirt with tights underneath, the white blouse and red tie, neck button never buttoned, soft cardigans in the winter with darker and thicker tights, kept Conway up nights in grade school. He couldn't draw, but a few times—sitting on his bed on lonesome afternoons, Duncan at some after-school activity, Mom volunteering at the church, Pop at work—Conway tried to draw Alessandra in her uniform, filling pages in spiral notebooks, never getting it right. When it went on for too long he'd try to draw her naked. He was even worse at that, giving her saggy old lady boobs and jutting hips, lumpy legs, a blocky circle head balanced on a peanut of a neck. He'd tear up the drawings and deposit them in garbage cans around the neighborhood, pieces here and pieces there, on different corners.

No sign of Alessandra. He had the radio off now and was thinking about how Ray Boy made it all sound so easy. He drove by Alessandra's house. He remembered where her family lived because he'd walked by their house every day as a kid, hoping that one day the shade would be up in Alessandra's window and she'd be changing, giving him a private show, a little striptease, putting her hair up and puckering out her lips, spraying Binaca on her tongue.

He thought about knocking on Alessandra's door and telling her his whole sob story, about how life had been since Duncan died: fucking up, going off the rails, Rite Aid.

An actress. She'd reach out with sympathy? She'd offer her shampoo smells and Binaca breath to him, a shelf-stocker, a shitheel in a dirty booze-stinking shirt and thrift store coat, living with his old man in a flop house of failure and regret? She'd do that? Doubtful.

She was what, impressed by Ray Boy, by his turn-around? Maybe that's why she was talking to him. Maybe she had some Hollywood sense of this guy deserving a new start.

Conway drove away, passing Stephanie Dirello's house. Her whackjob mother was outside, sweeping up the front walk in her housedress.

———

McKenna called and wanted to get a drink at Murphy's Irish. Conway headed straight there. McKenna was waiting for him in the same booth as the night before. They slapped five. The bartender brought over shots and a pitcher. "Here's to forgiveness," McKenna said, already seeming half-lit.

They put back the shots.

"How's Marylou?" Conway said.

"Don't want to talk about it."

"I get you in trouble?"

"Let it be. What's the deal? Where we at?"

Conway talked about his most recent run-in with Ray Boy, keeping his voice low, saying this was the way it was going to go down. McKenna nodded along, his eyes glassed over. Conway wanted to know if it'd work.

McKenna said, "More shots." He stood, wobbly, and bellied up to the bar, ordering two double shots of Jack. He brought the shots back, balanced on his palms, doing a little crabwalk for kicks, and put them on the table in front of Conway. "Tomorrow I take you back to the range." Then he started singing "Home on the Range."

"I'll need, you know, I'll need another—"

McKenna shushed him dramatically. "You'll need another slice of carrot cake."

Conway laughed. "I'll need another slice of carrot cake."

McKenna, even drunker than Conway had realized, leaned over the drinks. "Carrot cake equals pistola, sí?"

"Sí, sí, Señor McKenna," Conway said.

McKenna took his shot. "Spanish, junior year, Ms. Polanco," he said, reaching under the table, grabbing his crotch. "I had such a boner for her. I'd sit there, the whole class, just staring, drooling on my desk. You think she's up to now? I wish I had her number."

"She was so hot." Conway sipped his whiskey.

"Remember, remember," McKenna slurring, "we thought she was fucking that senior. Frankie Mazzo."

"Maz had pictures." Conway thought about Alessandra again. "You remember Alessandra Biagini?"

"From Kearney?"

"Yeah, and I went to MPB with her."

"Tight little body. She was in all the plays. You used to talk about her non-stop."

"Never really had the guts to talk *to* her. Not since grade school anyway. I'd see her outside Kearney when we'd drive over there in the afternoons, and I'd want say something, see if she wanted to go to the city or something."

"Standing outside Kearney, those chicks in their uniforms, Christ. I remember that one smelled like vanilla perfume. Fuck was her name?"

"Mary Parente."

"Mary Parente!" McKenna's eyes rolled back in his head. "Jesus Christ. You didn't even have to get that close to smell her. You could smell her across the parking lot."

"I saw Alessandra. She's back."

"You're what, interested? How'd she look?"

"Good. Great."

"Better act soon before you wind up in Shawshank."

Conway was still sipping his double shot, not making a dent in it.

"You want a straw?" McKenna said. "Drink up."

A couple of hours later, Conway and McKenna left the bar. They stumbled back to the Civic. Conway was thinking seriously about driving home. McKenna said do it and bring him along. Conway got behind the wheel and turned the car on. McKenna got in the backseat, sprawling, yawning. "Take me home to Pop, driver," McKenna said. "I want to see Pop. I want to tell Pop he's the greatest."

"Here we come, Pop," Conway said. He put the radio on, McKenna pounding the back of his seat.

McKenna said, "Driver, drive. Take me to Pop. I need to have a consultation with Pop. I need Pop's advice."

"Pop's in. Pop's seeing patients."

"We need more booze."

"We do," Conway said, feeling like he was back in high school. "And we need Ms. Polanco and Alessandra."

"Ms. Polanco!"

Conway took the car away from the curb, almost ramming into a parked Pontiac Firebird across the street. He felt like this wasn't going to end well. How could it? Sirens in the rearview, telephone pole in the front seat. But he kept driving, tunnel vision all the way, the radio guiding him. McKenna was shouting along to the music. It was an old Nirvana mix, played a hundred thousand times in this car and on the stereo in his room, but it wasn't skipping and it felt new tonight. Conway was moving his head, wiping the window, thinking, *Don't let me get pulled over don't let me get pulled over don't let me get pulled over.*

Conway parked at a hydrant outside a bodega on some dark and forbidding corner. Nothing looked familiar. He couldn't even read what block it was. They went in, bought two twelve-packs, and came out, half-embracing, half-gut-punching each other, twirling the twelve-packs like they were basketballs. McKenna dropped his and a few of the beers broke in the box, splashing a sudsy mix of glass and beer out the handle-holes.

"This is like fucking Afghanistan!" McKenna said.

Conway snorted, thinking this was just a gluey hallucination now, not even real.

Back in the car, driving again, Conway opened a beer in his lap. He brought it to his mouth on the sly, everything feeling slo-mo weird.

Home was in front of them now somehow, behind a telephone pole and an extra high-seeming curve. Out of the car then. Leaving the doors unlocked. They stumbled through the front gate, beers in pockets, McKenna with three under each arm, his box gone soggy. Conway balanced his twelve-pack on his head and tried to make the key fit the hole. Pop was there behind the curtain, looking fish-eyed like in a carnival mirror. He opened the door.

"Pop," McKenna said. "Good old Pop."

Pop said, "You boys should be ashamed."

"The bozo shawl bead claimed," McKenna said. "You're right, Pop." He reached out and patted him on the shoulder. "You're a hundred percent correct."

Conway brought the twelve-pack down to his chest and cradled it. He led the way inside. Pop yapped at them, but Conway took McKenna right to his room and closed the door. He put the box down, popped a beer, and sucked down half. Pop was on the other side of the door, reminding him that he was twenty-goddamn-nine. But Conway felt fourteen the whole time, getting hammered, closing the bedroom door, his old man yelling at him. He completed the picture: turned his stereo on loud. *Road to Ruin*. The whole house shaking. Let the cops come.

McKenna sat on the bed, opened a beer with his teeth. It exploded, foam dribbling on his lap and the twisted blankets under him.

Feeling like maybe he really was fourteen again, Conway remembered things in flashes: coming home drunk one night and seeing Duncan and Davey Ignozzi, a kid they'd known since he moved to the neighborhood after the Mets won the Series, making out. They both had their shirts off, a crazy hot summer night, the pavement seeming to cook the city, and they both had the same creamy skin, the same frosted nipples, no hair in their pits. It took Conway a second to understand what he was seeing. "Take a picture," Duncan had said that night after noticing him. Conway had gone to his room then and turned on the stereo, finding an airplane-sized bottle of Johnnie Walker Red he'd stolen from Pop in the stash-box under his bed and drinking it down.

Another flash: Pop coming into his room the night Duncan was killed. Ghost-faced. Eyes looking gone, like there were only the whites. His lips quivering. His hands shaking. Conway didn't believe what he was saying straight off. He went out to the kitchen and saw his mother at the table with a quart of Aristocrat vodka, pouring herself shot after shot in a Golden

Nugget mug. She'd been on the wagon for a few years before that and made no hesitation to fall off five minutes after the cops called with news of what had happened to Duncan.

In this room, at twenty-two, Conway had stabbed himself in the arm with a cheapo switchblade. Right above the wrist. The knife went down to the nerve and he lost feeling in his hand for over four years and still had a numb, pins-and-needles feeling in his fingers on days the weather was bad. He was drunk and had just been broken up with by a girl named Kristy Caggiano, who he'd started dating in college. He stabbed himself in front of Kristy, who was reading him a letter she'd written about why they were done. When the blood started spurting out, things went hazy, but he remembered Kristy getting him outside and in her car, Pop not knowing what was going on, and then she dropped him at the door of the Victory ER. He woke up the next morning in the cold glow of the hospital. A nurse had said, "You glad you're alive?"

"Not really," he'd said.

"Well, you are," she'd said. "Alive. You should be happy."

"Thank you," he'd said. "But I'm not happy."

They made him talk to a psychologist before he left the hospital in a sling. And since his father couldn't pick him up, and since his mother was nowhere to be found, it was McKenna who showed up in his Maxima, slurping orange soda and gin.

"Dude," he'd said. "You almost died."

Yet another flash: Duncan and him sharing the room back before Duncan moved his stuff into the basement. They'd sit on the bed playing Battleship or Yahtzee, Z100 on, or listening to *Nevermind* on cassette, Duncan saying in a hundred years people were still going to have pictures of Kurt Cobain up on their walls, that Nirvana was the best band ever, that Conway had a lot to learn about music. Other days Duncan had made Conway listen to The Replacements, The Pixies, Sebadoh, always in this room, always sitting Indian-style on the floor, Duncan sometimes taking out a one-hitter and smoking, finally passing it to Conway an afternoon when nobody else was around.

Pop banging on the door jerked Conway back into the present. He wasn't fourteen. He was twenty-nine, drunk as shit, and he had failed at everything.

Conway opened the door, said nothing.

"Turn that shit down," Pop said. "Now. We got neighbors for Chrissakes. *Disgraziato.*" Italian always meant Pop was at his maddest.

Conway turned the volume down to one. "Sorry," he said.

"You boys should be ashamed."

McKenna was lying back on the bed now, not sleeping, but the beer had spilled out next to him.

"You're how old?" Pop said.

"I'm young," Conway said.

"You're not young."

"Please get out. Leave me alone."

"This guy's got a wife, no?" Pop motioned to McKenna. "She's not gonna worry?"

"Go." Conway put his hand on Pop's shoulder and gave him a slight push.

"You keep your hands off me."

Conway pushed harder and Pop fell back over the threshold onto the kitchen linoleum, landing on his ass and hands, grunting, his supposedly bad leg curled up under him.

"You're fine," Conway said. "You're not even sick. Go be fine in your room."

Tears showed in Pop's eyes. He worked himself up to his hands and knees. "You're gonna go to hell for treating your old man like this."

Conway slammed the door and locked it. He plugged his headphones into the stereo and turned the volume back up, sitting with his back against the dresser, letting the music blast a hole in his head.

———◆———

Next morning, Conway got up and went to work. He left McKenna asleep on his bed, said nothing to Pop as he passed him at the kitchen table drinking coffee out of his green plastic cup, buttering a heel of Italian bread. He walked straight to Rite Aid, looking, he imagined, like a dried-up turd with his hair all over the place, his four-day beard, his chapped lips and rank clothes. He got there and Stephanie came right at him, bright in her pharmacist whites, and she tried to convince him to go home and rest, she'd cover for him.

"I'm not going home," Conway said.

"What's going on?" Stephanie said. "You okay?"

Conway wasn't yet hung-over. He was still drunk. His temples pounded and the world seemed wavy and bright. "Fine."

"You don't look fine."

He mimicked her. "'You don't look fine.' Mind your own business, Steph, huh?"

"Listen, Con, I think you need to go home."

"You're ordering me?"

Conway walked over to the register, the one he was meant to man, and the front doors whooshed open and Alessandra Biagini walked in. Stephanie was right behind him. She pushed past him and met Alessandra with an embrace. "It's so good to see you in here," Stephanie said.

"You too," Alessandra said.

"You remember Conway D'Innocenzio?"

Alessandra nodded. "We ran into each other yesterday."

"Conway's having a hard day," Stephanie said.

Conway was just staring at Alessandra, staring through her, images of her sitting in front of him at MPB mixing with images of her talking to Ray Boy down on the promenade in his mind's eye.

"You okay, Conway?" Alessandra said.

"He's just having a hard day." Stephanie lifted a fake bottle to her lips.

"I just need to pick up a prescription for my dad."

"Sure, I'll help you. One sec."

"I need some hydrocortisone, too."

"We'll pass right by it on the way to the pharmacy. I'll show you."

Still staring right at Alessandra, Conway said, "Fuck were you talking to him about last night?"

"Excuse me?" Alessandra said.

"You know."

"What are you saying?"

"I saw you. Talking to Ray Boy. About what?"

"You saw me?"

"I was down by the water."

"Leave it alone, Conway," Stephanie said. "You're drunk."

"You followed me?" Alessandra said.

"I saw you, that's it. You visit my brother's grave and then you chat up his killer?"

"Excuse me," Alessandra said. She backed up and made a move for the door.

"Fuck are you talking to this guy about? I need to know. You guys going to get coffee? He's a nice guy now? That it?" Conway was moving toward her as she back-pedaled, wanting to get right in her face, hoping his beery breath blinded her, hoping she would let down her guard and hug him and beg for forgiveness.

"I don't know what you're saying."

"Don't lie."

Stephanie said, "He's just drunk. Forget it. Don't pay any attention."

"Yeah, I'm drunk," Conway said.

Alessandra turned around. "I'll come back later, Steph." She tried to walk out the wrong set of doors, the ones that whooshed in, and had to hop over a small chain to get to the exit.

"I won't forget I saw that," Conway said.

The doors opened out, and Alessandra was gone, crossing under the El and turning the corner behind McDonald's.

"Real nice," Stephanie said. "Welcome back, Alessandra."

Conway took off his red apron and flung it down on the ground. "Who needs this shit anyway?" he said.

"Don't you go out there and follow her," Stephanie said.

Conway said nothing and walked out into the blazing glare, a D passing overhead on the El, cars honking out in front of the fire station as a fireman tried to guide a truck back into the garage. Conway looked over at where Alessandra had just been. Follow her? Fuck would he do that for anyway? Let her go. It was time to wake up McKenna and practice shooting.

7

Eugene hated mornings most. Especially Monday mornings. He hated waking up to the alarm clock buzz, five-thirty, the little clock vibrating on his dresser, and he hated sitting up in the dark and stretching. He hated his breath in the morning, the way he tasted it on his tongue and teeth. He hated limping to the bathroom, little squiggles of dust caught between the pink hallway rug and the wall, the rug threaded down to bare spots in the places where his feet fell.

He hated the bathroom: pink tiles and moldy grout and the sick glow of the light over the sink that hurt his first-thing-in-the-morning eyes. He hated showers this early, the most depressing thing ever, scrubbing himself with Irish Spring in the dark stall, the water pressure so hard that it felt like sandpaper against his skin, closing his eyes, the water sounding like bad weather.

He hated his body. He hated his body covered in soap. He hated getting out of the shower, stepping on the rose-colored mat, and drying off over the toilet. He hated the way the towels felt. His mother sprayed them with starch before washing them and line-dried them in the backyard over the fig trees and they were stiff like ironing boards, raw against his skin, full of holes with almost-serrated edges, nothing like the soft towels in Sweat's house.

He hated walking back to his room, getting dressed, crumpled boxers first, wife-beater, shitty uniform, clip-on OLN tie. He hated trying to do something with his hair. Other guys had fades and used gels. His hair was kinky, impossible to spike, and there was nothing to do except shave it or to plaster it down in a Caesar.

He hated breakfast with his mom, coffee and cereal and fruit, her reading the *Daily News*, trying to talk about the weather, WINS on in the background. He hated the smell of his mother in the morning, Jergen's lotion and Listerine breath. He hated the way she filed her nails without paying attention, doing everything at once: talking, listening, reading, eating, filing. He hated the clock his mother had up on the wall in the kitchen, some Disney bullshit that played movie theme songs every hour. At six, it was always *Beauty and the Beast*, Eugene wanting to rip the thing off the wall and stomp it to death. He hated how his mother handed him his lunch, still wrote EUGENE on it in black Sharpie with a flowery design underneath like he was in third grade. He hated the way his mother said goodbye, patting him on the head and kissing his cheek, him taking it, feeling retarded, her practically saying, "I hope my special little man has a special day."

Eugene hated the walk to the bus stop, six blocks, and he hated that he had to stop at the garbage bin by P.S. 101 and throw out the bag his lunch came in because then he had to just dump his sandwich and chips and drink in his backpack and sometimes they opened up and made a mess.

He hated how heavy his backpack was, big textbooks he never cracked, binders full of loose leaf, his sneakers on gym days. The zipper stressed so hard that its teeth pressed out.

He hated standing at the bus stop, under the El, waiting for the B1. He hated the cars driving by. He wished Sweat would just pick him up. He hated

the buses, the way they pulled up and wheezed, the way they lowered themselves to you, and he hated every bus driver on the route. He knew them all,
a fat black lady, a skinny Chinese guy, a not-Italian white guy with teeth like
brown pebbles, another not-Italian white guy with a bushy red chin beard
and dry skin around his nose. He hated showing the driver his bus pass,
taking out his flimsy Velcro wallet and flashing it, the driver always saying,
even after they got to know him, to take it out and hand it over and then
inspecting it closely as if he'd take the time to fake it, as if he'd be on the
fucking bus if he didn't have to be.

He hated the wheelchair lady that always seemed to be getting on the
bus the same time as him no matter when he got there. Getting on and off
buses was pretty much all she did with her life, as far as he could tell. She
was there in the afternoons, too. He hated the process of getting her on the
bus, the way the driver put on the hazards, stopped up traffic, got out with
a big ring of keys, went around to the back of the bus, and turned the rear
steps into a lift. It was sort of amazing the first time Eugene saw it but now
he was sick of it. The lift went up slowly, and Eugene stared at the lady's
peg-leg, her dirty wheelchair, her shopping bags, and her crusty hat with a
pigeon feather in it. He hated that the bus driver had to kick people out of
the handicapped section and then scoop up the row of seats to strap her in.
Wheelchair Lady gave the shit eye to everyone on the bus, like this was her
privilege and they should be happy no matter how long it took. Sometimes
it took ten minutes, the driver struggling with the straps, Wheelchair Lady
not cooperating, others standing around, checking their cell phones and
watches, cars behind the bus beeping. When it was finally done, the driver
fixed the rear steps, went back to the front of the bus and got it moving.
Inevitably, though, Wheelchair Lady would signal for a stop by Eighteenth
Avenue. She was never on for more than two or three stops and then the
whole process happened in reverse. Other OLN students didn't really get
on until they hit Dyker Heights so Eugene was alone in witnessing this, his
headphones on, blasting hip-hop, trying to drown it all out.

He hated the long ride to school, stopping at almost every corner, it seemed. He hated when other guys from the school finally did get on: Jimmy Tanico, Billy Morris, Chris Burke, Tony Volpe, Zip Maroney, Petey Salerno. Then he had to act with them, swagger, when all he wanted to do was let the music wake him up.

He hated arriving at school, boys gathered around outside the front gate, an army of buses coming from fifty different neighborhoods shivering at the curb, the juniors and seniors pulled up in their cars across the street, girls from Kearney and Fontbonne in their front seats putting on makeup, chewing gum, turning up the radio. Eugene hated making his way through the crowd, up the front steps, and passing under the sign that said THE TRUTH SHALL MAKE YOU FREE. Fuck truth were they talking about? He hated the glass case in the main alcove that was a monument to Chris Mullin, the school's most famous alum. Mullin's high school picture was blown up. So were his OLN team picture, a shot of him mid-three in a St. John's-Georgetown Big East tourney game, an action snap from his Golden State heyday, and—framed, signed, the centerpiece—a picture of him from when he was on Team USA, looking coked out, eyes hazy, that military haircut revealing an Irish nastiness in his features. There was also a ball he'd signed and a newspaper clipping about him dancing with some retards at a Ryken Club event.

Eugene hated passing by the main office and the theater on the way to his locker, Brother Dennis standing there, the old alkie with a nose that looked like it had been formed out of bloodshot Silly Putty, whacking kids in the arm, making like he was going to trip them, a real comedian. Aherne, the principal, had no real job for the old man so he made him patrol the halls. Eugene hated when Brother Dennis said something to him, maybe, "Mr. Calabrese, chin up, it's not the end of the world." Or: "Keep on the sunny side, Mr. Calabrese." He wanted to punch the old alkie in the nuts or reach through his chest like in *Temple of Doom* and pull out his shitty prune of a heart and mash it. Eugene hated not being able to do that, just walking past, nodding.

He hated his locker, above Tommy Valentino's. Tommy was tall, a B team basketball player who wasn't very good, and he was always hunched over his locker in the morning, spooning sugar candy from an envelope into his mouth with a wooden stick and washing it down with Gatorade. Eugene hated how he had to work around Tommy to get in his locker.

He hated the clocks in the school. He hated the color of the walls, broccoli green on top fading into bad teeth yellow near the floor. He hated the elevators. He hated the staircases, smelling like ammonia and sadness. He hated the OLN uniform and the way everyone wore it with little variation. He hated the teachers, the Brothers and otherwise, even his English teacher, who pretended to be cool, talking about Kanye and sneaking cigs out the back door at lunch. He hated the advertisements for school plays in the halls. He pictured the school from above, like from a satellite, and he hated the way it looked, squirrelly students and defeated teachers all moving through a maze. He hated that he couldn't just leave school and walk over to Owl's Head Park or the Sixty-Ninth Street Pier. He hated that he couldn't go to Constantino's to get a slice for lunch like the juniors and seniors. He hated classes—Global Studies, Religion, English, Math, Biology, Italian— and he had to zone out to make it through them, pretend he was listening to music, practice his Uncle Ray Boy's old tag in the margins of his notebooks. Eugene hated most things with a hate that tasted like broken glass.

This morning was no different. He hated with his eyes, with his mouth, with every motion he made, trying to turn his limp into a too-cool badass shuffle. Maybe teachers thought he was a dimwit joke of a kid, probably they were scared of him, probably—he liked to think anyway—they thought he was the kind of kid who could learn to build a bomb on the Internet and set it off during the school day.

He walked to Italian and sat in the back of the class even though Mr. Bonangelo had assigned him a seat up close. Mr. Bonangelo liked to keep troubled kids and troublemakers close to him. Eugene didn't know which Mr. Bonangelo thought he was, but he hated the front of the room, hated

Mr. Bonangelo breathing on him, hated his bad jokes. Mr. Bonangelo had a limp too, something about polio when he was a kid, and he was always using this to try to get in Eugene's good graces. But that made Eugene hate him more, the guy thinking they were what, connected somehow?

"Eugene," Mr. Bonangelo said, "please, up front now, son."

Eugene ignored him.

"You want another detention?"

Eugene trudged up to the front of the class, sat next to Billy Morris. Billy looked like he'd just smoked up, eyes gone red and heavy, a rubberbandy look on his face.

Mr. Bonangelo said, "That's a boy."

That's a boy.

Eugene folded open his notebook and started scratching lines in the margin with his pen.

Mr. Bonangelo cleared his throat. "Mr. Calabrese."

Eugene said, "What, yo?"

"'What, yo?'" Mr. Bonangelo said. He laughed. "'What, yo?' You must be kidding, Mr. Calabrese. Try again."

"What?"

"Try: Yes, Mr. Bonangelo, sir?"

Some kids in the back of the class laughed.

Eugene stopped drawing in his margins. He squared up, shoulders out. "Fuck you, yo."

Mr. Bonangelo's face turned the color of spoiled meat. "To Principal Aherne's. Now, Mr. Calabrese. Now." He was rattled, almost quivering with rage, limping around in front of the chalkboard frantically. He had his phone out and was punching in a number.

Other guys in the class were stirring in their seats, pressing Mr. Bonangelo to choke Eugene to death. Vinny Liozzi said, "It's worth losing your job, Mr. Bonangelo. Kill this kid."

Eugene stood up, put his books in his backpack, and got out of the room as fast as he could. Mr. Bonangelo stuck his head out the door after him. "Wait right there, Mr. Calabrese. I just called Brother Dennis. He's coming to accompany you. Make sure you don't take any detours."

Eugene stood still, staring at the floor. It was peach-colored with flecks of yellow and brown, and he'd never noticed just how ugly it was.

Brother Dennis came lumbering around the corner by the elevators, excited, acting as if his whole life had been leading up to this moment. "I hear Mr. Calabrese needs an escort," he said, coming closer.

"He does indeed," Mr. Bonangelo said.

"Well, then, I'm your man." Brother Dennis put a hand on Eugene's shoulder. "Come along, son."

Eugene flinched.

"Looks like we've got ourselves a real live wire." Brother Dennis nudged Eugene now.

Eugene said, "Keep your hands off me, yo."

"'Yo,'" Mr. Bonangelo said. "He says that a lot."

Brother Dennis aped him, too. "'Yo, yo, yo.' Tough talk."

"You want to know what this punk said to me, Brother?"

"I sure do."

Bonangelo slumped his shoulders, did his best Eugene: "He said, 'Eff you, yo.' Except he said the word."

"Disgusting talk." Brother Dennis shook his head.

"No way for a young OLN man to speak," Mr. Bonangelo said.

"Grounds for suspension, certainly. Maybe worse. What'll your mother think, young man?"

Eugene shrugged.

Brother Dennis guided Eugene down the hallway, past the auditorium, to Principal Aherne's office.

Martha, the secretary, was sitting behind a desk in the alcove outside of Aherne's office, filing her nails.

"Mr. Bonangelo was having some problems with our young friend here," Brother Dennis said.

"I'll buzz him," Martha said. She hit a button on the phone in front of her and bent over it to speak into the receiver. "He says go in."

Brother Dennis opened Aherne's door and showed Eugene in with a dramatic wave of his arm.

Principal Aherne was behind his desk. He closed a game of solitaire on his computer. "Mr. Calabrese," he said. "Well, well, well. Sit down."

Eugene sat down in the egg-brown wingback chair across from Aherne. Brother Dennis stood next to him, arms crossed. Aherne opened his desk drawer. He took out a clementine and peeled it. It smelled like someone had sprayed orange Lysol in the room. He piled the strips of rind in a used tissue. Eugene examined the other stuff on Aherne's desk. A picture of his hollow-cheeked mother looking like a zombie. Fax machine. Picture of his wife and three kids, the youngest a girl who had Down's Syndrome and always dressed like a ballerina. Box of Kleenex. A Derek Jeter bobble-head. A plaque remembering Brother Mathis, the old principal who'd lost his mind and wandered into Owl's Head Park one night too many in a row and been put in a home where he lived out his last days in a haze of soft foods and fat nurses in bright scrubs. An eight-by-ten picture of the Sacred Heart of Jesus hung behind Aherne on the wall.

"What was Mr. Calabrese's offense, Brother?" Aherne said.

"Would you like to tell him, son?" Brother Dennis said.

Eugene said nothing.

"Language unbecoming," Brother Dennis said to Aherne.

"What was the severity level?"

"Ten."

Eugene couldn't believe they were talking like this.

"Ten." Aherne rocked back in his chair, closed his eyes, and scratched his chin. "Ten. My, I hate to hear that." He paused, turned to Brother Dennis. "You can leave, Brother. I'd like to talk to Mr. Calabrese alone. Thank you."

Brother Dennis half-curtsied and left the office.

Eugene looked down at his lap, grinding his teeth.

"I'd like to speak frankly," Aherne said. "Okay? I understand that with your *affliction* you have a hard time of it. I get that. I do, Mr. Calabrese. I don't know what it's like to have a limp, to be different from everybody in that way. I'm not sure what that does to you. Maybe it makes you angry at the world. You know who else had every right to be mad at the world?" He stopped, put his elbows up on the desk, made a steeple out of his hands, and exhaled. He wheeled around and pointed to Christ's big, exploding heart. "Jesus Christ."

Eugene almost cracked up.

"You need to learn how to deal with your anger, Mr. Calabrese. You need to figure out how to channel it. Get involved in some clubs, sports. I'm not sure what sport you could play with your situation but I'm sure there's something you could do. Maybe you could get involved with the Ryken Club. Most of the students in that club have," he paused, considering his words, "an affliction."

Eugene couldn't believe he was being called retarded by Principal Aherne.

Aherne continued: "We'll work on this later. First, I want you to tell me exactly what you said to Mr. Bonangelo so we can deal with your punishment. Brother Dennis said your level of severity was a ten. That's very unsettling. What did you say?"

Eugene didn't hesitate. "I told Mr. Bonangelo, 'Fuck you.'"

Aherne rocked back in his chair again and let out a whoosh. He punched a button on his phone and lifted the receiver. "Martha, will you get Mr. Calabrese's mother on the phone?" He hung up and waited.

Eugene said, "My mother's at work."

"I think this takes precedence. This is a very serious situation. Do you understand, Mr. Calabrese? I've had students expelled for less." Aherne sunk half of the clementine into his mouth and spit the seeds into a crumpled Kleenex.

Eugene knew Aherne was bullshitting. No way they'd expel him. He was a paying customer.

"I'm stepping out for a moment, Mr. Calabrese," Aherne said.

To speak to his mother. Then what? She'd flip, leave work, make a big deal out of having to leave work, come to OLN, pick him up, bitch him out in the car, bitch him out at home, take away some shit that Sweat had given him, probably his iPod. She'd lecture him for the next month, every chance she got, about how far getting in trouble got you, about how he was letting her down, and then she'd forget for a little while and things would be okay, she'd stay out of his shit, and then it'd happen all over again. But part of him must have enjoyed it. Otherwise, why'd he say what he said to Bonangelo? He knew where that was going to lead him. Maybe he just wanted to test the limits, see how far they'd let him go before they did expel him or before his mother had to send him to military school.

Aherne came back in the room and sat down in his chair. He pointed to the phone on his desk, red lights blinking under the numbers. "Pick it up, Mr. Calabrese. Your mother would like to speak to you."

Eugene stood up and went over to the phone. He picked up the receiver.

"Eugene," his mother said, almost whispering, pretend calm. "I'm at work so I can't talk loud, you understand?" She paused. "But I'm very upset."

He pictured his mother getting red in the face, tears penny-thick on her lower lashes, trying to keep the conversation private, trying not to show the other girls at her office that her no-good son was in trouble again.

"I get what, two calls in an hour? One from Augie. One from Principal Aherne. Both saying essentially the same thing. Augie called the cops on you. He wanted to press charges. I had to talk him down. Now Principal Aherne says you might get expelled. For saying," lowering her voice even more, "'eff you' to Mr. Bonangelo. This how I raised you? I raised you to go to church and help old people. What are you trying to do, put me in an early grave? This is supposed to be a happy time, your Uncle Ray Boy back."

Eugene said nothing.

"You've got nothing to say for yourself?"

"I'm—"

"You're what? You better say you're sorry, young man. I swear. You better apologize to me, to Principal Aherne, to Augie, and especially, especially right now, to Mr. Bonangelo. Is that understood?"

Eugene knew what his mother wanted to hear. She wanted him to say, *Yes, Mom. I understand.* Instead, he said, "I'm not apologizing."

"You're not what? What'd you say?" his mother said.

"I got nothing to be sorry for."

He could see his mother taking the phone away from her ear, wiping tears from her eyes, making an I-can't-believe-this face. "I don't know who you think you are, Eugene. You got a lot to be sorry for. Principal Aherne's suspending you. I'm sending your Uncle Ray Boy to pick you up in fifteen minutes. You be ready for him. And by the time he gets there I better hear that you've apologized to everybody. I have to spell that out? You can save your apology to me for later. Make it a good one." She hung up with a huff.

Eugene put the phone down.

"That's one angry lady," Aherne said. "And she has every right to be. I gather she told you you're suspended?"

Eugene looked past Aherne at Jesus on the wall.

"Your suspension will be shorter, two days, if you apologize. It'll be longer, a week or more, if you don't. I'd aim for the shorter suspension. Permanent record and all of that. Not to mention your mother's forgiveness." Aherne buzzed Martha and told her to bring Mr. Bonangelo in when classes switched in five minutes and to ask Brother Dennis to cover for him. Then Aherne turned his attention back to Eugene. "Now I understand that your Uncle Ray's coming to pick you up." Aherne put his chin in the air. "Not the alum we're proudest of, as I imagine you're well aware. But I hope that he's honestly rehabilitated. I hope the system's done some good for him. He was, after all, just a kid himself when what happened happened. You should look at your uncle's mistakes, son, and learn from them. Believe me, you don't want to wind up in prison. Ask your uncle. You think he wouldn't like to have those sixteen years back? I guarantee he'd like to have them back. The prime of his life. His twenties up in smoke just like that."

Eugene had heard all of this before.

"If I can give you some more advice, Mr. Calabrese, it'd be to treasure your mother. Plan a topnotch apology. Buy her flowers. Wait on her hand and foot. Believe me, one day you'll regret you weren't better to her. She'll be sick, at the end of her life, probably not for a long time, but I guarantee you'll be sitting at her bedside, saying, 'I should've been better to you when I had the chance. I didn't realize how short life actually is.' And life is short. Ask Brother Mathis. You think seventy-eight is old? It passes like this." He snapped his fingers. "And then we have to stand before God and show Him what we've done. We've got to say, 'Here's what I did that's good.' But we've also got to say, 'Here's what I did that's bad.' And that list tends to be very long. 'I stole, I lied, I lusted, I treated my mother like garbage.' And there's no way around it, no lie you can tell that God can't see through. You spend your whole life making choices that will lead you up to Judgment Day. It's not too late for you to start making the right choices. Be good to your mother, exude kindness, be merciful, be forgiving." Aherne leaned back in his chair, impressed with himself, as if he'd worked on this little speech for ages.

Martha opened the door and Mr. Bonangelo was standing behind her. He slid into the room on his polio leg and stood beside Eugene.

"Mr. Bonangelo," Aherne said, "Mr. Calabrese here has something he'd like to say to you."

"I gather Brother Dennis has filled you in," Mr. Bonangelo said.

"He has."

"I've never, in all my years, been spoken to like that by a student. Just for the record. When I was going to school at St. Augustine in the Fifties, you even looked at a teacher cock-eyed and they'd beat the ever-loving crap out of you. Those were good days. I miss those days. One time, one time only, I spoke out of turn in class and Brother Clemente—how could I ever forget him?—put me in my place with a yardstick. I never spoke out of turn again. I did my work, never said so much as boo. What do you fear, Mr. Calabrese? Nothing. No one like Brother Clemente exists now. OLN is not St. Augustine's. We live in a time when you can say whatever you want and walk away from it. So, you apologize, that's fine. Principal Aherne and your mother have both convinced you it's the right move. But it'll mean absolutely nothing to me." Mr. Bonangelo let out a breath. He was sweating.

Eugene looked down at the carpet, swirls of gold and blue, the school's colors. He noted where the carpet was threadbare under his shoes, worn down under the pressure of all such tense sit-downs over the years, kids like him trying to kick into a tunnel world.

"Well," Aherne said, "you still need to apologize, Mr. Calabrese. For what it's worth. Make it sincere."

"'Sincere,'" Mr. Bonangelo said. "That's good. Yeah, make it sincere, Eugene."

Eugene picked his head up and looked right at Mr. Bonangelo. "Fuck you, yo," he said again.

Uncle Ray Boy was late. Eugene was sitting on a foldout chair next to Martha's desk. She was filling out some sort of invoice, glasses down on the edge of her nose, and Eugene was trying to see between the buttons on her black and red flower-print blouse. She was old, early fifties, and he could see the bottom sides of the padded cups of her yellowing bra and wrinkly swaths of skin that looked like pinches of cottage cheese.

Things had not ended up well in Aherne's office. Mr. Bonangelo lunged at Eugene after he said "Fuck you, yo" for the second time in an hour. Aherne got between them, knowing that Mr. Bonangelo would lose his job no matter what if he put a hand on a student. Eugene dared him to do something. Brother Dennis barged in after a few seconds and dragged Mr. Bonangelo to safety. Aherne looked at Eugene like he'd just fingered his cat's asshole. "You, young man, are in deep, deep trouble," Aherne said. Then he walked him to his locker to get his backpack and jacket.

Eugene was thinking that he'd honestly upped his chances for expulsion, as unlikely as it still was. Mr. Bonangelo had been guilty of entrapment or some shit and he was sure Aherne would take that into consideration. Not that he wanted to come crawling back to OLN. Being expelled was okay with him, though it would break his mother's heart. His grandparents, too.

Uncle Ray Boy came through the door, still wearing the same clothes, purple-black bags under his eyes, back stooped.

Eugene stood up.

"You're the uncle?" Martha said.

"I am," Uncle Ray Boy said.

She buzzed Aherne. He came out of the office and stood in front of Ray Boy and Eugene. "Ray," he said. "I hope you're doing better."

"I'm good," Uncle Ray Boy said. "You?"

"I'd be better if your nephew would've made this simple."

Uncle Ray Boy didn't look at Eugene. "My sister told me."

"Well, I'm afraid that's just the tip of the iceberg. Things went downhill after I spoke to Eugene's mother. He's in much deeper trouble. I'll be calling her back soon. There's a possibility we'll have to expel him. He's done something worthy of such action."

"Whatever you need to do."

"I suggest you have a talk with your nephew. Warn him against such behavior. Let him know where being a troublemaker gets you. You know best."

"I'll talk to him."

Eugene couldn't believe Uncle Ray Boy was just going along with this, wasn't tearing Aherne a new one. Nothing tough came out of his mouth. Only you're-better-than-me shit.

"You seem like you've turned things around some, Ray," Aherne said. "That's good. I'm very happy for you. I'm happy God granted you a second chance. Eugene might not be so lucky. He's headed down a bad road."

Uncle Ray Boy was nodding. "I'll have a talk with him," he said.

Aherne turned to Eugene. "Your future is uncertain. Think of ways to repent, son."

Uncle Ray Boy led Eugene out of the office. They walked out of the building under THE TRUTH SHALL MAKE YOU FREE and headed for Grandma Jean's Camry, which was parked up on the curb. Eugene got in on the passenger side, and Uncle Ray Boy got under the wheel. A copy of *The Village Voice* was folded on the dash. Eugene noticed that it was open to a story about Uncle Ray Boy and Duncan D'Innocenzio. A picture of Uncle Ray Boy from back in the day was side-by-side with his mugshot. And Duncan's junior yearbook picture took up the bottom of the page. Uncle Ray Boy plucked the newspaper from the dash and put it in the backseat. Eugene figured it was better not to ask about the article.

"That was bullshit," Eugene said.

"What?" Uncle Ray Boy said, pulling away from the school.

"The whole thing. What Aherne said."

"What'd you do?"

"My mom didn't tell you?"

"Yeah, I don't know."

"Said 'fuck you' to a teacher."

Uncle Ray Boy kept his eyes on the road.

Eugene said, "How come you didn't say anything to Aherne? You just let him talk to you like that?"

Uncle Ray Boy said, "Like what?"

"Just like you were nothing. Like he was so much better than you."

"You got a lot to learn."

"I always thought you were tough."

"You wanted to be like me?"

"What you did to that fag, who cares?"

Uncle Ray Boy pulled the car over by Owl's Head Park. He was gripping the steering wheel so tight his fingers were quaking-red. "They're all gonna want me to help straighten you out," he said. "They're gonna want me to tell you how shitty prison was. How sorry I am. I am sorry, Eugene, but I'm not gonna do any of that. You're my nephew, what's that mean? Blood? What's blood mean when you're dead? I don't give a fuck about you, about your mother, about my parents, about anything. Just let me be dead."

Eugene got out of the car and limped into the park. He took cover behind a tree and watched Uncle Ray Boy pull away. Eugene could see now that there was something very wrong with his uncle.

Sweat was still in school, so Eugene walked to Constantino's for an early slice. He didn't know what Uncle Ray Boy would tell his mother, but that didn't matter yet. For now, he was free. Free to roam between Bay Ridge and Gravesend. Or to go somewhere new. There was so much Brooklyn he hadn't seen.

The slice was cardboardy, orange with grease. Leftover from yesterday. Eugene ate from the crust in and left a circle of picked-clean dough.

He took out his phone and texted Sweat: *Hit me up later.*

No response, the phone probably off at the bottom of Sweat's locker. He'd gotten in trouble so much for carrying it around that Brother Dennis always checked in the mornings to make sure he put it away before classes started. They were on different schedules, and it was possible that Sweat hadn't even heard about what had happened yet.

Eugene played pinball in the corner by the window under the neon beer signs, and the Mexican guy behind the counter, apron over his shoulder, watched him, like, *Why aren't you in school?* Eugene stripped off his tie and stuffed it in his backpack.

He went through three bucks in quarters on the machine and then left Constantino's.

It was weird to be walking around on a Monday morning. Not much was going on. Old ladies humped shopping carts up Fifth Avenue, stopping at banks and markets. Construction workers and traffic cops goofed at Dunkin' Donuts. Old alkies shuffled into The Dodger, McTierney's, The Wicked

Monk, and Brushstrokes, playing touch video games and starting off the day with a glass of beer or a Bloody Mary or straight whiskey.

Eugene's phone started buzzing non-stop. His mother. Uncle Ray Boy must've called her as soon as he got home. Eugene powered it down, put it at the bottom of his backpack.

8

Alessandra was in the city at Café Torino with a director named Lou Turcotte she'd hooked up with through a friend on Facebook in the gin haze of two, three the night before. The guy was casting a small indie drama set in Brooklyn, and she chatted to him that she was born for one of the parts. He said he'd e-mail her a script, and he did first thing in the morning, just a few pages. She glanced at it. It was really bad. No way the guy was from Brooklyn. But she needed work, anything, and maybe a movie part would get things going. They sat at a sidewalk table and he ordered them espressos. He was dressed the part: sunglasses, ascot, sport coat, beard. She was dolled in her low-rise super skinny jeans and a long-sleeve chambray shirt, her vintage taupe coat folded over the back of the chair.

"What I'm thinking," Lou Turcotte said, "is that Angie—that's the part looking at you I think you'd be good for—is fed up, just about to explode, tired of her life. When Angelo comes back to the neighborhood, she's sort of starstruck."

Alessandra said, "Angie and Angelo?"

"Yeah. I'm going for the authentic vibe. You're Italian, right?"

"I'm Italian."

"So Angie, she's led a sheltered life, never been out of the neighborhood. Angelo, he's a mobster, he goes all over the place, Jersey, Italy, Vegas, killing, gambling," lowering his voice, "making love to whomsoever he chooses. He's back because his mom's dying. Real prodigal son situation. He walks in with pastries, sees his mother hooked up to ventilators, starts shooting holes in the ceiling."

"Shooting holes in the ceiling? Why?"

"That's what this guy does when he gets upset."

Alessandra almost lost it. "This is the lead you want me for?"

"Look at you. You're beautiful. I mean, you're a Brooklyn girl."

"Where are you from?"

He took his time answering. "Connecticut. My grandmother's from Brooklyn, though."

"Right."

"Listen, I'm gonna get this movie in at Sundance. No bullshitting."

"You're gonna keep this title?" Alessandra said, looking down at the pages he'd sent her.

"*Fuhgeddaboudit*? No. No way. That's a working title. Tentative as hell. I'm open to suggestions."

"Okay, that's good. I'll do it, I guess."

"Really? Great. Great. I'll get you the rest of the script."

Alessandra put out her hand and they shook on it. Lou Turcotte had the hands of someone who'd never worked a day in his life. They were moisturized, his nails manicured. "When do we start?"

"Well, that's the hitch. Gotta raise some money. My mom's got some doctor friends. They said they'd kick in. My dad, he's affiliated with these start-up-your-business kind of guys, they say they'll help. It's gonna happen, don't doubt that. The ball's rolling, Ali."

"Alessandra."

"The ball is rolling, Alessandra. It's in my court and I'm ready to hit some shots." Lou was getting cheesier and cheesier, mixing up clichés. Alessandra wondered just how bad the rest of the script actually was.

"Okay, well keep me updated." Alessandra stood up.

"Would you like to accompany me for a celebratory drink? I can text Beau, get him to join us. Beau's gonna be playing Angelo."

"Beau?"

"Beau Benjamin. Quite the young actor."

"Beau Benjamin?" Alessandra smiled chin-to-eyes.

Lou Turcotte was texting Beau Benjamin. "He'd love to meet you. Angelo and Angie out on the town."

"I don't think so," Alessandra said. "Not now. I've got some things to do. But be in touch about the film." And she walked away from the table, up Thompson, wanting to put her head in her hands, thinking, *I've stooped lower.*

She didn't have anything to do, anywhere to be. She figured she'd just walk around the city, get lunch, go to a museum, avoid Brooklyn. The run-in with Conway D'Innocenzio earlier in the day had unsettled her, made her feel like things had corkscrewed way out of control. And trying to get with Ray Boy Calabrese—or whatever she'd been trying to do—had been a sick mistake.

She stopped at a bodega and bought a pack of American Spirits and a Pellegrino.

At lunchtime she ghosted after Dojo on St. Mark's. The place no longer there. She remembered afternoons cutting Kearney when she'd take the train into the city and have an avocado, lettuce, and tomato sandwich and sparkling water at the Dojo and then take in a movie at the Angelika. St. Mark's had turned into a yuppie wonderland, Coney Island High gone, Kim's moved, no-better-than-Hot-Topic boutiques and a chain frozen yogurt shop replacing the diviest of the dives, basement leather shops, dust-dark vinyl-only record stores up craggy stone staircases, shithole bars. The Keyhole Cocktail Lounge was still there, thank Christ, and she remembered nights she'd hang out there senior year, playing the jukebox, drinking free, Stefan, the owner of the joint, an old drunk who was famous for serving anyone, serenading her.

She stopped at the Keyhole for a drink, gin-and-tonic with double limes, and struck up a conversation with the shoulders-hunching-into-titties bar-tender. Whiskers hung from a flabby mole on the bartender's cheek, and her eyes were black and deep. Stefan died three years ago, she said. Just went plop behind the bar one night and everyone kept drinking for three hours before they realized he was dead and not just asleep.

Alessandra left the place depressed.

She got the 6 at Astor Place and took it uptown. She smoked cigarettes in Bryant Park and picked up a paperback at a drugstore.

People made movies all the time. Maybe the next Cassavetes or Scorsese was around. Lou Turcotte wasn't him, but she had to start somewhere. There was *Law and Order*, off Broadway, off-off Broadway. The city was humming with plenty of work. She'd be in Gravesend once a month maybe, for dinner with her father and Aunt Cecilia, to do a favor, drop something off. Real promise overwhelmed her.

She was feeling better about everything, excited to find a place, even if it was only with sad, sweet Stephanie Dirello. She could still pull out of that anyway. Say she found a nice studio. Went back downtown, East Village, West Village, wherever. Say she found one today. *Sorry, Steph. Dumb luck. Stumbled into it. Come visit.*

Hell, maybe she'd stay in the city all night, find someone to go home with, no ex-con hate crime-perpetrators to tempt her for lack of better options.

But, first the Met. Still an afternoon to kill.

She took her time at the museum, lingering at *Joan of Arc* for forty-five minutes, just sitting on a small bench, legs crossed, staring deep inside of it, Joan of Arc's eyes in the painting alive, wondering how the painting stayed so alive-looking for so long. She remembered the first time she'd seen it, on a high school field trip, and how she'd lingered then, too. The other girls scooting past, drunk on the energy of being outside of school, seemed uninterested. Marie Gennaro joked that the painting gave her the creeps. But Sister Erin, the youngest nun at Kearney, stood in front of it as if she were praying. She said to Alessandra on the bus home, "It's just beautiful, isn't it? Stays with you." And Alessandra knew what she was talking about and nodded.

The rest of the museum was a blur of tourists and forced air. Other paintings interested her, but there was nothing else like *Joan of Arc*.

Alessandra remembered the time she'd seen Ed Harris and Amy Madigan down by the bathrooms. It was the week before she was leaving for L.A. Mid-summer. She'd tried to make conversation, tried to say, "I want to be an actress." But nothing came out. She just stared, mouth open like a gag had just been removed, eyes gone fuzzy, tongue sandpapery.

Her father had wanted her to go to Italy that summer before college, to spend a month with some cousins in Naples, but she'd refused, spending her days in the city, doing bogus extra work, haunting the museums and cafés, drinking at the Keyhole.

She should've gone to Italy, had always regretted not going.

Feeling bad, she called her father to check in, said she'd run into some friends and was going to be crashing with a girlfriend from L.A. Her dad didn't seem happy, already used to the company, but she brushed it off, pretended to be in a too-crowded place where she couldn't hear him.

"Okay, I love you," he said.

"Love you too, Daddy."

And then the actual blankness of the day blindsided her.

She ate a baguette in Central Park and watched some hipster-slash-hippie play guitar with a case open on the ground in front of him full of nickels and dimes. He wasn't singing. Just strumming. Poorly.

She sat down on a bench, dreamed of Lou Reed-style romance, a perfect day, sangria, animals in the zoo, a movie too and then home.

She stopped at a wine bar called Zulaz, which she'd heard about from a friend of a friend, had a glass of pinot noir and a small square of dark chocolate dusted with sea salt.

On the subway back downtown everything was headphones-on quiet. People were getting off work, going home with sacks of groceries from Whole Foods and Trader Joe's. She wished she had a home here to go to. To hell with a studio. Something in a brownstone, with a let's-drink-this-rosé-and-chat kind of roommate.

Back off at Astor, she picked up *The Village Voice*, figuring she'd see about apartments. Craigslist was a better bet, but maybe she'd find something old school this way. She sat at Starbucks with a small coffee and flipped through the pages from back to front, seeing very little about apartments, a couple of out of reach places maybe, but nothing else. Instead, she noted movies she wanted to see, albums she wanted to download, restaurants she should tell Lou Turcotte to meet her at if he was footing the bill.

Folding the paper open to its center now, the main headline screamed at her: THE MURDER OF DUNCAN D'INNOCENZIO, SIXTEEN YEARS LATER. Duncan's high school yearbook picture stared up at her. Such a cute kid. That genuine smile, Duncan not miserable-looking, not being ironic. Little streak of red in his hair. Next to it were side-by-side pictures of Ray Boy. He was sitting on his stoop in the first, wearing a wife-beater, hair greased back. The other was his mugshot, Ray Boy's face drawn in, his eyes hollowed out, like he was being sucked inside himself.

Alessandra didn't want to think more about it all, but she read the article anyway, the writer saying that Duncan's murder was committed before the Hate Crime Act got passed in 2000, otherwise Ray Boy, Teemo, and Andy Tighe might've gotten sent up for life. She was saying their sentences should be revised and they should be thrown back in jail according to the new law, that it was a goddamn crime they were out walking around. They couldn't even get a plaque up at Plumb Beach for Duncan, but these guys had their whole lives ahead of them, she said. It was a rallying cry. No comment from Frankie D'Innocenzio.

Alessandra folded the paper and put it on the chair next to her. She finished her coffee and just sat there, watching people through the window.

A sick feeling crawled up in her.

The picture of Ray Boy, the mugshot, it was like looking at the Devil.

Seven Bar was a hipster dive on East Seventh. Alessandra plugged a few dollars into the jukebox and put on X, David Bowie, and The Cramps. She sat at the bar and ordered a double gin-and-tonic. The bartender, a blond girl with pin-up tats, rockabilly jeans, a tied-in-the-front blouse, and Bettie Page hair was a welcome relief from the Gravesend brand of bartender. Alessandra felt like she could sit here all night. Anyhow, the place was open until four. If she didn't find someone to go home with, she'd get an Irish coffee or two and go to a diner when Seven Bar closed.

The bartender bought her back after the first drink and introduced herself. Amy Falconetti from Flushing. "You live near here?" Amy said.

"Been in L.A. for a long time. Just got back home to Brooklyn. I'm Alessandra."

"Alessandra, that's pretty. So what's L.A. like? I've never been."

"Better than you'd expect. But still kind of shitty." Alessandra sucked down her second gin-and-tonic and rattled the ice around in her mouth.

Amy bought her another one.

"No," Alessandra said.

"Owner's an angry Ukranian midget," Amy said. "I'm sure."

Alessandra tipped big.

They got to talking about music. Amy complimented Alessandra on her picks, especially The Cramps, and talked about how goddamn much she loved Lux Interior. Alessandra told her about some great shows she'd seen out in L.A. at the Wiltern and the Hollywood Bowl: Social Distortion,

Wilco, Nick Cave and the Bad Seeds. Amy talked about her record-buying problem. She loved vinyl, 180 gram vinyl, and it was costing her. She lived with all her records in a small basement apartment in Flushing. She only really came into the city to work and see shows.

The bar started to fill up, and Amy left her to drink. Hipsters, kids from NYU, bikers, old weirdoes from the neighborhood filed in. They ordered pitchers of PBR or the house beer. Some kids got the Dirty Hipster special: a shot of Jäger and a PBR. The booths filled in. The jukebox got backed up. A kid trying to look like Edward Scissorhands played pool on the ratty table in the back with an entourage of giggly Japanese girls.

Amy came over and said, "Fuck my life." She backed Alessandra up with another on-the-house gin-and-tonic. "We'll do shots, me and you, when things calm down."

Alessandra grinned dumbly, gin hazy. She was just sitting there, drinking, watching Amy, the action of the bar swirling around her like some ribbony dream. Her phone rang a few times and she silenced it. Her old man. Stephanie. Ugh.

At midnight the bar was packed, sweaty guys shoving up behind her, ordering over her shoulders. She had to pee a few times and tipped her stool forward to show it was taken. If someone snagged it in the time she was gone, Amy made sure to kick them off.

She was going home with Amy when the bar closed, that was clear, taking the subway to Queens. Or maybe they'd stay in the bar, dance to the jukebox, get cozy on the pool table. Alessandra let her mind wander.

Amy's alarm clock sat on top of a stack of magazines next to a bookcase. It was just past noon. Alessandra, guessing they hadn't actually gone to sleep until about eight, was still tired. They were lying in a curl of blankets, both naked, a record player at the foot of the bed skipping against the middle ring of *Rain Dogs*. The mattress was on the floor. Alessandra sat up, put her head in her hands, the gin still twisting in her temples. She looked over at Amy, sleeping belly down, tats all down her back and thighs, lots of ink, hundreds and hundreds of dollars' worth of work. Her breasts were pressed against the bed. Her breaths were short and sweet, the tats rising and falling. Alessandra thought about waking her up by kissing her neck and ears, but decided against it. Amy probably had to go back to work in a few hours.

She got up and walked through a maze of vinyl-filled egg crates to the kitchen. The refrigerator was close to empty. Black bean veggie burgers, pickles, leftover to-go Indian food, a bottle of Kombucha, Seven Stars yogurt. She opened the freezer: two bottles of Smirnoff, ice trays, cans of Trader Joe's coffee. She popped an ice cube out of one of the trays and sucked on it. She looked through the cabinets for Tylenol, found none, drank two glasses of tap water.

It felt good to be walking around Amy's apartment naked.

She went over and thumbed through a crate of records. *Wrecking Ball*, *Soul Journey*, *Phases and Stages*, lots of other great stuff.

Framed sketches filled the walls. Rough drafts for some of Amy's tats. Alessandra wondered if Amy had drawn them herself or had someone else do them.

She went back to the bed and sat down, checked around for her phone. She picked it up and saw she had ten more missed calls. All from her father. Christ.

No movement from Amy.

She got up, got dressed, and found the pack of American Spirits in her coat. She went up the small flight of steps at the front of the apartment, opened the door, and was out in a little courtyard. She smoked and felt totally relaxed. Opening her phone again, she decided to call Stephanie, see if she could get a ride home. It was a bitch taking the subway from Queens. Especially where she was on Kissena Boulevard. Probably take two hours easy.

Stephanie picked up. "Alessandra?"

"Hi, Steph." Her throat felt glassy. "Sorry I missed your call yesterday."

"It's okay. I was just looking at some apartments online."

"Nice," Alessandra said, trying to lay on the charm. "You working now?"

"No, I go in later."

"I was wondering, if it's not too much trouble, only if it's not too much trouble, if you could come pick me up in Queens. It's a pain to get the subway from here. Car service'll cost me God knows how much. You got a car, right? You mind?"

"I got my mother's car. I don't really drive it much."

"She'll let you take it?"

"I think so, yeah."

"Let me give you the address." Alessandra told her where she was on Kissena. Couldn't give her solid directions on how to get there. "Just look it up on Google Maps." Alessandra said thanks so much, really, finished her smoke, and went back in to Amy.

Amy was up, still naked, putting a new record on the turntable. *Wonderful Wanda.* "Almost thought you cut out on me," she said.

"I'm getting a ride soon."

Amy put on a T-shirt and boxers. "I had a good time last night. Really."

Alessandra sat on the edge of the bed. "Me too. I'm glad I walked into your bar."

Amy came over and kissed her. "This is sweet. We're talking so sweet to each other."

"I mean it," Alessandra laughing now, tucking her hair behind her ears.

"So come back tonight. I'm working again. Shift starts at seven."

"I just might do that. Got to see how things are with my dad."

"How long until your ride gets here?"

"I don't know. She's looking up directions. Forty-five minutes maybe. An hour."

Amy sat in her lap. "Can I make you some breakfast?" She started to kiss her neck.

Alessandra put a hand between her legs.

"I've got yogurt. Probably some granola."

They went back to the bed, kissing. Amy stripped off Alessandra's clothes as they tumbled backward. They hit the sheets in a headachey swirl, all limbs and kissing. Amy tasted like gin and the morning. Alessandra rubbed between Amy's legs, caught her breath in the hollow of her neck, heard it building up inside of her, felt her body bucking.

Stephanie showed up a little more than an hour later. Amy had made a French press, and they were sitting at the table, sharing a cigarette and drinking coffee. Alessandra left when Stephanie called her, kissing Amy one last time, thinking maybe she would go back to Seven Bar, exchanging numbers, e-mails.

Stephanie was double-parked. She looked moronic behind the wheel, not quite sure how to grip it, sitting up straight, way too perky for Alessandra in hangover, just-got-laid mode.

"Hey," Stephanie said, "you have a friend that lives here?"

"A new friend, yeah," Alessandra said, getting in, lighting another cigarette.

"My mother wouldn't like you smoking in here."

"I'll keep the window down. She won't know."

Stephanie drove like she was in an old movie, hardly looking at the road, her hands at twelve and seven, the whole thing feeling like it had disaster written all over it.

"You get here okay?" Alessandra said.

"Mostly." Pause. "So, who's your friend?"

"Just someone I met last night."

"A girl?"

"Yeah." Alessandra laughed. "A girl."

"You're a," Stephanie's mouth having trouble making the word, "lesbian?"

Alessandra, deciding to have some fun with her, thinking—seriously—that this might save her from having to live with Stephanie, said, "Oh yeah. Big time. You didn't know?"

"You don't look like one?"

"Don't look like a lesbian? What do lesbians look like, sweetie?"

Stephanie's eyes were off the road for a good ten seconds as she gave Alessandra a once-over. "You know, butch, tough, manly."

"Keep your eyes on the road, Steph, will you?"

Stephanie focused on the traffic in front of her, intensified her grip.

"Will this get in the way of us living together?"

"I don't know. I've never met a lesbian."

"You've never met a lesbian?"

"I don't think so."

Alessandra said, "What about Ms. Berry, tenth grade chemistry?"

"Ms. Berry?"

"Sure."

"And Nurse Loretta."

"No."

"Absolutely. And, you ask me, Sister Clare."

Stephanie let out a breath. "I thought for sure you were trying to get with Ray Boy Calabrese the other night." She stopped. "You like it, being a lesbian?"

"It's peachy." Almost making herself crack up now. "You ever consider it as a life choice?"

"Oh no, I've never—" She stopped and pulled the car over into a bus stop. "Can I tell you something?"

"Sure," Alessandra said.

"I've never even," her voice falling to a whisper, "I've never even kissed anyone. Probably never will."

Alessandra felt bad now. Stephanie had turned this into something serious. "Oh, sweetie."

"I've always liked Conway, but he's never liked me like that. I'd love to get married, but it won't happen. I'm already old."

"You're so young."

"Look at me."

Alessandra said, "I'm not a lesbian, Steph. I was just kidding with you. Sometimes I'm just, you know, open to different experiences."

"Oh. I thought we were being honest with each other. I thought we were having, like, one of those moments."

"I'm sorry."

Stephanie pulled back out into traffic and headed for the BQE. They were quiet the rest of the way.

Alessandra's father was sitting in his recliner reading a book called *Chicken Soup for the Widow's Soul* when she got home, dollar store reading glasses—taped where they'd broken in three places—crooked low on his nose.

"You were out all night," he said.

"I just spent the night with some friends."

"I called."

"I know. I'm sorry. My phone was off." She went over and kissed him on the head.

"Your stuff got here." He pointed to the two large boxes over by the staircase. "You got bricks in there?"

"Mostly clothes." She went over and looked at the boxes. "I'll just take the stuff out little by little, if that's okay."

"Maybe you'll just leave it all in there if you're so anxious to get a new apartment."

Alessandra wasn't in the mood for this. She ignored him. "I need to take a shower. I'll be back down in a little while."

She went straight to the bathroom, turned the water on hot, the water pressure so good here if nothing else, and got out of her clothes. She looked at herself in the mirror, a faint blushy patch where Amy had kissed below her belly button, and then got into the shower.

9

Conway did some more time at the range. McKenna had brought along his piece, the thing rubbery and clean. Conway's aim was still off. McKenna stood next to him drinking coffee spiked with gin from a Styrofoam cup. He was less interested now in how Conway was shooting and more interested in procuring another pint of gin. He wondered aloud if it was possible to brew coffee with gin instead of water and determined that it was, that it might even be good for a drip coffeemaker to be run through with booze. Conway was taking sips from McKenna's cup and feeling warm and loose. When they decided to leave the shooting range and go to The Wicked Monk, which McKenna was pretty sure opened at ten, it seemed like it had been the plan all along.

McKenna ordered gin, straight, a pint glass of it. The bartender, an Irish girl who was all hips and wore her black hair piled on top of her head, her gleaming neck fantastic to look at in the morning, acted like a couple of homeless guys had just shuffled into the bar.

"You just off the boat?" McKenna said. "I want gin, plenty of it."

"I'm sorry for my friend," Conway said, knowing things with Marylou must have gotten even worse. McKenna had snuck away when they were at the range, talked to her on the phone, and had come back pounding gin.

"I don't care you're sorry," the bartender said. "One more word out of line and you're done."

"Let us buy you a drink."

She poured the gin, bottom rack stuff, and pushed it in front of McKenna. No coaster, no napkin. "I don't need you to buy me a drink in my bar. What do you want?"

"Bloody Mary, thanks."

She made a Bloody Mary, not a good one, from mix with the same shitty gin she'd given McKenna, canned olives spiked through with a plastic spear floating in the black-flecked film on top.

"I wanted vodka," Conway said.

"You got gin," she said, turning away. She cleaned up behind the bar now, doing all the routine early morning things they were interrupting. She punched a few songs into the Internet jukebox, turned the overhead TV on with no sound, collected stray bottles, wiped down tables, swept the floor.

Conway wanted to ask McKenna about Marylou but held back. He'd been like this once before, senior year of high school, obsessing over Tanya Voloktin, who'd dumped him for Jimmy O'Halloran. Tanya was different though, a high school thing, and out of his league with her pouty Russian lips and knock-you-on-your-ass body. This was his wife. They'd been together a long time, ten years, had a kid, and Marylou wasn't Tanya. Instead, Conway tried to steer the conversation back to Ray Boy.

"You know," McKenna said. "I got heartburn. A fucking headache. Let me just drink my gin for a sec."

He was right. It was getting old. Do it or don't and get on with your life.

Conway's phone vibrated in his pocket. He flipped it open and looked at it. Stephanie again. She'd been calling and calling. He decided to pick up finally. Stepping away from McKenna, he went back over by the bathrooms, the Irish bartender sneering at him as he passed.

"So, did you quit this morning?" Stephanie said. "Is that what happened?"

"I don't know," he said.

"You don't know?"

"What I said."

"You're scheduled to come in on Wednesday."

"You're the manager now?"

"I just don't want you to get fired if you're not gonna quit."

He let out a breath. "Thanks, Steph. I'll probably be in Wednesday."

"'Probably.' Are you okay? I just wanted to make sure you were okay, that's why I'm really calling. I wanted to see if you were feeling better."

"I'm okay, Steph. I mean, the world's shit and I'm a piece of shit, but I'm okay."

"I think you should take some time off. Maybe get some help."

"Some help."

"Why don't you talk to Father Villani? He's a good person to talk to. Confess. Start over."

"Confess?" Conway said.

"Maybe get involved in the church. Volunteering, you know? Bring Communion around to old people in the neighborhood, the way they bring it to your dad sometimes when he can't make it to church."

He closed the phone and went back over to McKenna, who had ordered another tall gin and was slurping on it. "This bartender," McKenna said, the Irish girl out of earshot now, "is a fucking class A cunt."

"Take it easy," Conway said.

"You want to fix your problem? Put Ray Boy in a car with this pretty bitch for a few hours. She'll be like a praying mantis, eat his face off, or his head, or whatever the fuck."

Conway laughed.

McKenna said, "Marylou left me, went to her mother's in Staten Island."

"I hope it wasn't because of this shit."

"It's been a long time coming." McKenna's voice was gin slurry. "A looooong time. Ever since the shooting. I had the shrink and then desk duty and then they made me leave the force. Everything just fell to shit. Haven't been a good dad to Nicky. Marylou, she just keeps getting colder, it's hard."

"I didn't know, man. Not all of it."

"You got a one track mind, that's it. It's why you work at a fucking Rite Aid, why you stopped playing guitar, why you don't know what's happening in my life."

"Dude."

"It's understandable. Understandishable." McKenna smiled, eyes glossy, mouth bent drunkenly. "I don't know what I'd be like if my brother got killed like that. Fucks you up. You're fucked up in your way, I'm fucked up in my way. Me shooting that guy, that was bad. I mean, it won't be like that for you with Ray Boy I hope, but it might be, maybe that's why it's so hard for you to go through with it, because you know deep down that taking a life takes something out of you no matter what."

"That guy you shot was a bad guy. He charged you with a knife." Conway paused. "Ray Boy's a bad guy."

"True. Ray Boy's bad, he ran your brother out into fucking traffic, no amount of prison's gonna make up for that. And that guy charged me, yeah, he did. In that hallway with the bike rack and the piss yellow light and the old lady next door watching out her peephole. That fucker charged me, wanted to slam that knife into my chest. I couldn't get my gun down, couldn't take out his legs, fired into his chest when he was this close," McKenna demonstrating a body length with his arms, "and he went flying back, just dead. But it takes something out of you, whether it's right or wrong."

Conway's phone rang again. He looked at the screen. Stephanie. He silenced it. He wasn't sure what to say to McKenna, so he kept quiet and hoped McKenna would just keep going. It was a relief to hear him talk.

"I don't know what I'm saying. I already said, 'Don't do this,'" putting on a school marmish voice, "I already said, 'It's not worth it.' I already said all that bullshit. Truth is, of course I understand why you need to do this. But I'm telling you, you're gonna live with Hell inside of you. It's gonna crawl up in you. Not purgatory. Hell with a capital H."

Conway didn't know what to say. He'd been determined and that was starting to fade. A couple of days ago, he would've said, "It doesn't matter. I've got to do it." But now, now he felt like there was a reason he wasn't able to go through with it. Like it was Duncan trying to warn him that everything McKenna was saying was true.

McKenna ordered another gin and Conway got another Bloody Mary and they sat there in silence, staring with empty eyes at the TV.

Finally, McKenna broke the silence. He said, "You're lucky you don't have kids, Con. It's a whole other business when you have kids. I'm happy you don't."

"I'm happy, too. I wouldn't be a good dad."

"No, you wouldn't. I'm not a good dad. Good dads are hard to come by. Pop's okay, but he's a disaster. My old man beat me with a belt, fucked his secretary, ate veal cutlets five days a week. Veal, that's a baby cow, man. A calf. You know what they do to those fucking things? They raise them in a box. What kind of example is that?" McKenna paused. "I'm no better. I make Nicky watch TV while I do fantasy football, fantasy baseball, whatever on the computer. Used to be *World of Warcraft* but I got banned. I mean, I should take the kid outside, go up to schoolyard and play stickball, something. I remember growing up, you remember Dino Randazzo and his old man? Giannozzo his name was. Every night they were in the P.S. 101 schoolyard having a catch. Until it got dark. Dino had this nice new glove and Giannozzo had this old beat-up thing, looked like he'd made it in the middle of bad weather back in Italy. And they'd just throw the ball back and forth, back and forth. Sometimes Giannozzo would tell Dino how to do stuff, but it wasn't really about that. All that practice, Dino never even got that good at little league. His father was at every game though, cheering him whether he fucked up or did okay."

Conway said, "I can't even remember what Pop was like before Duncan died. I remember he smoked cigars. I remember he sat out on that lawn chair in the yard. I remember he went over and had beers with Polack Steve, who worked for Sanitation, on Friday nights."

"Let me tell you something. The day Nicky was born, I should've been overjoyed. I should've been there at Marylou's bedside. I wasn't, man. I was at a fucking bar. Her mother kept calling me, saying, 'Get to the hospital.' One more, I kept telling myself. Then the guys found out my kid was on the way and they kept buying me rounds. I was so drunk I didn't even go to the hospital. Woke up in the back of my car. It all started right there. That was before I shot the guy, too. It's just in me."

"Pop hasn't been great, but I've been a bad son."

"You do for him."

"I do, yeah. But I don't want to. Everything's pulling teeth. And now, these last couple of days, I'm lucky I didn't kill him the way I spoke."

They were quiet again. It wasn't even noon. On a Monday. Pretty much every self-respecting person was out in the world working. Hauling trash, conducting trains, butchering meat, fighting fires, teaching, doing construction, whatever. And here they were. Fucked. People to pity. Not even noon on a fucking Monday. No wonder the Irish girl gave them that Spaghetti Western death stare.

Conway let his mind wander. The other day, on the way to Hawk's Nest, he'd thought about running away to Nova Scotia if things went well. He had always wanted to go there. He'd seen a spread on it in *National Geographic* one time in the OLN library and he thought it looked like the end of the world, peaceful desolation, and he started dreaming of it as some sort of paradise. He started thinking again that, however this went down, maybe that should still be his goal. Get there and get right. Try to live.

Conway took the bus home, a little wobbly. He'd left McKenna at The Wicked Monk, where the bartender, sensing that he was mostly harmless, took a shine to him and started to bust his balls. McKenna probably had some far-flung notions that Irish would let him fuck her, but Conway knew there was no chance for that. The girl had simply adjusted and was starting to treat McKenna like a regular.

Hyun was on the bus again. Running numbers. Always running numbers. Whatever that meant. Conway thought it sounded like something people did in the Twenties and Thirties but not now. And Conway wanted to know, if it was illegal, why did he ride the bus? He also had questions about Mr. Natale. A legend in the neighborhood, Mr. Natale had to be at least seventy now. He always wore a vintage DiMaggio or Mantle jersey and track pants, a gold chain dangling in the cottony tufts of his chest hair. He had ties to Gotti and Gaspipe Casso and the Genovese family. The rumor was that he'd been the one, back in the Seventies, who'd shot Eddie Russo outside the Loew's on Eighteenth Avenue.

But Conway said nothing. Drunk but not drunk enough.

Another call came from Stephanie and he ignored it.

He got off the bus and walked home. Readying an apology for Pop. He could see the way it would play out otherwise. He'd say he was sorry because he didn't want it to be like everything McKenna had described.

Maybe it'd be different, though. Maybe some shit would be healed between them. It was worth a shot.

To Conway home didn't feel like home anymore. It felt like a subway station at four in the morning. Sketchy. Uninviting. He opened the door and took off his shoes. The house alarm was set, thank God he noticed, and he shut it off, punching the password, 71239, Pop's birthdate. He went into the kitchen, guessing Pop had wanted him to trip the alarm as some sort of punishment or something, figuring he wouldn't remember the password.

The TV was on in the living room. Conway could hear it, some early afternoon game show with its buzzes and blips, Pop probably only half-watching, in and out of sleep, rocking in his recliner.

Conway started a pot of coffee, thinking he'd bring a cup in to Pop as a peace offering. As he spooned Folgers into the percolator, he noticed out of the corner of his eye that the bathroom door was closed. He guessed Pop was in there. He turned the flame on under the percolator, rust-brown from ages of burnt coffee and too-hot gas.

In the living room, Conway waited for his father and the coffee. The TV was blaring, so loud Conway hunted for the channel changer to turn it down. No luck. He remained in noise.

The coffee was boiling, bubbling up at a rapid pace. Conway shut the gas and took the percolator off the stove and put it on a wood block. He poured two cups, non-dairy creamer and sugar for Pop, black for him. He went over and knocked on the bathroom door. He had been in there a long time now. "Pop," he said, "I made coffee. You coming out?"

Nothing.

Conway tried the door. Locked from the inside. Fuck. He went straight to worst case scenario: Pop dead on the toilet or in the shower or slumped over the sink. He pounded the door. "Pop, open up. Come on."

A chance remained that Pop was merely giving him the silent treatment. Fuck else could it be?

"Come on, Pop. Open the door."

He wanted to call McKenna, felt like he couldn't face this alone, but he thought better of it. He rammed the door harder now, with his whole body, leading with his shoulder and following with a hip-check and a kick.

The slide lock finally snapped, taking some wood with it, and the door opened in. Pop was in the shower. It looked like he'd fallen forward going to put the water on. He'd hit his head on the edge of the tub and opened a large gash over his forehead. Conway figured it must've happened hours before. The bottom of the tub was layered thickly with blood. He didn't move fast. Didn't even think to call 911. He went over, picking up Pop's limp wrist, felt for a pulse, and confirmed what he already knew: Pop was gone.

Conway kneeled over and stroked his father's back, trying not to touch the blood. "I'm sorry," he said. "I remember more from before Duncan died, that was a lie. I remember that game we used to play, you'd hide that snow globe in the basement and I'd have to find it. I remember you getting out the BB gun that time we saw a mouse in the kitchen and me sitting next to you on the stairs all day waiting for the mouse to show so you could shoot it."

He didn't cry. His face felt shattered.

"I'm sorry, Pop," he said again.

He kept saying it.

How Pop fell was a thing Conway really didn't want to imagine but he couldn't help the scene from coming to mind. Distraught, wandering around the house, Pop had decided to take a shower. Getting in the tub, no mat, he was reaching for the water on unsure legs—that right leg had been bothering him for years—and he lost his footing. He fell forward. Hit his head. Everything went starry. Blood covered his eyes. Or maybe it was more difficult than that. Maybe Pop had a heart attack and passed out. Or, worse yet, maybe something had snapped in his hip when Conway pushed him the night before. Maybe he fought through the pain, not wanting to go to the hospital.

Whatever had happened, Pop deserved better.

Conway thought about calling McKenna again. He decided not to. He decided not to call anyone. He went to the bedroom, got a clean white sheet, and covered Pop up. The blood started to seep through the edges of the sheet pretty quickly, so he got a comforter, the thick beady yellow one from Pop's bed, and put that over him, too.

The TV was on low, something that wasn't normal in the house, Conway flipping through the channels and settling for some reality show on MTV. Not *Jersey Shore*, but something like it. Tanned, cut guidos making asses of themselves in a pool in Hollywood or Miami. Cut to the confessional room: one of them saying, "I'm a lonely person. A very lonely person."

Conway sat in Pop's recliner, nervously tapping his foot against the floor.

Telling people about this would mean a lot of attention. There'd have to be arrangements made. A service. A funeral. It was too much.

He'd closed the door on Pop.

And now he closed his eyes.

It was Tuesday afternoon when he woke up. He'd slept for almost a full day. He thought Pop dying in the shower might have been a dream, but he got up and saw the bathroom door closed and knew that it wasn't.

He heated up and drank the whole pot of yesterday's coffee, all the way sober for what seemed like the first time in days.

His phone rang. Stephanie. He picked up. "What, Steph?"

"Is this a bad time?"

"No."

"I just wanted to check in."

"You can't do this."

"Why don't you meet me somewhere? I think you need help. I think you need to talk to someone."

Conway thought about it. Maybe a distraction would be good. "Where you want to meet?"

"How about the Roulette Diner?"

"Fine."

"Should I pick you up?"

"I'll walk. I'll meet you there in an hour."

He closed the phone, put the percolator in the sink, and blocked the bathroom door with a chair. Not that anyone would be coming in the house. Even if Pop started to stink, there were no too-close neighbors to smell it. The whole house was theirs. Conway started to think of it as Pop's casket. Maybe, after everything was done with Ray Boy, Conway would just burn the house down with his father's body in it and hit the road for Nova Scotia.

The Roulette was a pretty far walk, over on Sixteenth Avenue. Conway's head was a blur. It was gray out, low fifties. He walked under the El on

Eighty-Sixth again and listened to train sounds. People walked around him, mostly Chinese, some Russians, with grocery bags and foldable shopping carts and babies in their arms and cell phones, hustling to and from banks and markets. He passed the Optimo on Bay Parkway where he used to buy porn magazines. He started when he was twelve, going in there trying not to look like a scumbag. The Indian guy behind the counter, he could really give two shits, but Conway went through the motions anyway: putting that day's *New York Times* down on the counter with copies of *Hustler*, *Leg Show*, *Barely Legal*, whatever else looked legit. The Indian guy got to know Conway pretty well, tried to make small talk with him, but Conway never wanted to strike up a friendship. He couldn't help but imagine the guy picturing him at home, jerking off over the toilet with one of the magazines balanced on the tank. Pop used to go to that place for lottery tickets and tall boys too, so that was another reason Conway had wanted nothing to do with the Indian.

Before Duncan died, Pop used to go up to a coffee shop on Twentieth Avenue for foil-wrapped bacon-and-egg sandwiches and coffee two or three times a week. The building where that coffee shop was now was split between a Russian Internet cafe and a pho joint. Conway passed it and remembered going to the coffee shop with Pop. It was called Jolly's, the name in red-script neon in the window, and it was owned by a fat Sicilian named Carlo who everyone called Jolly. Conway and Duncan would sit in the glossy wooden booths with Pop and they would unwrap their sandwiches and Pop would read them stories from the *Daily News*.

Another place he passed, a Gold's Gym now, used to be a garage where Pop worked as a mechanic. Pop told many stories about that place, how he was the best mechanic in the neighborhood for the few years he did it, how Chevy wanted to hire him for the place they had on Coney Island Avenue, and then Pop would take out his business cards and show them: FRANK D'INNOCENZIO, MECHANIC, CLIPPER JOHN'S GARAGE, 1982 86TH STREET. Conway probably still had one of those cards, tucked away in a drawer or closet somewhere.

On Eighteenth Avenue, right before the El turned away up New Utrecht Avenue, was the funeral home where Duncan had been laid out. CAPELLI'S, the letters in somber white tiles on the black storefront. Under that: *A family funeral home, est. 1963.* Pop had gone to school with the guy who ran it, Fabrizio Capelli, and he'd given Pop an old buddy's discount on Duncan's wake. It cost eight grand. Eight grand. That number had always astounded Conway. He couldn't believe it cost anything. Who would charge a friend that much money to lay out and bury his son? Then there was the church and ugly Holy Garden on ugly Long Island. Early on Conway was aware how people will charge you for anything and wring money like blood from the wet cloth of suffering.

Conway remembered being in the funeral parlor. Duncan laid out. Open casket because most of the damage had been internal. People bending over him. Flowers everywhere. Hands on his shoulders. Smell of formaldehyde. Grizzled old men patting the back of his hand, their hairy knuckles brushing his nose. Wailing ladies in mourning bear-hugging him, their flowery perfume the worst smell of all. Duncan looking so young with rosy cheeks and a glass-smooth chin. The whole thing like being inside a memory that wasn't real. Conway remembered Pop that day, gone in the eyes, ghostly, top button undone on an unpressed suit, ready to collapse, finally—all these years later—collapsing in the shower. Maybe the shock of losing both sons now—Conway dead to him after all—was simply too much to let a man stand straight anymore.

The neighborhood was the story of Pop's life, even more than it was the story of Conway's or Duncan's. He had gone to school at Most Precious Blood. Had been raised on Bay Thirty-Eighth. Went to Coney Island on weekends and holidays. Rode the bus. Scratched lotto tickets outside the Optimo. Got his newspapers at Augie's. Bought Duncan and Conway Spaldeens at Jimmy's. Got pizza at Spumoni Gardens, sitting on a bench outside and munching on a square slice, chasing it with a chocolate ice and maybe bringing a pint of spumoni home. He'd met their mother at a mixer in the Most Precious Blood basement. He'd walked his Nonna and Nonno to church every Sunday morning. He'd gone to his brother Ralphie's on Stillwell every Sunday for a touch of Johnnie Walker Red. He never strayed far from the neighborhood, unless he took a bus to Atlantic City from Bay Parkway or went to some bullshit family event in Jersey. When he went to Duncan's parent-teacher conferences at Our Lady of the Narrows, it was the first time he'd ever been in Bay Ridge, just a couple of neighborhoods over. No reason to go, he'd always said, just a bunch of goddamn Micks. He'd never been to Manhattan, never been to the Bronx for an in-the-flesh Yankee game, had no desire to visit Queens (hell for?), and—only after Duncan died—made a trip to Holy Garden on Long Island where he'd bought two plots back in the Seventies because they were dirt cheap. After Duncan's death, his range got even smaller. Home. Church. That was it.

Conway saw Pop everywhere and in everything.

Even the Roulette Diner, when he walked in, reminded Conway of Pop, who had taken him and Duncan there for pancakes after church two or three times. The place was glittery, with Naugahyde booths and mirrored walls, and the servers looked desperate in their dress-up best.

Stephanie was at a booth by a window overlooking the parking lot. She had makeup on, black squiggles around her eyes, a thick inkiness in her lashes, rouge blotted on her cheeks. She was slurping on a milkshake and watching a Hasidic Jewish family outside, husband, wife, four kids, load up their hulking green Olds: carriage, bags of groceries from Pathmark, a stack of library books.

Conway sat down.

Stephanie leaned across the table and tried to read his eyes. "You don't look okay," she said.

"I'm just tired," Conway said.

"You need help. You need to talk to someone."

"You keep saying that. I'm talking to you. Here. Now."

"I'm a start, but you need professional help. At least talk to Father Villani like I said. I talk to him all the time. He's a very gentle man. He gives good advice."

"You're what, thick? I'm not talking to Villani."

A tense silence hung in the air. The waiter came over and Conway ordered a Dewar's to settle himself down. He was shaky from all the coffee he'd had. Stephanie said what the hell and ordered a gin-and-tonic.

"I drink now," Stephanie said.

"That's nice."

The waiter brought their drinks back and put them on yellow cocktail napkins covered in recipes. He asked if they wanted food and Stephanie ordered disco fries for them to split.

Stephanie said, "Did you used to come here as a kid?"

"Just a couple of times," Conway said.

"I used to come here with Nana Dirello all the time. She'd get me a Belgian waffle and a milkshake."

"Pop brought us here two or three times, me and Duncan. I was just thinking about it."

Stephanie winced at Duncan's name. "I'm sorry, Conway."

"For what?"

"Ray Boy Calabrese. Everything. I know that's what's going on. Ray Boy's back and—"

"Really, Steph, you don't know anything."

"I know how you feel."

"You know how I feel?"

"I'm sure I do."

Conway downed his Dewar's and rattled the ice around in the bottom of the glass. "Do me a favor and change the subject."

"I don't know what to talk about." Stephanie sipped her gin-and-tonic through a coffee straw. "What do you want to talk about?"

"Tell me about Alessandra."

"What about her?"

"You've seen her since she's been back."

"A few times."

"Just tell me about her. Anything."

"Well, I thought we were going to live together. Just me and her. I was finally gonna get out of my house. I was excited. But today she calls me for a ride. Wants me to pick her up in Queens. Something about she can't take the subway from there because it'll take too long. I pick her up at another woman's house." She lowered her voice. "Alessandra's a lezzie or at least part-lezzie."

"So this was her girlfriend?" Conway said.

The waiter brought back the platter of disco fries and set it between them. Conway ordered another round of drinks. Stephanie reached out for a gravy-slathered twist of fries and started munching.

"Just a girl," Stephanie cupping her hand over mouth, "she slept with."

Conway, angry, grabbed a couple of fries and stuffed them in his mouth, but they tasted pasty and he spit them out into his cocktail napkin. He needed his scotch. He pictured Alessandra fucking some other blurry-faced girl, using what, a strap-on the way they did in girl-on-girl movies he'd seen? Behind the girls, he saw Pop, curled up and bleeding on the floor, dead. And he saw Ray Boy sitting in the corner of the room, watching, his hoodie snapped low over his brow.

"What's wrong now?" Stephanie said.

"That makes me mad."

"She said she wasn't really a lezzie, that she was just open to different experiences, but she was acting like a lezzie."

The waiter brought the drinks back and Conway practically huffed his Dewar's, spilling it out the sides of his mouth and down his shirtfront. "It's just another thing."

"You're in love with her?"

Conway held back. Didn't say anything. He couldn't talk about the dreams he'd had about Alessandra all through grade school and high school. Not to

Stephanie. He was still picturing Alessandra and the anonymous chick, Pop
dead on the floor, Ray Boy peeping the whole thing.

Stephanie's face went flush. "Why do you love her? I don't understand.
You don't even know her." She lifted her gin-and-tonic and drank some with
a quivery flourish.

"Take it easy, Steph. Maybe don't drink so much."

"'Don't drink,' he goes. I'm *finally* drinking."

"Why are you upset?" Conway said, grinding his teeth, not believing—
with all he'd been through—that now he had to talk Stephanie down.

She rubbed her chin with the heel of her palm. "You love her, you don't
even know her."

"I know her. From school, you know that. I don't love her, it's just . . . I
don't know, a thing. It doesn't matter. It's not real."

"How come you don't love me? I've known you forever. I've never left. I've
been here the whole time."

Conway grasped what was going on and couldn't really believe it. Steph?
"I can't, I don't really, I just don't think—"

"Forget it! Just forget I said anything! Please."

People were starting to look at them, the waitstaff concerned, other
patrons whispering about whether this was a break-up or just some domestic
spat.

"Let's get out of here, Steph," Conway said. He left forty bucks on the
table, more than enough to cover the bill, and led her outside.

There was nowhere to go. Conway had talked Stephanie down and had convinced her they should find somewhere quiet to talk. Just talk. Somewhere
quiet wasn't her house. They both knew that. Not with her psycho mother.
And, Conway explained, it definitely wasn't his house with Pop sick, resting,
not up for any kind of company.

They were driving under the El in Stephanie's mother's car. She looked
like a cartoon duck behind the wheel, elastic like Christopher Lloyd, her

hands never seeming to settle in the right places. Conway wanted to ask her to pull over and let him drive, but he resisted.

"How about down by Nellie Bly?" Stephanie said.

Conway said, "Just park there?"

"I guess, yeah."

"Stop at that liquor store on the corner of Bath and Bay Parkway first. Let me get something."

She barely missed hitting a parked car as she made a right turn onto Twentieth Avenue, went through two red lights before she got to Bath Avenue, and almost rear-ended a car service guy idling his Lincoln outside the liquor store. Conway jumped out, ran in, and bought three short dogs of wine and a quart of scotch.

He came back to the car, opened one of the short dogs, and sucked it down in a snarling fit.

Stephanie said, "Gosh, I think you have a problem."

"Golly gee, you think?" Conway said. "Have some." He passed her the short dog, and she sniffed it.

"Don't think I should. I'm already a little buzzed. It's not smart to be driving like this."

"Just taste a little."

She took a mouthful and swished it around before swallowing. "Not as gross as I thought it'd be."

"Let's go over by Nellie Bly."

She took them to the strange little amusement park buried on Shore Parkway. The slide you went down in potato sacks was the only thing Conway remembered from his own trips there as a kid. A junkyard fence surrounded sad carousels and bumper cars and gloomy splash pits and other worse-than-street-fair-quality rides. It made Coney Island look like Disney World.

Conway saw a couple of Hasidic families playing a shoot-the-clown-in-the-mouth water gun game through the fence.

The street was filled with close-together parked cars. No action otherwise. A squashed gloom hung in the air. The rush-heavy Belt thrummed nearby.

Stephanie had parked behind an abandoned white van, the hood torn off, the wheels flat and looking like lumpy black feet.

"Looks like they changed the name of the place," Stephanie said. "Adventurer's."

"Christ, that's terrible."

"I always liked the name Nellie Bly."

"I always pictured some old black-and-white lady with an umbrella," Conway said, slugging wine and then passing it to Stephanie.

She took a drink. "I'm sorry for before."

"Don't be."

"I know I'm ugly. I know you don't want me. I know you have other things on your mind. Ray Boy. Alessandra." She paused. "I'm not pretty. I've never been pretty. I tried to wax my upper lip once, I did, but it just made it worse."

"You're really nice, Steph. We've always been friends."

Stephanie seemed like she was about to gag but then she regained her composure. "You come down here ever as a kid?"

"Few times, I think. Nothing special."

"This was another place Nana Dirello brought us. I remember being pretty sketched out by it. All amusement parks are pretty sad but this was sad in a different way. Now it's another kind of sad."

"Everything's some kind of sad."

"I guess."

They sat there and passed the wine back and forth. Conway almost wanted to tell Stephanie about Pop being dead at home, about how he was going to kill Ray Boy and then torch the house with Pop in it. He almost wanted to confide in her.

She was getting really drunk now, he could tell. The cheapo wine wasn't agreeing with her. Her eyes were loopy. Her lips twitched.

"Kiss me," she said. "No one's ever kissed me."

"Never?"

"Never."

"I don't think so, Steph."

Stephanie whimpered. A tangle of spiderwebby snot dangled from her nose. "Please, please, please."

"Like you said, I got a lot of things on my mind. I just, I just can't."

"Close your eyes. Pretend I'm Alessandra. Can't you do that?"

"You don't really want me to do that," he said.

"Why not?"

"It's too sad. Too strange."

"I don't care. It's what I want."

Conway said, "Fuck it. Fine." He closed his eyes and leaned in, imagining Alessandra, that Hollywood look, the scarf, the black hair, olive skin, bright smile. It was working. Then came the kiss. Stephanie didn't know what to do. She didn't open her mouth. He had to push his tongue between her teeth. Clammy taste of rotgut wine and disco fries and gin. Stubbly feel of her upper lip. Dead fish stillness. Conway's image of Alessandra shattered. Instead, he pictured Stephanie as she was: glasses, mustache, trembling drunken mouth. He pulled away.

"I'm sorry," she said. "I don't know how to kiss."

"It's okay," Conway said.

"Maybe we could do something else."

"No, Steph."

"We could have sex. I've seen movies. I could just—"

"Stop."

"I could just turn around and you wouldn't have to look at me. I don't really have to know how to do anything. I just want to know what it feels like."

"This is crazy. You're crazy."

She reached over and touched his arm. "Let's," she said. "Please."

"That's what you want? Fine." He jerked around in the passenger seat—there wasn't a lot of room to move—and got his jeans and boxers down. He wasn't hard, couldn't imagine that it was going to happen, but he popped the buttons on her shirt and felt around inside the cup of her bra. "Take your pants off."

She struggled to get them down and then just sat there, her hands across her thighs. She was wearing pink underwear that didn't really qualify as underwear. They were bloomers, not soft and cottony, but towel-thick and streaked with lint. Her bush spilled into the crack between her thigh and where the bloomers cut into her skin.

"How?" she said. "There's not a lot of room here."

Conway said, "Take your underwear off and climb on top of me."

"Do we need, like, do we need protection?"

"I'll pull out."

Stephanie pushed her underwear over her knees. Conway saw her bush. It was like certain yards in the neighborhood that hadn't been maintained. The only thing missing was windblown debris and a plastic statue of the Virgin Mary.

He opened the scotch, clicked off the cap, and took a good five second pull. He wiped his mouth with his sleeve and passed the bottle to Stephanie. She sipped a little.

"We don't have to," Conway said.

"I want to. I do."

He took the bottle, replaced the cap, and put it on the floor by his feet.

"I do," she said again.

"Come on then." He reached next to the door and reclined the seat.

She scrabbled around to get in his lap and then landed there awkwardly, her doughy legs cradling him, her head down.

He reached up and lifted her bra over her tits. They were horribly white, her tits, freckled and pimply, with strange, big nipples that looked like cut-open half-grapefruits. He closed his eyes and played with them, trying to get hard. He thought of Alessandra.

Stephanie panted like an out-of-breath dog.

When Conway finally got something going, he spit on his hand and rubbed her puss open and then pushed himself in.

She grunted, fell onto him, trying to move rhythmically but failing, grinding in a sloppy circle, her puss gluey and tight.

Conway pounded upwards. Alessandra was moving on him in his mind's eye. And she knew exactly what to do. She didn't just flop around. She touched his neck and his chest, said things, smiled, her hands up in her hair and then back on his chest.

He finished quickly, forgetting to pull out, and pushed Stephanie from his lap.

She settled in the driver's seat and collected her clothes. "I'm sorry," she said.

"Don't be sorry."

"You finished?"

"I did. I didn't pull out."

"That's okay?"

"It'll be fine. Just sit up. It'll be fine."

"I'm sorry if it wasn't good."

"You deserved better than that for your first."

"I'm glad it was you."

Conway curled up and looked out the window, anywhere but at Stephanie, who was shaking, he could feel it across the seat. They were both bottomless in her mother's car on the street outside what used to be Nellie Bly, now Adventurer's, on creepy-as-fuck Shore Parkway, and Conway felt like a dead criminal, in the ground for years like landfill garbage, ashy bones you wouldn't even spit on.

10

Eugene's Monday was one for the ages. Phone off, he walked the streets of Bay Ridge and Sunset Park. He saw some sweet Puerto Rican girls, sitting on stoops, headphones on, drinking soda, and watched them from a safe distance. Then he circled back and went to the Sixty-Ninth Street Pier and just stared out at the water. The Statue of Liberty. Some big ass cruise ship passing under the Verrazano. Rats on slimy black rocks. Sketchy fishermen with red buckets and warm beers climbing over the railing to cast out. The rotten egg stink from the Owl's Head Wastewater Treatment Plant. He bummed a cigarette off a Chinese guy in a Lakers Starter jacket and flip-flops. When the guy spoke up, it sounded like metal banging against metal. Dude wanted something in return, but Eugene couldn't tell what, so he took off and snagged a light in the park.

When Sweat got out of school, they hooked up and drove back to Coney. Sweat's cousin's buddy, this dude Cesar Cisneros, told them about a girl

named Knee Socks, eighteen, and they went to her, and Sweat screwed her
first and Eugene got sloppy seconds and he discovered that she was called
Knee Socks because she wore these ratty skull-and-crossbones knee socks
from Target.

Eugene asked Sweat's advice about Uncle Ray Boy on the way out of
Coney. "I gotta get him back on track. Fuck am I gonna do?"

"You're gonna get kicked out of school," Sweat said.

"They won't kick me out."

"I think they're gonna."

"Fuck that. My uncle used to be the shit. What happened, you think?"

"Dude probably got butt-fucked so hard his brain's a mess. Some big
motherfuckers in jail. Cocks like *Lord of the Rings* axes."

"No way."

Eugene figured his mother was out looking for him and wondered if she
would call the cops. Sweat's would be the first place she'd look, so he had to
be careful there. But he had to go there because there were no other options.

Sweat snuck him into the basement through the lift-open doors in the
backyard. There was a crawl-space under the stairs, next to the rack of homemade wine that Sweat's dad was so proud of. Eugene had tried the stuff once
and thought it tasted like motor oil.

Sweat came down every hour with reports. Eugene's mother had called.
She was worried. She had Uncle Ray Boy out looking around the neighborhood. The image of Uncle Ray Boy driving around the neighborhood looking
for him made Eugene laugh. Sweat said his mother acted like it was the end
of the world but she told Eugene's mother that he definitely wasn't there.

On the next two trips, Sweat brought him down a smuggled slice of
Grandma pizza, some porn magazines, and an old school Gameboy.

Eugene put on his iPod and listened to Ice Cube, Dre, Snoop Dog, Wu
Tang.

Sweat's mother came down at ten and did a load of wash. Eugene could
hear her clomping around. He peeked through the keyhole and saw her

leaning over the washing machine in frumpy boxers and an oversized sweat-shirt. Her knockers hung to her waist. When she was done, she huffed up the steps. Sweat came down fifteen minutes later with a pepperoni stick, a blanket, and two frilly pillows from the upstairs couch.

Eugene put his head down and tried to sleep. He couldn't. He played the Gameboy until his eyes got sandy and, even then, what must have been sleep didn't feel like sleep at all.

When Sweat left for school the next morning, Eugene snuck out the lift-open doors into the cement-bright backyard and hopped a fence into a neighbor's side alley. Sweat's block was somewhere he didn't need to be. Eugene's mother knew him well enough to know he'd turn up there at some point even if Sweat's mother wasn't lying about him not being there when she called.

He hopped fences, came out a few blocks away on Fourteenth and Seventy-Eighth. His limp made him stand out. He was afraid some cops with nothing to do would spot him and give him shit for not being in school.

Trouble was he didn't want to be found by anyone—not the kind of found where he got dragged home to his mother and some bullshit punishment, where he had to go back to OLN on his hands and knees, begging not to be expelled—but he wanted to, needed to, find his Uncle Ray Boy.

Uncle Ray Boy had no haunts that he knew of. He wasn't sure he'd even been out-out since he showed up in the neighborhood, but Eugene figured if he went anywhere he'd go to The Wrong Number. Teemo bartended there. Say Uncle Ray Boy was looking for Eugene and needed a break, a cold beer (did the poor fucker even drink anymore?), he'd almost certainly go where his old wing man was pulling on-the-house drafts.

So Eugene headed to The Wrong Number.

It was a long walk, and it was damp out. Eugene felt the weather in his leg. He watched the ground as he walked. Counted cracks in the sidewalk.

Catalogued cement etchings. *Yanks '96 World Champs. Sarah Ruggiero is a Cumbucket. New York Giants, Babeeeeeeee!. MAX LOVES MARIE. DREX WUZ HERE.*

Eugene remembered more stories about his uncle's glory days, how—according to Andy Tighe—they'd scale rooftops to tag places you could only see from the El, how they'd tag subway tunnels, how they'd go to Borough Park and throw bottles at Hasidic Jews, lean out the window and shout, "Heil Hitler!" That was some funny shit right there. Eugene had heard these stories from people all over the neighborhood—Andy Tighe and Teemo since they'd been out, yeah, but also brothers of guys he went to school with and guys he just ran into in the 101 schoolyard or over by Lafayette or even in Coney who somehow knew he was Ray Boy Calabrese's nephew and wanted to share a tale.

Another thing he'd heard courtesy of Andy Tighe was how Ray Boy had fucked this girl on the hood of his car at a red light on Eighty-Sixth Street. Andy Tighe was in the backseat when it went down. He said the girl—just some chick from Kearney who Ray Boy had picked up that afternoon—slid over, put her head in Ray Boy's lap, and started sucking him off while he was driving. He stopped at a red light and the girl kept slurping on it. Ray Boy threw the car in park, pushed the girl off, got out of the car, yanked her out the driver's side, carried her to the front of the car and plopped her down on the hood. He ripped off her dress and just started having at her right there while cars stacked up behind them. The best thing, Andy Tighe said, was that the girl was really into it, that she didn't give a fuck, that she was writhing around, playing with her tits, moaning. People on the sidewalks stopped to watch. Trains rumbled by overhead. The light changed a few times. Cars were honking, skirting around them, drivers leaning out their windows about to say something and then just being stunned into silence. It went on for like fifteen minutes and then Ray Boy pulled out and shot his load across the windshield. "Hand to fucking God," Andy Tighe had said when he told Eugene the story outside HSBC one day. "Big glops of jizm right on the windshield."

That was the guy Eugene wanted to know.

The other things Eugene had heard about Uncle Ray Boy flooded his mind. How he'd gotten blown on the Wonder Wheel by Sissy Taibbi. How he'd punched out Wajahat Hussein outside Loew's just for being a goddamn Paki. How he'd run around the neighborhood waving an American flag when the Gulf War started and thrown eggs at an Optimo run by some Arabs. How he'd beat up a Mexican who worked at Deno's for saying something out of line against Andy Tighe. And there were secret things he knew about his uncle as he was. He knew Uncle Ray Boy collected comics. *The Punisher. X-Men. Batman.* White boxes stuffed with comics in glossy slips filled a closet in Grandma Jean and Grandpa Tony's basement, and they'd never let Eugene look through them. Eugene also knew that Uncle Ray Boy had kept a poster of Alyssa Milano in a Devils jersey over his bed. He'd seen pictures with it in the background and one day, when he was trying to break into the comic closet, he'd come across it, folded away in a box Grandma Jean had just thrown in the corner next to the water heater. Also in the box was Uncle Ray Boy's Most Precious Blood yearbook, signed by everyone, girls leaving their beeper numbers. A Velcro Yankees wallet with fifty bucks and a naked girl's picture folded in a Snickers wrapper was underneath that, an *Out for Justice* ticket stub in the outer pocket.

Eugene stopped on Twentieth Avenue to get a bagel and coffee. He was starting to feel sorry that he'd run out on Uncle Ray Boy the day before. It wasn't that he didn't think Uncle Ray Boy would've turned him over to his mother. He would have. But if Eugene had just taken a few more minutes, talked to him, made him see, if he wasn't so stressed from the Bonangelo and Aherne bullshit, who knew what might've happened? Uncle Ray Boy might've said, "You know what? You're right. Enough with this act." And then they might've driven off, and Uncle Ray Boy might've shown him the ropes, all the good old ways.

Leaving the bagel shop, Eugene saw a Russian guy in a black tracksuit leaning against a telephone pole. He had a goldfishy face. The guy looked at him and smiled and then he started limping around, making fun of Eugene. "You have a very funny walk," the Russian said.

"Fuck you, yo," Eugene said, feeling his face go red.

"Fuck me! Fuck me!" The Russian came over and petted Eugene's head like he was a mangled stray.

Eugene swatted his hand away. "What the fuck?"

"You are very tough. Why aren't you in school?"

"I'm off."

"You're playing hooky, yes?"

"I'm off. Who are you?"

The Russian leaned in and whispered. "I have a job for you. You interested?"

"A job?"

"I give you something, you take it somewhere. I pay you fifty dollars. Yes?"

"You're going to give me fifty bucks to bring something somewhere?"

"Yes, exactly."

"What is it?"

"No questions. And you don't look."

"Why me?"

"You have a very good face. I trust you, yes? But you also look like you're not afraid of the danger."

"The danger?"

"A little risk, huh?"

"You're just standing there, you say, 'I'm gonna give this kid a job?'"

"Exactly."

Eugene shook his head, confused.

"Very simple offer," the Russian said. "Give a very simple answer. Yes. No."

Fifty bucks would help. Maybe the Russian was legit. Shit like that had to happen. Eugene had seen it in the movies. Guys like this, they got kids to carry shit because if kids got collared it wasn't a big deal. They got a slap on the wrist. They didn't know what was in the package. They were doing a job for this guy who offered them fifty bucks and said don't peek. What kid was gonna turn down fifty bucks? Fifty bucks meant armloads of candy, Gatorade, baseball cards, cigs, porn mags. For Eugene, it meant surviving on the lam for a couple more days. "I guess," Eugene said.

The package was small, a manila envelope sealed with duct tape. Eugene turned it over in his hands looking for a sign of what it might be. He'd decided not to open it and take off with whatever was inside. Could've been drugs, cash, anything. But it was more trouble than it was worth to get these guys, whoever they were, after him. It was a much better option to go through with the job and get in their good graces. If they kept wanting him to do stuff, the dough would pile up and he could buy whatever he wanted. The Russian had given him a ten dollar down payment and he was getting the remaining forty on the other end. Going through with it would make him a little saint to these guys.

He looked down at the address the Russian had written on a torn piece of brown paper bag. Over on Cropsey by the Shell. The Wrong Number would have to wait. But he'd go there afterward with his fifty bucks and maybe Teemo would serve him.

Eugene was back in his neighborhood now so he had to be especially careful. If his mother had called the cops, Six-Two might've been out in numbers looking out for an on-the-loose kid.

He walked with his head down, stayed close to buildings, hugged corners, ducked low when he saw blue-and-whites.

On Cropsey, Eugene stopped at a deli and got an Arizona Grapeade and then continued to the address. The place was next to a crouchy church, a ramshackle little house converted into an old man's club. Alkie-nosed dudes with hairy ears sat outside on folding chairs. They played rummy on metal tables and whistled. A thousand year old boombox at their feet blasted WCBS.

One of them, smoking a cigarillo, with a mole that looked like bloody birdshit on his cheek, said, "Help you, kid?"

Eugene held up the package. "I'm supposed to drop this off." He was starting to think he knew who this place belonged to. Mr. Natale. The guy was a legend—he'd smoked Eddie Russo, stood by Gotti, done hard time, made his sauce in jail like *Goodfellas* with the razor-sliced garlic, had been the basis for a character in *Donnie Brasco*, was old school mobster royalty— but Eugene never knew where his base of operations was.

"Inside," Bloody Birdshit Cheek said, nodding his head in the direction of a propped-open door.

Eugene walked in, package under his arm. The front room was a small kitchen. A fat guy, four hundred pounds at least, in a wife-beater with swirly discs of hair on his shoulders, stood in front of a stove, rolling *braciole* on a cutting board with one hand and stirring gravy with the other. Eugene held up the package. The guy, breathing heavily, waved him in the direction of a back room.

A long, dark corridor that smelled like the VFW hall where Grandpa Tony used to take him led Eugene to a no-windows room where Mr. Natale and five others, double-thumb cigars poking out of all their mouths, were engaged in a poker game. Eugene only recognized two of the other guys: Hyun the Numbers Runner, who he saw on the bus home from school three, four times a week, and Mike Hickey from Eighty-Third Street, who was Philip Benvenuto's cousin—People called him Hockey Head. A cloud of smoke hung ribbony over the table. Two guys sat on stools behind Mr. Natale with their arms crossed. A cash drawer filled with hundreds and fifties rested on a scattered pile of red and black chips in the middle of the table. Had to be nine, ten grand there. Maybe more.

Eugene couldn't get anyone's attention. He stood there and took it all in. Mr. Natale was wearing a DiMaggio jersey, the top two buttons undone, and dark glasses. He looked like an actor playing a mobster. Swollen cheeks. Dark eyes. Serious mouth. Chomping on his cigar until it was a spitty stump.

The guy next to Mr. Natale, hooded eyes, drooping mouth, dealt a new hand.

Mr. Natale said, "I fucking lose again, I'm going apeshit."

Everyone around the table laughed. "You won't lose," Hooded Eyes said. "I'm dealing here. I'm on your side."

"You better deal me a good fucking hand, I'm telling you."

"Here comes a winning hand, Mr. Natale."

Mr. Natale noticed Eugene then. "You got something for me?" he said.

Eugene went over and handed him the package.

"Ilya sent you?"

"Yeah."

"'Yeah?'"

"Yes, sir."

"You're Ray Boy Calabrese's nephew, huh? I hear your uncle's back around."

"He's back."

"He used to do some jobs for me, too. Before his misfortunate occurrence."

Eugene had never heard that, but he wasn't surprised.

Mr. Natale reached into the cash drawer and grabbed a fifty. He handed it to Eugene. "Extra ten for being expeditious. You got what, a bad limp?"

Eugene tucked the fifty into his jeans. "I got shot when I was a kid."

"Even more impressive you were so expeditious." Mr. Natale paused, took the cigar out of his mouth. "You know what *expeditious* is?"

"I don't."

"See, I'm a fan of words. These ten dollar words especially. I read the dictionary. For fun. Ten words a day. I got one of those word-of-the-day calendars, too. I'm learning new words constantly. *Expeditious* is like speedy. I guess it's hard for a gimp like you to be speedy, but you were. You dealt with your job in a manner that was efficient."

"Thank you, Mr. Natale."

"You know of me then?"

"Who doesn't? You're famous."

"Famous? Famous?" He patted Eugene on the shoulder. Hard. "I love this kid. Famous." It was a scene from *Goodfellas*. Eugene was Henry Hill. "You believe this kid? I'm famous. You write? You want to write my life story?"

"I don't write."

"Okay, kid. Good job. Get out of here. Come back here tomorrow you want to do something else for us."

Eugene nodded and limped back down the corridor. He passed the Gravy Stirrer. Then he went outside, the clammy gray sky seeming a stupid kind of bright after being in the smoked-out back room, and he nodded at Bloody Birdshit Cheek and the Folding Chair Crew. They all nodded back. He felt electric.

Sixty dollars made him a king. He'd never had so much money in his pockets. He'd made some decent dough for his confirmation, but his mother had snagged it and opened an account for him at HSBC that she claimed was his but she was the only one who could make any transactions. He wanted to blow it all on Lutz or Quincy or Knee Socks.

Instead he went to The Wrong Number and bellied up to the rail like an old pro alkie. Teemo was behind the bar, watching a rerun of *Center Stage* on YES. Eugene said, "Can I have a screwdriver?" *Screwdriver*: the word was gristly in his mouth. Booze screwed into juice, that sounded good. Eugene also wanted to order a kamikaze, whatever that was.

"A screwdriver, huh?" Teemo said, his eyes laughing.

"A big one."

"How about just the juice part?" Teemo poured orange juice from a can with a peel-off label into a pint glass flowered with fingerprints. He brought it over to Eugene and set it on the bar.

Eugene tried to pay with a ten.

"On the house, Eugene," Teemo said.

"You seen my Uncle Ray Boy in here? I'm looking for him."

"I haven't seen him since the other night."

Eugene suddenly realized that Teemo could maybe know his mother was looking for him, but then he stopped worrying because nobody would guess he'd be at The Wrong Number. "I need to talk to him," Eugene said.

"Your uncle's different now, you know that?"

"I know."

"That guy everybody loved is dead."

"I'm gonna help him."

"You're gonna help how?"

"I'm gonna make him be like that again."

Teemo, leaning over to Eugene, said, "You got heart, kid. That's cool. 'I'm gonna make him be like that again.' You do that."

Eugene said, "I'm working for Mr. Natale now."

"Your mom know that?"

"No. I just started. I was at his card game today. I brought something to him."

"Ray Boy used to do some stuff for him, too."

Eugene nodded.

Teemo said, "On the sly. Your grandparents didn't know. But Mr. Natale screwed him over. Forget it—I shouldn't tell you. It wasn't anything big."

"Tell me. Please."

"It was nothing. He had Ray Boy knock off this doctor's office. Heard the guy, this doc who owed him on gambling losses, had a safe with fifty grand. Lady at the office told Mr. Natale. She was on his jock, one of his goomars, and the doc didn't know. So Ray Boy went in, no experience with safes, cracks the thing, gets the code, I don't know. That was your Uncle Ray Boy back then. Talent. He's sixteen, seventeen. Cracking safes. At this point, he's been working for Mr. Natale almost two years. Small fries to start out, dropping things off, picking things up, getting food, surveillance. And then some strong-arm stuff. Breaking legs. Threats. Like Rocky at the beginning of *Rocky*. Then Mr. Natale has him do this, says he'll give him ten percent of the dough, if it's there. He brings it back to Mr. Natale, honest, could've maybe run off, said there was less in there than there was, but he brings back the full amount. And Mr. Natale says five hundred's what he's getting for his work. Five grand's what he was promised. Ray Boy's going crazy on the inside, but he can't let it show. He's gonna what, complain to Mr. Natale? He'll wind up face down in the fucking Gowanus Canal."

Eugene took it all in. Maybe this was the way to get Uncle Ray Boy back. The promise of revenge. It was crazy to think about, way over the top to imagine taking on Mr. Natale, but why not? Eugene was already on the lam, and maybe Uncle Ray Boy—in the right frame of mind and given the right circumstances—would really hit the road with him. Live motel to motel, crime to crime. Sounded like heaven. He thought about the pile of money at Mr. Natale's card game—nine, ten grand, however much it was—and thought about going after it with Uncle Ray Boy, guns blazing, like that episode of *The Sopranos* when Jackie Jr. robbed Eugene Pontecorvo's card game, except they'd do it right.

"Looks like your little brain's working in there," Teemo said.

Eugene said, "I really need to find my uncle."

"I see him, how can I tell him to touch base?"

"I don't know. Not my phone. I'm avoiding my mom."

"Trouble at the house?"

"School."

"Fucking OLN. I don't miss that place at all. Aherne still a douche?"

"Big time."

"I always hated Brother Dennis the worst. That guy was definitely a kid-fucker. Always giving us the once-over like he was imagining twiddling our dongs. Place was full of fruits. Should've gone to Ford, Lafayette. But then you gotta deal with an army of *tizzuns*."

"Fuck Brother Dennis. And Bonangelo."

"Bonangelo, that fucking gimp."

Eugene looked down.

"Kid, I'm sorry," Teemo said.

"I don't give a shit," Eugene said. He backed away from the bar.

"I'll let Ray Boy know when I see him." Teemo turned around and went back to watching YES.

Eugene walked outside. Fucking Teemo had to go and say that. *Gimp.* He was talking about Bonangelo, sure, but later when he was telling Andy Tighe or whoever that Ray Boy's nephew had come in, he'd probably say, *You know, the gimp.*

A corner store up the block from The Wrong Number was piping out Middle Eastern music. Eugene walked there and bought a forty of O.E. and some Swedish Fish. The guy behind the counter had a beard that almost connected to his eyebrows and was wearing a pit-stained white shirt. The hair on his arms was like used Brillo. He didn't even look up at Eugene.

Eugene left and sat on the curb outside. He tilted the forty back, taking a long slug, elbow raised, crinkling the brown bag between his fingers. When he held up Mr. Natale's card game, when he fixed his Uncle Ray Boy, maybe then people would stop thinking of him as a gimp.

11

Stephanie pulled up at the bus stop across from the Cavallaro schoolyard on Bath Avenue, about a block from Conway's house. Conway told her he needed to stop and pick up a few things at the grocery store. "You okay?" he said.

"I'm fine," she said.

"You sure?"

"I'm good. You?"

He nodded. "I'm not coming back to work. I can't."

"I figured that."

"Listen, I'm sorry. I shouldn't have—"

"I wanted you to."

Conway said goodbye, took what booze was left, and got out of the car, figuring it was better just to end the weirdness. He watched Stephanie pull away. He was sorry for how things had gone down between them, but he wasn't in his right mind with all that was going on. Ray Boy. Pop. She had to know that, some of it at least. He thought more about how it would be to leave all of this behind, finally kill Ray Boy, burn the house, go to Nova Scotia. Fuck was in Nova Scotia anyhow? He saw land. Lots of it. Wind blowing tall grasses. Cliffs. Gray water. Gray skies. No one else around. He saw miles and miles of peace.

It was almost dark. Not wanting to go back to the house just yet, he sat on a bench in the schoolyard and stared across at the Allstate office where a girl named Ludmilla used to work. He wasn't sure who worked there now, but he knew Ludmilla had been transferred to a Brighton Beach branch six years ago. He'd been obsessed with her, used to stare at her through the window, sit on this bench with a cup of steaming coffee from Augie's or Jimmy's and just watch her. Her desk was closest to the window. Depending on the light and the time of day, it was easy to see through the window from a distance, harder up close. Ludmilla always had a pencil behind her ear. She seemed to be constantly on the phone. Her hair was blonde like the cocktail waitresses in Atlantic City, down to her shoulders, and he imagined that it was feathery. He could draw her face from memory. Dropkick blue eyes. Button nose. Purplish birthmark over her mouth. Skin the color of lemon ice. Lips to end the world. For hours Conway would stare at her. She'd push her hair back behind her ears. Take the pencil out and write something down on a lined yellow pad. She'd put her hair up in a pony-tail with a tie. She'd type on the computer. Tender pecks. Posture perfect. Three buttons open on her blouse. She'd scratch her throat. Blow her nose. Sip from a bottle of water with Russian writing on the label. Eat salads from tinfoil trays, slurping up greens as if they were noodles. Conway had wanted to change his insurance just so he could go in there.

The way the light was hitting the window now, he couldn't see in. But maybe no one was at the desk where Ludmilla used to sit or maybe the desk was done for, retired.

He should've gone in there all those years ago. He should've asked her out. Maybe things would've been different. Maybe he would've kept making music because she liked it. Maybe they would've gotten sushi every Friday night on Eighty-Sixth Street, walking back to her place (maybe she lived in one of those nice new condos on Twenty-Fourth Avenue) under the El, holding hands.

Conway had always been a first-class fuck-up. No hope and no balls was a rotten combination. And the way he'd dealt with the whole Ray Boy situation defied logic. For years, he'd dreamt about getting revenge on Ray Boy, but he did nothing to prepare. He didn't learn to shoot, didn't lift weights. He thought it didn't matter. Maybe what he really wanted was for Ray Boy to still be Ray Boy. Maybe what he really wanted was to die at Ray Boy's hands, be overpowered by him, fail in an ultimate and final way.

He was being honest with himself now. That *was* what he'd wanted. For as long as he could remember.

But Ray Boy couldn't give it to him. Ray Boy had turned the tables. The son of a bitch felt sorry for what he'd done to Duncan.

No one understood Conway. No one ever had. He didn't understand himself.

He wanted to see Alessandra, wanted to apologize to her. She didn't know what he was, hadn't been home for so many years. Maybe she'd forgive him. Picturing her while he was fucking Stephanie had made him feel closer to her, like they'd bonded somehow.

Before going back to Pop's coffin, he'd stop at her house, see if she'd talk to him.

Mr. Biagini opened the door. Fur poured out of his ears. He wore slippers patched together with duct tape. His nose was damp-looking. He reminded Conway too much of Pop.

"Mr. Biagini." Conway folded his arms across his chest. "It's Conway D'Innocenzio."

Eyes adjusting, Mr. Biagini glanced at him sideways. "Sure, sure. Come inside."

Conway stepped inside. "Alessandra home?"

"She's home, my daughter. Not for long, though. Got places to be. Too good for her old man, for the old neighborhood. Just got here and already she's talking about moving out."

"She's upstairs?"

Mr. Biagini nodded. "I'll call up to her," he said. He went to the stairs and put his hand on the railing and leaned forward, his chest punching out, as if it were taking all his energy to call up. "Alessandra, you've got a visitor down here."

Her voice came from the top of the stairs. "A visitor?"

"Conway. From school."

Conway heard Alessandra huff. "One minute," she said.

"Get you anything?" Mr. Biagini said.

"No, sir. Thanks." Conway sat down on the couch. Mr. Biagini sat across from him on a recliner. The TV was on low. News. Mr. Biagini picked up the channel changer and flicked around. "How is everything?" Conway said.

"Huh?" Mr. Biagini strained forward.

"Everything's good with you?"

"Good? What's good? Waiting around to die, that's it."

Alessandra came downstairs a few minutes later. Her hair was wet, crayon black, glossy. Conway could see beads of water on her neck. Her shirt clung to her. She was wearing gym shorts, and she was barefoot. Conway pictured her in the shower.

"What are you doing here?" she said.

Conway said, "I wanted, I just wanted—"

"What?"

"Could we talk somewhere, just me and you?"

"About?"

"I just . . . I need to, I just want to," he lowered his voice, "apologize."

"Apologize here and then get out."

"I need to talk to someone. I thought maybe I could talk to you. I was drunk when I saw you, I'm sorry. I'm just, it's this, it's . . . with Ray Boy out, thinking about Duncan, I don't know, I just, I'm sorry how I acted toward you. I was way out of line," Conway groveling now, "and I just hope you'll forgive me. I don't want you to think bad things about me. I'm not a bad guy. I didn't want to give you that impression. I'm not like the guys around here."

Alessandra clenched her jaw. "I'll give you five minutes."

They went in the kitchen and Alessandra put on espresso and turned the small clock radio next to the microwave to WCBS, cutting down on the burning silence. They sat across from each other at a Formica table with one of those flecked tops. A few issues of the *Daily News* were folded open to crossword puzzles, horoscopes, the Metro Section, Mike Lupica's column. "How's it being back?" Conway said.

Alessandra took out a cigarette and lit it. She blew the smoke over her shoulder. "You kidding?" she said.

"I just . . . I was just wondering if it was weird being back."

"Yeah, it's weird. Next question."

"Los Angeles—"

"You want to make small talk, that's what you're after?"

"I'm sorry. It's hard for me to talk about any of this. I've never talked to anyone about any of it. Hardly anyone."

The espresso bubbled over. Alessandra got up and took the Laroma off the burner. She poured the espresso and rubbed the rim of her cup with a lemon wedge. She came back to the table and put the cup in front of Conway. He spooned sugar into his espresso from a small bowl on the table and stirred.

"I don't know what you're hoping for here," Alessandra said. "You want me to say you're forgiven? I already said it."

"We used to know each other."

"You can't help who you grow up with. We were kids."

"I've been a wreck since Duncan. My whole life fell apart after that."

"I always felt sorry for you."

"I don't want you to feel sorry."

"What do you want?"

Conway thought about it. He wasn't sure what he wanted and he wasn't sure why he was with Alessandra now. Did he really think this was going to play out like a bad movie? She'd forgive him, they'd fuck, and then they'd run off to Nova Scotia together? That wasn't going to happen. So what was he hoping to accomplish? He didn't know. Things weren't neat like that in real life. "I don't know," Conway said. "Nothing."

"I wish you'd go."

Conway toyed with the handle of his espresso cup. "Remember that time in Ms. Lacari's class? You kept turning around and passing me notes, asking me who I liked, what my job was gonna be when I grew up, what my favorite color was?"

"I don't remember that, no."

"You kept turning around, smiling. You'd put these little balled-up notes on my desk. Your handwriting was all bubbly. The notes smelled like you. Ms. Lacari yelled at you and you blushed. Made you read your notes in front of the class."

"Conway, you were a nice kid. We were friends. What else do you want to hear?"

"I don't know. I liked you. I see you again now, and I still like you. You're beautiful. No one I've liked has ever liked me back. Not really."

"You should really go."

"I heard you had a girlfriend now or something."

"You heard that where?" Alessandra stood up.

"Stephanie."

"You saw Stephanie?"

"She said you had a girlfriend. That true?"

"I think you should go. Really."

"I'm not going." Conway slurped down the rest of his espresso. "I want you to hear me out."

Alessandra went over to the rotary phone on the wall and started the long act of dialing. "I'm calling the cops," she said. "You're not out of here in a minute, I'm calling the cops."

"Don't," Conway said.

"Daddy!" Alessandra said. She dialed the nine and then started on the one.

Mr. Biagini came into the kitchen. "What's wrong?"

"Conway's—"

Conway ran over and took the receiver from her hand. He ripped the cord out of the base on the wall. "Don't call the cops please," he said. "I just want to talk to you."

"Kid, leave," Mr. Biagini said.

"Mr. Biagini," Conway said, his hands out. "You know, I'm just . . . I'm desperate."

"You ripped the fucking phone out of the wall," Alessandra said. "Psycho."

"I ripped the cord out." He paused. "I'm sorry. I shouldn't have done that."

"I should've known, soon as I saw you," Alessandra said, "what you were, what you are."

"What? I'm not, I'm just . . . I'm not bad. I'm good."

Alessandra still had the receiver in her hand. She was waving it around. Conway played out a scenario in his mind: Grabbing the receiver and smashing it over Mr. Biagini's head, Mr. Biagini letting out a defeated sound, part wail, part deflated oomph, and collapsing to the floor. Alessandra would shriek. Conway would hit her in the face, as if his hands weren't his own. He'd grab her T-shirt at the neck and rip down and it wouldn't be easy to rip. His hands would be leading him. His mind would tell him to stop, this was wrong, very wrong, but he wouldn't be able to stop because his hands had all the power. He would finally make the shirt rip. Alessandra wouldn't be wearing a bra. Her nipples would be hard from standing barefoot on the cold linoleum. She would be screaming in a way that he had never heard someone scream. Primitive. Guttural. He would hit her again. Feel her teeth under his knuckles.

Then he would put his hand over her mouth. She would try to bite him. She'd be crying, snot stringing out of her nose. "Please," she'd say. He'd get her shorts off. No underwear. He'd hit her again. He'd push her over the table. Take her.

But that wasn't happening. It was just some fucked-up fantasy. Conway didn't really want to rape-rape Alessandra, but he almost got a hard-on thinking about it. What was really happening was pathetic. Alessandra was coming after him with a phone receiver, trying to chase him out the back door like he was a moth that had gotten in by mistake. She swung the receiver. He raised his hands to block the blow. Mr. Biagini picked up a broom from the corner and started to swat at him. "You get outta here now," Mr. Biagini said. "My daughter tells you to leave, you leave."

Conway said, "I just—"

"No just," Mr. Biagini said.

"I don't know who you think you are," Alessandra said.

Conway opened the back door and skittered across the threshold. "I'm sorry," he said.

Alessandra said, "You don't know what you are. I'll tell you: You're a psycho."

"You got a screw loose," Mr. Biagini said.

The door slammed in Conway's face. He looked at the house, the red bricks, the awning over the door, and he felt paralyzed, empty, unable.

Walking away from Alessandra's house, Conway looked down at the sidewalk. Crack-lumpy. Weed-stitched. Candy wrappers like ripped flowers dotting dirt squares where the city had put in shitty little trees. Fire hydrants that resembled squat patrolmen. Telephone poles with the copper wire picked clean, probably by some kid who sold it over at One Stop Salvage. He crossed the street as he passed Stephanie's house and kicked into a run. Conway lifted his head and had a thought about the neighborhood: it had never let him do anything right.

He was close to home, just up the block. As he got closer to the house, he saw a dark, hooded figure sitting on the front stoop, head down. It was Ray Boy, hoodie drawn over his forehead, staring at the ground. Conway looked all around, as if there would be witnesses to this meeting, as if people would imagine that they were somehow in cahoots, as if that *Village Voice* reporter might leap out from behind a telephone pole and question the ethics of this encounter.

Ray Boy didn't get up. He just sat there.

Conway approached him. Maybe Ray Boy had been fucking with him all along. Or maybe he'd reneged on their deal, gone bad. What would it take to make him what he once was? Probably not much. Some prodding. A reminder that he ruled the neighborhood before prison, before the shit with Duncan.

Ray Boy said, "We doing this or what? I can't wait anymore."

"We're doing it," Conway said.

"When?"

"Whenever I want."

Conway couldn't tell if Ray Boy was smiling, but he could see his yellow teeth, filmy, a gap in the back where he'd lost a tooth, maybe had it yanked in prison.

"I'm saying now," Ray Boy said.

"You don't get to say," Conway trying to walk past him up the steps, "get it?"

Ray Boy reached out and gripped Conway's leg. "I do get to say. And I'm saying now. We've played games enough. I'm gonna make you do this, I've got to. Down to the last thing. I gotta hold you at gunpoint to make you kill me, I'll fucking do it. No more waiting. You can fail at anything else you want, but you can't fail at this." His eyes cut through Conway. "Hear me?"

Conway nodded.

"Where's your car?"

"Up the block."

"Walk."

Conway didn't move. "I don't have a gun anymore."

Ray Boy let out a breath. "Christ."

"Can I do it with something else?"

"Something else? You're kidding, right? You want to go inside, get a fucking butter knife?"

"No, I'm just saying, how am I gonna do it?"

"I've got a shotgun at the house in Hawk's Nest. You'll use that. You'll hold it up," Ray Boy miming how to hold a shotgun, "and blow a hole in my chest. Sound good?"

"I've got to go inside. Get something."

"Then we're getting in your car and going upstate."

"I know."

"I'm coming in."

Now it was Conway's glance digging into Ray Boy. "You can't."

Ray Boy said, "Hurry up."

Conway walked up the steps and went inside, shutting off the alarm. He thought about resetting it. What would Ray Boy, not knowing about the alarm, do then? Conway could just set it and hole himself up in the house. Scared. A pussy to the bitter end. If Ray Boy tripped the alarm, the cops would come. They'd haul Ray Boy away, that was it. They wouldn't go inside, wouldn't go near the bathroom. Didn't have a reason to. No one knew about Pop. Conway's fingers hovered over the buttons. He looked out the little window in the door at Ray Boy, sitting on the stoop, his back still to the house. From behind, he kind of looked just like some guy waiting for his buddy. Could've been McKenna. Conway didn't set the alarm, though. He walked into the kitchen and looked under the sink. He found the tin box full of matchbooks that Pop kept there—from the Golden Nugget, Benny's Fish & Beer, Villa Roma, Peggy's Runway, Amendola's, some of them so old he wondered if they'd even ignite—and pocketed a few. Then he looked for lighter fluid. There was some around, he knew, because one afternoon Pop had taken out two yellow bottles and was ready to give them to the garbage—the bottles twenty years old at least, Pop never wanting to go out in the back and grill and never wanting Conway to either—but he kept the bottles, just kept them, because it was such a waste to toss them. Conway found them turned over in a dish basin full of old rags under where the pots and pans were. He put one bottle down on the kitchen table and uncapped the other. Sliding the chair out of the way, he opened the bathroom door and looked in at Pop. All that blood. Poor Pop. To die like that. Conway stood back and sprayed the lighter fluid in an arc onto the blankets covering Pop. Next he made a trail out of the bathroom and sprayed the kitchen table and the curtains on the window over the sink. He went into his bedroom and sprayed his records, his cassettes, his stereo, the bed, all his clothes. Nothing was coming with him. Nothing at all. In the living room he doused the carpet, the lamp, the TV, the recliner. Pop's room was full of ghosts. He sprayed the ghost of his mother and Duncan's ghost and the ghost of what Pop used to be and he wanted to spray himself because he felt like a ghost, but he didn't do it. He dragged a line of lighter fluid close to the tips of his black Converse sneakers and cut the flow. He was almost out of fluid in the first bottle. He took the cap off and poured the rest on Pop's bed. He got the second bottle and went to what used to be Duncan's room in the basement. Pop hadn't changed much. Conway never went down there. A framed Nirvana poster hung over the bed. A cassette of Sonic Youth's *Daydream Nation* was out on the desk where Duncan had left it. The desk was covered in other things that screamed Duncan. A VHS copy of *A Streetcar Named Desire*. Vonnegut's *Cat's Cradle* with *DI* written on the spine. Fanned out issues of *Entertainment Weekly* and *Premiere*. An eight-by-ten picture of James Dean. Conway sprayed everything. He walked upstairs and went back to the kitchen, continuing to spurt the lighter fluid in a trail on the floor behind him, and he opened the gas burners on the stove so that the gas didn't come on but he could hear it hissing. He sprayed the stove and then he made a trail back to the front door. Looking out the window at Ray Boy, he considered dragging the motherfucker up the steps and starting the fire on him. Guy wanted to die so bad, let him die that way. But Conway didn't do it. Couldn't. He leaned over and flicked a match and then twisted it until the other matches in the book sizzled to life and he was holding a ball of fire in his hand like a witch, feeling the flame licking his palm. He tossed the fire at the trail of lighter fluid and watched a quick glow open up in the center of the house. He walked outside, closing the door behind him, and told Ray Boy to move fucking now.

12

Lou Turcotte was on the phone, jabbering on, sounding like he had a toothpick between his front teeth. He said, "I think this is a great opportunity. A great opportunity. For you. For me. For Beau. You understand? The things we could do here. Enormous potential. You, you've got that star quality."

Alessandra was still shaken up from Conway coming over. It was way worse than anything she had anticipated. She saw something pass over Conway's eyes in the kitchen, something that said he might be dangerous, not just a harmless, sad-sack doofus with a dead brother. Her hands were unsteady. She had smoked her last American Spirit down to the filter. She was trying to roll one of her dad's cigarettes now. She was uh-huhing Lou Turcotte. She hated guys that talked in this phony Hollywood-speak.

"What I'm saying is, I guess," Lou Turcotte said, "we need more money. Not boatloads. Just a little. Few grand. You know anyone who'd want to invest, that'd be just terrific. Maybe you yourself want to invest? Something to think about. Get that producer credit. Looks good, someone's considering you for a role down the line, they look at your resume, they say, 'Oh, she's a star and a producer. Sign her up. That's special.'"

"Breathe, Lou," Alessandra said.

"You think you might want to invest?"

"I can't, I'm sorry."

"It's okay. Keep your eyes and ears open. Maybe you meet a rich doctor, maybe he wants to put down a few grand, more than that. We get twenty grand, we're set. The things I could do for twenty grand. The bells and whistles."

"You change the title yet?"

Lou paused. Alessandra could hear him shuffling through papers. "I'm thinking *Brooklyn State of Mind*," he said.

"That's terrible, Lou."

"Okay, I've got a whole list. We'll find something else. For now, I'm gonna work on finding investors. I'll touch base soon."

Alessandra closed the phone. She took a long drag off her cigarette, the cheap tobacco burning the back of her throat. She'd spoiled herself with the pack of American Spirits and now it was back to the bottom shelf. She was sitting Indian-style on her bed with the window open a crack to air out the smoke. She thought about Conway ripping the phone cord out of the wall mount. Looked like a kid throwing a tantrum but with some genuine psycho action behind his eyes. He'd been an inconvenience up to that point, but now she was afraid he'd cross the line, keep coming back, begging, maybe get violent. One perspective was you had to feel sorry for him, no matter what. And maybe she should've been nicer, more understanding. But she had no patience. Not an ounce. She was almost thirty.

She turned on her laptop and plugged in her headphones and listened to her favorite Deer Tick song, "Twenty Miles," on repeat. She blew smoke out the window.

When she heard a thumping over the music, she looked up. Someone was knocking at her door. Conway, she thought. Stormed back into the house and just came up to her room. But it couldn't be. The knocking was gentle, not harried-weird, no pathetic edge to it. She got up and opened the door, deciding it was probably just her father, checking on her.

Stephanie was standing there, tears stitching her eyes. "Your dad let me in, said come on up."

"What's wrong, sweetie?" Alessandra said. She put an arm around Stephanie's shoulder. Stephanie was wearing a tattered XL St. John's sweatshirt. She'd put make-up on again, poorly, and it was running down her cheeks.

"It's nothing."

"Come in."

Stephanie sat on the edge of the bed and put her elbows on her knees and dropped her head in her hands. "It's really nothing. I just . . . I had no one I could talk to. My mother, my mother's just a total nut. I can't . . . I mean, I can't even be around her right now. I had to call in to work."

"Did something happen?"

"I don't know. I mean, nothing I didn't want to happen. It just wasn't, it wasn't, nice."

"What are you saying, Steph?"

"Just. Nothing. Really."

"You can talk to me."

Stephanie looked up, her cheeks zippered with inky mascara. "Me and Conway, we did it."

"You did it?"

"Like we went all the way."

"I know what you mean. When did this happen?" Alessandra sat next to her and rubbed her back.

"Just," Stephanie crying again, hiccupping, "this afternoon."

Alessandra made the chronology in her head: Conway having sex with Stephanie and then coming to see her. Disgusting.

"I guess," Stephanie blubbering, "I guess I sort of threw myself at him. I've always liked him, and I wanted the experience, and I wanted it to be with him. Because what if it never happened? Or what if it happened with someone I didn't care about? I wanted it to be Conway."

"Was he rough?"

"He wasn't, I don't know, he wasn't rough per se. But he wasn't gentle. It was, he was, I don't know. He wasn't thinking about me, I know that, which was okay, I told him not to, but it still hurts."

"Oh, Steph."

"And he didn't use, he didn't use protection. He said he'd," her voice going to a whisper, "pull out, but he didn't."

"You'll be fine."

"But what if? I could just hear my mother. 'Puttana! Disgraziata!'"

"You can get a Morning-After Pill. It's still soon enough. You can probably get one pretty easy."

Stephanie put her head back in her lap. Alessandra rubbed her neck and shoulders. She took her brush off the nightstand and ran it through Stephanie's hair. Poor girl had probably never had her hair brushed. It was full of knots and tangles.

"I feel awful," Stephanie said. "How can I ever go back to church? How can I look at Monsignor? Puttana. That's all I am."

"Don't say that. You didn't do anything wrong."

"I did. I did a lot wrong. I should've known better."

"He shouldn't have taken advantage—"

"He didn't. I practically had to force him."

Alessandra put down the brush and worked on separating a clump in Stephanie's hair with her fingers. "Your hair, it's . . . it's tough."

"I'm a mess, I know." Stephanie stood up, ripping her hair out of Alessandra's hand, and started to pace, taking off her glasses and wiping her eyes with the backs of her hands. The whites were bloodshot, streaky. The pupils pretty, Alessandra noticed, brown, mocha almost. Stephanie's face was square-shaped. Pimples under her chin. Peach fuzz glowing on her ears. Poor, poor girl.

Alessandra said, "You're not a mess."

"What can I do? This is gonna be my life until I die?"

"Tell me more about Conway." Alessandra wanted to know the dirt, wanted to know exactly what kind of degenerate scumbag she was dealing with. "You sure it was consensual?"

"I told you. It was. He didn't want to. I had to convince him. I told him pretend I was—" Stephanie stopped talking. Stopped pacing.

"Pretend you were what?"

"Another girl."

Alessandra chewed on this. Didn't take much figuring. "Me?"

Stephanie nodded, and there was something in her nod that made the whole goddamn world just seem like a double-awful place to Alessandra. All of Stephanie nodded. Her mustache. Her pimples. Her clumpy hair. Confessing. "I didn't mind. I closed my eyes, too."

"Steph—"

"I wanted to feel like you for a little while. Nothing weird. I just wanted to know what it was like. To be pretty. To have someone want me."

"He went along with this? He pretended?"

"I think so. I felt like you. I felt like he was with you and like I was you."

Alessandra was skeeved out, wanted Stephanie to leave, but she couldn't tell her that. She couldn't tear this girl down any further.

Stephanie said, "You're upset? Please don't be upset. I couldn't take that on top of everything else."

"I'm not upset."

"You are."

"I'm, it's, I . . . I just want you to be okay, I want you to feel better. I don't want you to feel bad about yourself. There's no reason."

"I'm a *puttana*. Even worse."

"Stop saying that. Please." Alessandra stood up. "I hate that word, always hated it. You're no *puttana*," struggling with the word, something her father used to say about girls up on Eighty-Sixth Street, girls on the bus in short skirts, any girl showing skin. "You're not that, so stop saying it about yourself."

"I'm sorry."

"You think I felt that way when I left Amy's house this morning?"

"I don't . . . I'm not . . . I don't know. Did you?"

"Course not. Why would I? Feel shame? Over doing this very human thing. Anybody makes you feel guilty about this stuff is just trying to keep you down. Your mother, she's gonna think you're what, a whore? Fuck her, Steph. Really. Fuck her. You don't need that. Nobody needs that. You're just a human. You did what you needed. Fuck your mother. Fuck Conway. You're a beautiful person," Alessandra laying it on thick, "you really are. I don't say that lightly. You need to start feeling that about yourself. Fuck Conway for not realizing that."

Stephanie laughed, spit dangling at the corners of her mouth. She said, "Fuck my mother," almost choking on it, and then she stomped her feet. "And fuck Conway. That chooch." She paused. "I drank a lot today, too. I've never done that."

"It's okay."

"I hope I'm not pregnant."

"You'll get the Morning-After Pill."

"That's not, you know. Morally, I'm not sure I can."

"You'll do what you have to do then."

"I'm sorry I've wasted so much of your time."

"It's not a waste."

"How are you? How's—what's her name?—how's the girl from Queens?"

"I haven't talked to her again yet."

"I might have to throw up."

"That's okay. Bathroom's down the hall."

"My mouth already smells like puke and I haven't even thrown up. You think that means I'm pregnant?"

"You wouldn't be sick so soon."

"I'm gonna use the lavatory." Stephanie left the room and walked down the hall. Alessandra heard the door open and close and then she heard Stephanie retching, like she was sticking a finger down her throat and trying to make herself throw up, almost like vomiting would cancel out the chance of pregnancy. Alessandra pictured what Conway was doing now. Guy was dirt. Such a shame. She had no doubt he'd been fucked up by Duncan's death, but she didn't feel pity for him now. To do what he did to Stephanie, that was just a dirtbag move, dead brother or not. And it bothered her to think about him picturing her like that. Just so sickening. And then to come to her house, angry, like she owed him something.

Stephanie came back out, and she said, "I can't puke. I feel like I have to, but I can't."

Alessandra tried for a laugh, but it came out more like an exhausted growl.

"You smell that?" Stephanie said. "I smelled it when I was in the bathroom. Now I really smell it."

Alessandra got a whiff of something—maybe—a smell that reminded her a bit of California in the summer. Something burning. Like when you blacken bread in the toaster oven and it rinds up into heat-smoky curls.

Stephanie went to the window and opened it. Dampness swirled in, carrying a hard burning smell. "Something's on fire." She pressed her face to the glass and tried to see over the rooftops.

Alessandra came up behind her and made out a billowy trail of smoke behind the telephone wires. It was coming from what seemed like a few blocks away. "There it is," pointing, "what's that, two, three blocks?"

"Oh yeah," Stephanie said. "More," wiping her mouth and then her eyes, "four maybe. Let's go check it out."

"Steph, I think you should go home, get some rest."

"I'm going over there. Gotta see whose house it is. Could be Mr. Nicola's. That old pyro. That's right over by Conway's house, too. Maybe God struck him down, smote him." Stephanie scrambled out of the room, saying, "Come on." The gossip in her pushed the Conway stuff out of her mind. Stephanie was not-so-secretly like every old bag in the neighborhood: up in everyone's business.

Alessandra followed her, rolling a for-the-road cigarette as she walked. She was curious.

Even her father wanted to know what was going on. He followed them out of the house, struggling to lock the front door, as Alessandra pulled on one of her mother's long coats over her shorts and T-shirt.

"You're gonna get sick out here," her father said.

"That's a myth," Alessandra feeling the dampness in her bones. "You don't get sick from weather."

"'Myth!' Listen to this one. Now she's a weatherman."

"I think that's true," Stephanie said. "I think I saw it on TV one day."

"Oh, bullshit!"

They walked up the block, following the smoke. Sirens were screaming, the fire department fast behind this. Could be a car, Alessandra thought. Could be anything. She remembered, as a kid, guys starting a fire in the middle of the avenue out of abandoned sawhorses, blocking traffic, throwing fireworks into the blaze.

"It's probably that Henry Nicola's house," her father said. "Bastard's a menace."

As they got closer, it didn't take Alessandra long to realize that it was in fact Conway's house. She looked at Stephanie. Stephanie's expression said she'd realized it, too. Her father said, "Frankie. I hope he's okay." Alessandra was thinking about Conway—snapped, all the way off the deep end—but now she thought of his poor old father.

Two fire trucks were pulled up on the curb outside Conway's house. They had a nearby hydrant open, going full blast. Firefighters scrambled around, unspooled hoses, hooked one to the hydrant and another to the truck. Alessandra watched their black boots, their greasy jaws, their spiderwebby jackets. Fifty, sixty people stood on the sidewalks, in robes, pajamas, work clothes, watching, huddled together. A couple of cops, chests puffed out, kept the crowd back. An ambulance buzzed down the street the wrong way, parking close to the trucks.

They stood across the street, as close as possible, and Alessandra felt a pang on her cheek from the burning. The flames were lighting the sky, swishy swabs against the clouds.

"I don't believe this," her father said. "Poor Frankie."

Alessandra said, "I hope Conway didn't—"

Stephanie said, "He wouldn't." She went and talked to a cop, wanting to know if everyone got out. She came back, shaking her head.

"What'd he say?" Alessandra said.

"Said no one's in there probably, no one's come out. Pop's got to be in there."

"They'll get him if he is."

"I hope."

The firemen had their hoses going now and they were trying to keep the fire from spreading to the houses on either side but it leapt to Chrissy Giordano's three-family frame house on the right and took a black bite out of the siding before they got it under control.

The air was heavy with smoke.

Alessandra rolled the cigarette around between her fingers, flattening it. She went around to people in the crowd, trying to bum a light. She got one from a blonde Puerto Rican lady in a pink robe with green curlers in her hair and drawn-on eyebrows. Alessandra thanked her and pulled in smoke. The lady said, "Just awful. Weird people, though."

"Weird how?" Alessandra said.

"You know, just weird. Guy's almost thirty, lives with his old man. That's weird, you ask me."

Alessandra nodded.

"I'd see that boy in the Rite Aid," the lady continued, "picking up my prescription and I'd say to myself, I'd say, 'Something's not right here.' Just the other day I was saying to myself, 'Something's off with this one.' The way he was lumbering around. I thought maybe," lowering her voice, "he liked boys like his brother. Who knew? I mean, I could just tell something was off. And now this."

Alessandra said nothing. She remembered that: whenever something went wrong, whenever someone lost it, everybody else started talking about how they could just tell something was going to happen. It was sickening really, the way they got off on it.

"Who are you, doll?" the lady said, now wanting the straight dope on Alessandra.

"Just passing through," Alessandra said.

The fire kept burning, spitting embers up into the air. The Puerto Rican lady caught one on the front of her robe and palmed it out, threatening to sue.

Next to her, a wrinkled old Chinese guy with white spots on his chin perked up. He said, "Sue who?"

"The city," the lady said. "The city goddamnit."

Alessandra went back over by Stephanie and her father. "Crazy," she said.

"This is my fault maybe," Stephanie said.

"You're not serious."

"I don't know."

The firemen charged into the house with axes and pulsing, waist-high hoses, like a scene from *Backdraft*, except none of these guys looked like Kurt Russell or Billy Baldwin. Alessandra tried to imagine what was going on in the house's inside parts: the firemen smashing down doors, looking for people to save, getting jumped on by flames.

It was almost an hour before one guy, a pug-nosed Irishman with grit on his face and bloodshot eyes, came out carrying a body wrapped in sheets and towels. It wasn't Conway, Alessandra could tell somehow. Something about the way the Irishman carried the body made it clear that it was Conway's father. And then the guy put the body on a gurney and one of the sheets dangled loose and the crowd saw Pop. He was crispy, but it was definitely him.

"Oh, what a shame," someone behind them said.

"Poor Frankie," Alessandra's father said. "Didn't hurt no one. Had no enemies."

Stephanie wiped her eyes with the heels of her hands. Blubbering again.

Alessandra wasn't sure what she felt. Pity. Remorse. Nothing. She thought about Amy, thought about taking the train back into the city, and going to Seven Bar. That'd be sure to wipe some of this mess away. Frankie D'Innocenzio dead, Stephanie Dirello and her old man gone to pot, Fire-starter Conway on the loose—Yeah, she needed respite, escape. Maybe she'd stay on Kissena Boulevard for a few days.

It wasn't easy to get away, but she said she had to go, something came up with a role she'd been offered in an indie movie, and her father said, "Now? This time?"

"That's the way it works," she said. "This business."

Stephanie said, "I understand." But she clearly didn't. She honestly believed, Alessandra thought, that she'd somehow driven Conway to this, that she was such a bad lay he'd had to go burn his house down afterward. Alessandra really hoped Stephanie wasn't knocked up.

She saw them putting Conway's father into the ambulance and took a few steps back. She passed the bullshitting Puerto Rican lady and nudged her way through the rest of the crowd, their necks arched, eyes wide, some taking pictures of the scene with their iPhones and BlackBerrys.

Back at the house, she got dressed. Tight jeans, loose flannel button-up falling off her shoulder on one side, red flats. She listened to The Cramps on her iPod and thought of Amy, not Steph, not Pop, not Conway. She put on rouge and eyeshadow and mascara and lipstick and dabbed a little ginger oil in the hollows behind her ears and under her pits. Then she brushed her teeth and rinsed with Listerine, cleaned her ears with Q-Tips, plucked her eyebrows, and studied her face in the vanity mirror.

She texted Amy: *You working?*

Amy said she was, to come on down or come on over or do whatever she needed to do to get there. Alessandra put on her coat and walked to the El, wispy trails of smoke still sitting over the neighborhood.

—✦—

Seven Bar was packed again, same crowd, and Amy was dancing around behind the bar, popping PBR tabs, pouring shots, pulling drafts. Alessandra squeezed between two hipsters dressed like hunters and waved at Amy.

Amy nodded in her direction, stopped what she was doing. She brought over a gin-and-tonic and passed it to Alessandra. "Crazy right now," she said over the noise.

Alessandra said, "It's okay. Thanks for the drink." Since there was no room at the bar, she went to a booth in the back and watched some college kids shoot pool. The girls were dressed in leg warmers and vintage ruched mini-dresses, the guys in retro T-shirts and pre-worn jeans and trucker caps. Roxy Music blasted from the jukebox.

It would be a few hours before Amy was free, she realized, and she wasn't sure how she'd pass the time. She twirled her swizzle stick in her drink and played with the corners of her napkin. She listened to the conversations the college kids were having. Classes. Movies. Music. She checked her phone. Her father had called. Steph, too. Updates probably. She powered off the phone and tucked it in her pocket. She wanted to empty her mind.

13

Eugene needed a gun, numbers filed off, that kind of thing. Untraceable. Sweat—he'd know how to score one. It was about three, little after maybe, and Sweat should've been out of school, driving home. Unless he had detention. Eugene wondered if they'd turned on the hot lights and questioned Sweat. *Where's your buddy Eugene?* he could picture Aherne saying. *We know you know where he is.* Like they were police. Like it was an interrogation. Pathetic.

Eugene took out his phone and turned it on. He ignored the blippy message saying he had voicemails and fought the urge to scroll through his texts, even if there might've been one from Sweat. Instead, he sent Sweat a fresh message: *Hit me up.*

Sweat got back to him immediately, Eugene's phone buzzing and bumping. He picked up.

Sweat said, "Where you at?"

"I'm over by The Wrong Number, that bar. You know it?"

"Aherne gave me serious shit today. Your moms was over here, too."

"Fuck them." Eugene paused. "Come by here."

"I gotta go pick up some cannoli and shit for my grandma. Then I'll be over."

"Whatever. I'll wait." Eugene ducked down an alley next to the corner store where he'd bought the O.E. and Swedish Fish, the music even louder now, and he turned over a milk crate and sat on it. He finished the forty and threw the bottle against the brick wall in front of him.

A Dumpster at the far end of the alley reeked of days' old garbage. A carpet of trash—wrappers, bottles, plastic bags—was all around it.

Eugene paced back and forth in the alley, examining the graffiti on the walls. Used to be an art to it back in Uncle Ray Boy's day. Now it was all half-assed.

The broken glass from the forty was pebbly, and Eugene kicked at it.

Sweat pulled up fifteen minutes later, powdered sugar on his chin. Eugene got in the car and slapped Sweat five like he was tagging him into a wrestling match.

"You know anybody get us a gun?" Eugene said.

Sweat cinched his face and smiled. "Why you need a gun?"

"I got plans."

"Plans to go all Columbine in OLN?"

"I look like a sicko?"

"You look fucked up, homes."

Eugene jabbed Sweat in the arm. "I did a job this morning."

"Kind of job?"

"Got picked off the street by this Russian in a tracksuit. Says, 'Deliver this.' Gives me a thing. Who knows what's in it? Winds up I deliver it to Mr. Natale."

"Enzio Natale?"

"You know another Mr. Natale?"

"Face-to-face with him?"

"Walked right into his card game, made the delivery, left with some hard-earned cash."

"You're a courier now?"

"I got bigger dreams."

Sweat drove away from the curb and alternated between looking at Eugene and looking at the road. "Kind of dreams?"

"The kind I'm gonna need help from your fat ass with."

"My old man told me some shit about Enzio Natale—"

"Hold up." Eugene sniffed the air. "I smell some snatch in this car? You gonna go snatch on me before I even explain?"

"Explain then."

"Mr. Natale's got this card game. I was there during it. Lot of dough on the table. My bet's they play all the time. They're in there that early today, they're probably just sitting in there all the time. What else they got to do? Guy's got all these other people working for him, he oversees these card games."

Sweat said, "So what?"

"You remember," Eugene said, "that episode of *The Sopranos* when Jackie Jr. and those guys hold up Eugene Pontecorvo's card game?"

"How'd that end?"

"Not if we do it right."

"They're gonna know. You can't just put on a mask. You're you. They're gonna take one look and say, 'Oh, it's that kid with the . . .'"

Eugene thought about this: it was true. He couldn't really hide under a ski mask. They'd know it was him. But who cared? Wasn't like he was going to hang around the neighborhood. He was going to be forever on the run with Uncle Ray Boy. And Sweat had nothing to lose because they didn't know him. Could be any porker from anywhere. Eugene sniffed the air again. "Stinks like snatch in here," he said.

"You better quit it with that snatch shit."

"They don't know you. No one's gonna say, 'That's Sweat Scagnetti.' You got nothing to lose." Sniff, sniff.

Sweat firmed up. Eugene could see he was about to fold. Sweat said, "That dude Cesar probably help us out."

"Call your cuz, tell him to hook us up with Cesar," Eugene said, waiting for Sweat to take out his phone and punch numbers. "Now. And we need money. I got some, but we need more. You got money?"

"I got hundreds." Sweat steered with one hand, dialed his cousin with the other.

Their past dealing with Cesar Cisneros had been quick and easy. Sweat's cousin had told them to ask Cesar if they were in the market for new girls. So they did, they went to Cesar, a forty-five year old with bushy red hair who wore a sweatband on his head and ripped corduroy pants, and Cesar had directed them to Knee Socks. Cesar operated out of the back room of a thrift shop on Mermaid Avenue. He mostly sold drugs and guns, but he also dealt in exotic birds.

Sweat and Eugene went into the shop now—place was called Sutton's— and walked past racks of dirty jackets and dusty bins of LPs and ruined alarm clocks and moldy rubber children's toys. A Chinese lady with an eye patch and a perm nodded them in the direction of Cesar's office.

Cesar was sitting behind a desk piled high with porn mags and spiral notebooks, writing on a napkin. He had a couple of monster parrots perched on bars over his shoulders. One was the color of the New York Mets, blue and orange, and said "Fire away" when they came into the office. The other was yellow, and he was silent.

"Remember you boys," Cesar said.

"Yo," Eugene said.

Cesar smiled. "Let me finish this right here," nodding down to his napkin, yellow, from Wendy's, "I'm going good. I write rhymes. Gotta just go where the flow takes you." He continued to write, bopping his head. "Like to write rhymes about birds. Fuck rhymes with cardinal?"

Eugene said, "Don't know."

"How about you?" Cesar looked up at Sweat. "You gifted with words?"

Sweat shook his head.

"You motherfuckers are useless. Let me figure this shit out on my own." He bopped his head some more, spit words under his breath. "How about I go, 'I was out looking at a cardinal, who was up in a tree guarding all . . .' And then I just let it bleed into the next line like such." He cleared his throat. "I was out looking at a cardinal, who was up in a tree guarding all," searching the air for words, "the berries from the crows who was trying to pick—" He tailed off. "Fuck it, I'll finish later. 'Berries from the Crows.' Good title."

"We're looking for a gun," Sweat said.

"Sure you don't want a parrot?"

"How much are the parrots?"

Eugene nudged Sweat. "We don't want no parrots."

Cesar stood up. "'We don't want no parrots,' he says. Something wrong with my parrots?"

"Fire away," the Mets parrot said.

"Nothing wrong with them," Eugene said. "Just parrots ain't what we need."

"How old are you?" Cesar said.

Eugene, without hesitation, said, "Seventeen."

"Small for seventeen. Tiny." He came around to the front of the desk and nodded in the direction of Sweat but looked right at Eugene. "He's fat, you got that limp, what you gonna do? What could you boys possibly need a gun for? You gonna hold up the lunch counter at your school? I say save your money and buy one of these here luxurious parrots. Teach 'em shit. Times tables. Poems. Motherfuckers are verbal as hell."

"We just need a gun."

Sweat said, "Something big."

Cesar showed crooked yellow-gray teeth that reminded Eugene of crumbling overpasses on the Belt Parkway. They looked like they'd been cemented together with grime. "'Something big,' the fat one says. 'Something big.'" Cesar closed his mouth and shook his head. "Too much. Ambitious beyond your means. I think you want a BB gun, that's what I think."

"We got money," Eugene said.

"You got money?" Cesar grinned again. "How much you got?"

"Enough. Show us what you got and tell us how much."

"You the boss now?"

"I'm just—"

"I'm fucking with you. You got money, I'm deaf to the rest of this shit. But, for real, you ever want an exotic bird, I'm your man on that front, too." Cesar went back behind the desk and opened the bottom drawer. He took out a large Nike shoebox full of guns and put it on the desk. He went through what they were and how much they cost. Eugene didn't give a shit what they were, the numbers meant nothing to him, as long as they wouldn't blow up in his face. He figured the more they cost, the better they were, so he settled on one that was almost two hundred bucks and made Sweat empty his pockets. "Good choice," Cesar said. "People take you serious with that one."

Back in the neighborhood, they were driving around, looking for Uncle Ray Boy. Eugene was slumped over in the passenger seat, Wu Tang thumping from the speakers. The gun was loaded and in the trunk under the spare tire. Cesar had given them a couple of boxes of bullets, too. They'd thought about going back to see Knee Socks but decided against it. Uncle Ray Boy was the priority. Eugene's block was a hot zone, but they zipped past his house a few times to try to catch a glimpse of what was going on. They saw his grandparents on the front stoop with a box of pastries, looking worried, out of it, forgetting that no one used the front door.

"I gotta go in," Eugene said.

Sweat said, "Go inside?"

"Got to. Maybe you park around the corner, I hop the fence in Henry Yu's yard, go into the basement, just try to hear what's going on."

"They catch you, you're fucked."

"They won't."

Sweat pulled around the corner and blocked Henry Yu's driveway, turning down the radio. Eugene got out and went into Henry Yu's front yard, activating a motion detector light, and then he went down the alley next to the house and hurled himself up onto the green-slatted, ivy-covered fence that backed up against his yard. He threw his leg over the top and pulled his whole body over, landing with a thud. He knew chances were good that no one would be looking out the two small windows at the back of the house on either side of the deck, chalky yellow shades always drawn, Virgin Mary statues on the sill facing out. He just had to hope no one entered or exited the back door on the deck. He stayed low and went over to the storm drain by the rusted jungle gym he used to play around on. He remembered sitting up on the high bars with Robbie Mariano one afternoon and talking about what they'd do if they had X-ray glasses. Robbie said he'd go stand outside Kearney and just soak it in, all the girls, being able to see through all their clothes. Eugene said he'd go to the bank and look inside people's vaults and then he'd plan a heist and know exactly which vaults were worth breaking into, which ones were loaded with cash and bonds and diamonds. He remembered going out there with his mom after the Yankees lost the Series in 2001, he was only six but he remembered it, and he was too young to be hurt or angry about the loss, but he remembered looking at his mother as she pushed him on the swing and seeing her cry. He lifted the drain cover and reached down into the hole. His mother kept a spare key for the basement under a rock at the bottom of the drain, and he took it out now. He stayed low and crawled to the basement door and used the key. He flipped the door open, shut it over himself, and walked down the steps into the dank basement where his weights and boombox were.

He could hear action upstairs right away. His mother's voice, loud. Grandma Jean and Grandpa Tony. Aunt Elaine. He climbed up the steps, soft-toeing it, and sat down, listening. His mother was saying they needed to get his picture up around the neighborhood.

Grandma Jean said, "That's the wrong tactic. We need to make him feel like he's welcome here, that he's not going to get in trouble."

"Not get in trouble?" his mother said. "I'm gonna beat his ass over here."

"See. Exactly what I'm talking about. I wouldn't come home either."

"He's lucky I don't beat him with a bat."

"You're assuming," Aunt Elaine said, her voice quivery, "you're assuming he's run away. What if?"

"What if what?"

"I don't know. He got kidnapped."

"Kidnapped. Yeah, right." His mother paused, paced around the kitchen. "And where's my piece of shit brother? I ask him to help me with this and now he's gone."

"We can't pretend to understand what your brother's going through," Grandma Jean said.

"No, we can't, can we? He's in and out, just like that. We mean nothing to him. My son means nothing to him. Middle of this, he leaves a note? A note? *Vaffanculo!*"

"Watch your mouth, eh?"

"Watch my mouth? I got my son missing over here, and you're worried about Ray Boy. Typical."

"Eugene'll be back. He's just scared. Your brother, on the other hand, he's a troubled soul."

"With this 'troubled soul' shit. I've given him the benefit of the doubt for years. But not now. I asked him to help me with this. 'Help me find your nephew,' I says. He goes running off back upstate or wherever."

"Maybe he's upstate, we don't know. Wherever he is, we've gotta give him room."

His mother started bawling. She talked through tears and spit: "Room? We're talking about giving Ray Boy room here? My son is missing! No one cares."

The Disney clock, the one Eugene hated so much, went off. "Circle of Life" from *The Lion King*.

He slid back down the stairs, part of him wanting to stay and listen, the other part knowing it was time to go. So Uncle Ray Boy had split. No big surprise there. Timing was bad, but Eugene had to bet he'd headed to the house in Hawk's Nest. Where else would he have gone? It wouldn't be hard to track him down up there and then to come back for the card game. Two things he needed to do before they went upstate, though. One was convince Sweat to continue with this. To drive upstate. Dude didn't like to miss meals at his house. The other thing was to scope Mr. Natale's joint a little more and get a feel for what else went on there. Eugene had a feeling that the card game was sort of never-ending, but who knew? What if they stormed in there and the guys were having a pasta dinner prepared by the Gravy Stirrer? There'd still be stuff to take, sure, but it'd be better if they hit the card game.

Eugene left the basement, locking the door, keeping low again, and returning the key to the storm drain. He went back over into Henry Yu's yard and scrambled out to where Sweat was waiting.

Sweat took some convincing, but not much. Eugene talked about bridges and trees, a chance to get the fuck out of the city. He said what he'd heard about Hawk's Nest: the Delaware River cut through the town, his family's house sat on a hill, the bar up the road was run by an Indian. Sweat didn't seem impressed by any of it, except the Indian and his bar. Eugene sniffed the air again—snatch, snatch—and that was really the end of it. Sweat texted his mother and said he was staying over at Danny Marcone's. Eugene punched him in the arm.

First they drove to Cropsey Avenue and parked across from Mr. Natale's club. Eugene told Sweat to keep the car running. "We're just gonna watch?" Sweat said.

"I guess."

"For how long?"

"I don't know."

"Dude, this shit's boring."

Sweat was right. No action in the club. No sign of Bloody Birdshit Cheek or any of the other old guys playing rummy outside. Place was quiet. Eugene's mind got to wandering and he imagined that the card game inside had grown, twenty guys hunched around the table, hundreds of thousands of dollars to be had. He pictured fat men too slow to chase him when he scampered away with their cash. He thought if they got up, huffing and puffing, he'd blow a hole in them and they'd deflate like dollar store birthday balloons.

"Fuck we doing here?" Sweat said.

Eugene said, "This is the place."

"I know."

"We gotta get some idea."

"Dark out. We're gonna drive upstate when?"

"We'll get some Dunkin' Donuts."

"They piss in the coffee over there."

Eugene watched the rearview mirror, hoping to see someone coming up the street, headed for the club. He wanted a sign that something was going on inside. He feared that there were other clubs he didn't know about, that maybe this wasn't Mr. Natale's home base, that there were other card games in other parts of the city. Little Italy. Downtown. Bigger stakes. Maybe the game he'd walked in on was a fluke. He was confused.

He saw a guy staggering up the street, stopping to lean against a telephone pole, walking with a twisty swish. The guy wasn't headed for the club, but Eugene noticed something over his head. Behind him was a two-story building—a Laundromat on the bottom, apartments on top—and in the sky over the building there was black, billowy smoke. It looked like the guy was part of the building and the smoke was coming out of the roof of the building. But really the smoke was coming from a few blocks away. It was starting to settle over everything. "Smoke," Eugene said.

Sweat turned and looked. "Fire. Something's up in blazes."

"We should stay here."

"Let's go look." Sweat pulled a U-turn and followed the smoke. Sirens blasted the night now. People were out on the streets, looking up at the smoke like it was an alien spacecraft hovering over the neighborhood.

The sidewalks and the streets were crowded. It was like a block party. Sweat parked outside Flash Auto, and they walked toward the house on fire.

Eugene put his hood on, cinched it around his face. He scanned the crowd for his mother, his aunt, his grandparents. "After this we go back to the club," he said.

Sweat nodded in the direction of a corner pizza joint, Mama Mia. He said, "Let me get a slice." They walked into the pizza place and there was a line, hungry fire-watchers, and it moved slowly, the Albanian guy in the sauce-stained whites behind the counter flustered by the sudden rush. When it was their turn, Sweat ordered two pepperoni slices and watched as they were tossed in the oven for reheating. Eugene ordered nothing. The slices came out hot, the pepperoni glistening, and the Albanian guy put them on two paper plates in a brown bag. Sweat ripped the bag off and threw it on a nearby table. Then they walked outside and Sweat folded one slice and took a big bite, orange grease cascading off the edge of the plate.

"Shit's really on fire," Eugene said, looking up.

Sweat mumbled, gnawing on crust.

Around the corner, the crowd was pushed up close to the fire trucks and police sawhorses like they were watching a movie being filmed. The house was burning bright and heavy.

Eugene said, "I know that house."

"Who lives there?" Sweat said, his chin grease-shiny.

"It's that dead fag and his brother's house."

"No shit."

Eugene couldn't believe it. He had the feeling that Uncle Ray Boy had set the house on fire, that his whole act had been building up to this. He'd waited for the chance, that was all. Let everyone believe he'd gone pussy and then he torched Duncan D'Innocenzio's house and split town. Had to be the story. Eugene smiled.

"You smiling for?" Sweat asked.

"Uncle Ray Boy did this," Eugene said.

"You think?"

"Hell yeah. Getting back at them."

This was perfect in Eugene's eyes. Might be a little tougher to get Uncle Ray Boy back to the neighborhood now. All eyes would be on him behind this. But at least Eugene knew that his uncle hadn't stopped being his uncle. Eugene could convince him about the card game. That was small. What really mattered now was going on the lam together. Eugene needed to prove what he was capable of.

A few feet to the left of them Eugene noticed Stephanie Dirello and pulled his hood tighter. Looked down at the ground. He backed up and Sweat followed him. "You see someone?" Sweat said.

"That lady. Stephanie. She knows my grandma from church. Watched me a few times when I was a little kid."

"One with the mustache?"

"Fuck. She sees me, she'll probably call it in."

"Maybe she don't know you're lost."

"Maybe."

"Who's that fine bitch next to her?"

"I don't know." Eugene checked out the lady Sweat was talking about. Tight body. Wearing a long coat and not much underneath looked like. Black hair. Not his type, but beyond pretty. Especially standing next to Stephanie.

"I'd like to climb up in that."

"Let's get out of here."

"I wanna watch the place burn."

"We gotta go back to Mr. Natale's, scope it a little more."

"That shit's mad boring."

"We got to. I don't want Uncle Ray Boy thinking we ain't prepared." Sweat shrugged.

They went back to the car. Eugene was glad he'd gone to see the house on fire. He felt hopeful. He pounded the dash.

Sweat sped through a light and made a left to get back to Cropsey.

"Shit's good," Eugene said. "Shit's real good."

14

For the second time in a few days Conway was driving to Hawk's Nest. Ray Boy was in the passenger seat, looking almost happy. The radio was off. Conway felt loose and empty, the booze he'd had with Stephanie keeping him level. He was a vessel, he knew that now. He tried to see the future through the windshield. Gun. Shovel. Woods.

Ray Boy turned to him as they drove over the Brooklyn Bridge. "Some people," he said. "Some people in the neighborhood think I got a bum rap."

"That so?" Conway said.

"Some people. Not me. I've been honest with myself over the years. Took me a little while, but I saw what really happened. Some people, they think it was involuntary manslaughter, that I shouldn't have done much time at all. But I know, Conway. I wanted you to know I know. I murdered Duncan. Straight up. I was on his ass for years. Just the way of it. Picking on him. Fucking with him. I don't know. It was some fucked up mission I had. I knew he was meeting up with dudes on the sly. I tricked him into coming out to Plumb Beach. We were gonna beat the shit out of him, that was it. He was scared." Ray Boy paused. "He was so fucking scared he jumped a rail into traffic to get away from us. That's not involuntary anything. That's murder. I'm not gonna say I'm sorry and I wish I could have it back. That's useless. Course I wouldn't do it if it was me now. I had sixteen years of jail, sixteen years to suffer behind what a stupid fucking kid I was. I don't believe in God, I don't believe in redemption, none of that shit. Why I got this tat. First few years in, I was the same guy who did what he did. Thought I got a raw deal. Then I started to realize things. I could've been out sooner probably, like Teemo and Andy, but I stayed stupid. By about Year Six I started to see and when I started to see I started to realize that you, you were it, all there was for me in the end."

"Fuck you saying all this for?" Conway said.

"I want you to know why you need to do this. I know what you're about. I know why you came at me the way you did on Saturday."

"I didn't—"

"You thought I was still me. You wanted to die the way I want to die. Secretly. Maybe not-so-secretly. You lied to yourself about it being a revenge thing. It was a kamikaze thing, you thinking I was strong enough just to kill you, you not being prepared."

"I want you to die."

"I know. But." Ray Boy opened the window as they barreled up the the FDR. He took a pack of cigarettes out of his inner jacket pocket and lit one, ashing out the window. "And I don't care what you do after you're done with me. I don't."

"I'm not a coward."

"You gotta understand I don't care about any of that. I need you to act on behalf of Duncan here."

Conway said, "I hate you. I always hated you. Duncan always hated you. Even in third grade. He didn't think you were friends, not really. You just weren't, I don't know, totally fucking evil yet."

"I got no excuses," Ray Boy said. "How I was raised, that kind of shit. I was just, I don't know . . . I was just the way I was. Put me in a time machine, let me go back and talk to that kid, let me tell him about jail and doing shit all wrong, wouldn't change a thing. Guaranteed."

"Duncan didn't deserve anything bad."

Ray Boy turned away. "You burned down your house back there, huh? Fuck was that about?"

"It was over. The house. Everything for me in the neighborhood."

"Your old man inside?"

"He's dead," Conway said. "Was dead before I put the house up."

"Huh."

"It's just a thing I did. Seemed better than a wake, a funeral, all that bullshit. This way, my father, Duncan, the whole thing, it's just right there, ash."

"I used to think, for a second, I used to think it was your father that was my end, that it was him that should be doing this. But then I realized he couldn't. He was already dead. I killed him, too."

Nothing about how this was going down made any sense to Conway. Here they were, talking. Accomplices. Almost like friends. "I did want to die when I came up to you on Saturday," Conway said. "Why I went after you the way I did, haphazard. I didn't expect any of this. I thought you'd be strong, bad."

"I'm gonna close my eyes," Ray Boy said, flicking his cigarette butt out the window. "I haven't been sleeping. I feel like I can sleep now. You remember the way?"

"I think so."

"Wake me up at the racetrack if you get confused—easy to make a wrong turn there."

"I don't think I want to die anymore," Conway said. "I'm no coward."

Ray Boy put his hands up against the window and rested his head against them. "I'm a coward," he said, closing his eyes. "I've always been one."

They were in the woods in Hawk's Nest, digging a grave for Ray Boy. To get there they'd climbed a craggy slope behind the house. Oaks and sycamores and sugarmaples and sweetgums spread darkly over the land in every direction. The smell of cold and soil hung in the air. The river was a hush down in the valley. Owls in the trees made sounds that reminded Conway of a tunnel. Crickets sizzled. Ray Boy had put on a headlamp and guided them there, holding a shotgun across his chest. Conway had a flashlight. It was smaller, slick in his hand, shooting a beam of light that made the world small. They both had shovels, new ones with the stickers still on the handles from Home Depot. They clawed into the earth, digging deep. Conway felt damp in his blood. He thought the half-blade moon over them was alive and watching. Ray Boy let out billowy breaths that painted the darkness. Everything seemed to glow dully, especially the shovels. Ray Boy wasn't talking now. He'd done his talking.

Getting to Hawk's Nest had been a blur of roads and bridges and lights, that traffic circle again, other cars seeming hazy and unreal. Ray Boy had slept until Monticello and then had pointed out directions, but Conway mostly remembered the way. The world around the house was all dark when they got there. The door had been left open from when Conway snagged Ray Boy on Saturday and the porch light was still on. A flurry of moths ricocheted around it. Conway had followed Ray Boy into the house, which was country quiet and mostly bare except for a mattress and a wood stove and a percolator and a chipped Formica table and some old water-bit vinyl records stacked on a wicker chair, and they had gone back to a narrow mudroom where there were boots by the door, tools on the wall, flashlights, everything they needed. Ray Boy had leaned over and pushed aside a beady carpet and then opened a long hatch that was notched into the floor and withdrawn the shotgun and some shells.

Never once did Conway think that Ray Boy would turn on him with the shotgun on the way into the woods.

He felt secure.

Digging now, he felt something else. The dampness in his blood had spread to his teeth and the backs of his eyes. He was shivery on the inside. He hoisted dirt and tried to imagine using the shotgun on Ray Boy and pushing his body into the hole and then covering him back up.

His phone rang in his pocket. He'd forgotten he even had it with him. It was McKenna. Probably he'd gotten word about the fire from some of his cop buddies and now he was calling to see if Conway was okay. He considered picking up but then silenced the ringer. He imagined that Stephanie would be calling soon, too. Poor Steph. To fuck her the way he'd fucked her, that was low. He put the phone down on the ground and smashed it with the shovel and scraped it off to the side of them.

Ray Boy looked up.

"I don't need it anymore," Conway said.

"Sure," Ray Boy said.

Conway looked at the shotgun, resting up against a tree. "You sure no one will hear the shot?"

Ray Boy said, "No one's that close by. Even if someone hears it, probably won't register. It's not an unusual sound up here." He moved down into the hole, which was deep enough to stand in now, and tossed out overflowing spadefuls of darker dirt.

Conway put down the flashlight and got into the hole with him. They were shoveling with their backs to each other.

"A little deeper," Ray Boy said. "Couple of more feet." He was doing enthusiastic work, making level walls, rounding the corners, back bent, sweating.

Conway was just chopping away at dirt, trying to get down further, sparking the shovel against rocks.

When they were done, when Ray Boy said it was enough, they both climbed out. Wasn't easy. Must've been six or seven feet deep. Three big mounds of pebbly dirt surrounded the hole. Conway put down his shovel and picked the flashlight back up. Ray Boy went over and leaned his shovel against the tree and picked up the shotgun. The way the headlamp moved was starting to spook Conway out. He kept thinking it was lights from a car.

"Make sure you take the shovels and lights with you," Ray Boy said. "Don't leave anything here. Don't mark the spot. Just cover me up. Try to use leaves and branches on top of the dirt so you can't see the shape of the hole. If you need to, stay at the house tonight and come back out here first thing when it's light to make sure nothing's obvious. Chances are no one will be out here, but just in case. Could be my family comes looking for me up here. Don't want anything too noticeable."

"Okay," Conway said.

Ray Boy came over with the shotgun. "You know how to use it?"

"Not really."

Ray Boy demonstrated how to pump and fire. "It's loaded already. Hold on tight. Be steady. It'll kick you back." He took some shells out of his jacket pocket and put them in Conway's pocket. "Should be hard to miss me, but you fuck up, here's extra shells." Then he showed him how to load the gun. "Got it?"

"Think so."

Ray Boy took off the headlamp and put it on Conway's head. "I'm going down in the hole."

Conway nodded. "Anything else?"

"I'm good."

Ray Boy handed him the shotgun. Conway took it and put the small flashlight on the ground, leaving it on. The headlamp would be more than enough. He held the shotgun out in front of him and tried to imagine making it work the right way. Ray Boy got down on his knees and climbed back into the hole. He sprawled on his back, eyes closed, arms out. Conway had the light on him. It was shaking, not steady like a spotlight. He was waiting for Ray Boy to say something, one last thing, an order, or an apology to Duncan, but Ray Boy was silent. Conway thought of Ray Boy's Duncan tattoo and wondered if he'd have to get one with Ray Boy's name and death date.

Conway pumped the shotgun and put it on Ray Boy. His hands were sweaty. His instinct was to close his eyes and not fire. But he kept his eyes open and pulled the trigger.

Ray Boy's chest exploded in a pulpy thump. The sound filled the woods, echoed around the trees. Blood fountained out of Ray Boy's chest. Gristle covered his face and legs. Conway had been someone else for a minute and done the job. Or maybe he'd just been himself. He didn't know. He thought about reloading and turning the gun on himself, eating the barrel, blowing the back of his head up to the moon. But he didn't. He was on some kind of sicko autopilot. He was not a coward.

He found his broken phone on the ground and threw it and the gun and the rest of the shells and one of the shovels down in the hole with Ray Boy, feeling nothing. He didn't look at Ray Boy's body again. He started to use the other shovel to fill in the hole with dirt from the nearby piles. He was sweating. His blood still felt damp. He heard the river and was very afraid he would hear other things—people, cars, sirens, shots, coyotes, ghosts.

When Ray Boy was under the dirt he looked in the hole again and was glad to see only dirt. The shape of a body was there but it was more like a shadow.

It took him a long time to fill in the hole alone. Couple of hours at least. The moon shaded rusty. The small flashlight he'd left just sitting on the ground sputtered out and died. Owls made tunnel sounds. He wiped his forehead with the back of his hand.

He looked at the square outline in the earth and proceeded to follow Ray Boy's directions. He gathered armloads of branches and dead leaves and spread them over the grave, tamping it all down with the shovel. He had no instinct to put a marker there. Not a cross. Not a rock. Nothing. When it was over, when the spot looked like the rest of the earth, he sat down and put his head in his hands and tried to feel something.

He picked up the shovel and the dead flashlight and trudged back to the house. The headlamp scattered the land in front of him. He pulsed down the final slope on his backside, rocks scurrying, and saw bats moving against the moon.

Inside the house he took off the headlamp and put it and the dead flashlight back in the mudroom. He washed the shovel in the kitchen sink, clumpy dirt backing up the drain so much that he had to break it up with his fingers and it felt glassy and cold. Brown residue edged around the sink. He pinched his fingers together and scrubbed. Dirt hummed under his nails.

The wood floor in the house was darkened with the dirt he'd trailed in. He found a broom in a closet and swept it all up and took off his shoes and set them on the front porch. Walking around in his socks felt strange in the quiet house. He'd never experienced this world of sound. The city was always a scratchy mess of noises. All night from his room he heard buses and cop cars and radios and boys down on the corner and sometimes fireworks. Here, apparently, it was just woods noises and the occasional shotgun and in the house it was your feet on the floor and the trembling walls.

The percolator on the stove reminded him of his grandmother's house, how he and Duncan would stand at her hips and watch the coffee brew up into the glass bulb, and how he loved the smell of it filling her house until she smelled like coffee and he smelled like coffee and the world was just coffee. They'd sit down at the table after that and his grandmother would pour coffee for everyone, Pop, their mom when she was just a mom, him and Duncan, and boxes of *sfogliatelle* and rainbow cookies would be open and there'd be fennel, grapes, paring knives. Their grandfather would say, "Eat some fennel." But he'd want a rainbow cookie and the good-smelling coffee even though he was too young to drink coffee. "Have a grape," their grandfather would say, and then he'd put a grape on Conway's plate and a piece of *sfogliatelle*. *Sfogliatelle* were Duncan's favorite. He could eat a whole one, maybe two. He loved the powdered sugar on top. He loved to dunk it in their mother's coffee on the sneak. Conway didn't love *sfogliatelle*. He preferred rainbows. Both he and Duncan yearned to know coffee.

Now Conway looked through the cabinets and found a dented can of Folgers and opened it and scooped some into the percolator and ran the tap through the spout and put it on the gas on high and waited for the smell.

He guessed he would do what Ray Boy had suggested, stay the night and go out in the morning to make sure he'd done everything correctly. If someone had heard the shot and thought it somehow out of the ordinary, maybe the cops would be banging on the door any minute. But it had already been two plus hours and he didn't think that would happen. It was late and first light wasn't that far off, and he might get lost on these small roads if he tried to drive out anyhow.

He sat at the kitchen table and explored the gold-flecked Formica with his fingertips. Almost the same as Alessandra's.

The coffee sputtered on the stove. He could smell that it was done and he searched around for a mug and found one with a picture of a hawk on it. He poured the coffee and sat at the table with it steaming in his face.

He finished one cup and poured another and went into sit by the wood stove. The glass on the stove door was sooty. Conway opened it and saw scoops of ashes and little curls of Sunday circulars. He wondered if he should burn this house down, too.

A high stack of newspapers was piled on the floor protector that the wood stove sat on. Behind the stack was a pyramid of logs. A black Fila shoebox was sitting on top of the logs. Conway rested his coffee on top of the stove next to the pipe and reached for the shoebox. He opened it and saw what he guessed to be Ray Boy's stuff. A marble notebook, a few pictures, a fake Rolex, a Don Mattingly rookie card, a pair of drugstore reading glasses, and a passport-sized album full of airplane stamps. Looked like Ray Boy had meant to burn it all but instead he always just wound up sitting there looking through everything.

Conway was afraid to open the marble notebook, guessing it would be some sort of confession or letter to Duncan. But he opened it anyway and it wasn't a letter or a confession. It was just pages and rows of numbers. He couldn't figure out what the numbers signified but then something signaled that it was likely a tally of push-ups and sit-ups. The notebook was just filled with neat little rows of numbers, written in pencil mostly and Conway could see where Ray Boy had erased and adjusted a number here or there.

The pictures were harder for Conway to take.

One was of Ray Boy with Mary Parente outside Bishop Kearney on a fall day. Conway could tell it was fall because Mary Parente was wearing her crimson Kearney cardigan with the sleeves halfway down her palms and there was a tree in the picture, the one from outside Kearney, and it was a fall tree with half-bare branches and a gray quality. Ray Boy was hugging Mary from behind, kissing her neck, looking at the camera. Conway wondered who was taking the picture. Probably Teemo or Andy Tighe. More in the picture revealed itself. Girls stacked on the front steps of Kearney behind them. One of those girls—it was fuzzy but Conway could make it out—was Alessandra Biagini. Crazy. She was talking to another girl, hands up, gesturing.

In the next picture, Ray Boy was sitting on the hood of a car with Andy Tighe, Teemo, Bruno Amonte, and Ernie DiPaola. McKenna had once asked him—right after Ray Boy got out and Conway was making plans to find him—why he hadn't just gone after Teemo or Andy right there in the neighborhood instead. What he'd told McKenna then was that it was all about Ray Boy, it'd always been only about Ray Boy, he was the strong one, the leader. Teemo, Andy Tighe, they might've busted Duncan's balls a little bit, but Ray Boy was the evil one, not just some neighborhood chump. And that was true. But what Ray Boy had said in the car was also true: Conway knew or thought he knew that Teemo and Andy Tighe weren't capable of the things Ray Boy was capable of. One of the things he thought Ray Boy was capable of was squashing his mission, killing him, making him a ghost like Duncan. The picture told it all: Bruno and Ernie at the far ends, Teemo and Andy Tighe with their arms around Ray Boy, Ray Boy in the center, legs wrapped around the hood ornament, the leader, everyone wanting to be part of his crew. And he had been strong enough to control Conway in the end. Just not in the way Conway would've figured.

A couple of pictures showed Ray Boy's family posed in front of a blue sky backdrop. Him and his sisters, his mother and father. Conway couldn't believe it. They'd all gone to a place, one of those places that made photos like this, and had a fucking family picture taken. Maybe a big version of one of these hung on the wall in Mr. and Mrs. Calabrese's house. Ray Boy, in the picture, wasn't smiling, wasn't anything. He looked like a snake against the blue sky, greasy, fake, like he didn't belong.

Then there was a faded Polaroid. A nudie shot of Mary Parente. It wasn't posed for. She was sitting on the edge of a motel bed. Conway knew it was a motel bed because of the drab quilt and anywhere-everywhere landscape painting on the wall over the headboard. Looked like she'd just dried her hair. She was sitting straight up, shoulders out, was in the middle of saying something.

Conway arranged three of the logs in the wood stove and stuffed newspaper pages under them. He found matches in the kitchen and came back and lit the crumpled pages and watched them flame up and lick the logs. It took a little while but the logs caught and the fire started to burn. Conway fanned out Ray Boy's pictures on the floor in front of him. He threw the blue sky family shots into the fire and watched them sizzle. Next was the one of Ray Boy and his crew and Conway took his time watching the fire eat it, the way fire-clawed holes took over and the picture just stopped existing. Next he tore Ray Boy and Mary Parente Kissing in Fall into little pieces and sprinkled them into the fire like a seasoning. He thought about keeping the nudie shot of Mary. He still saw her around the neighborhood sometimes. She worked in a bank, had four kids, kept a tight body, dyed her hair black, wore enough make-up but not too much. He'd always thought she was hot. She got on the same bus as him his freshman year and he used to sit there and just take in a deep breath as she passed in the aisle. She smelled of apricot lip gloss and vanilla perfume. Two buttons on her white blouse were always undone. She wore a wispy gold crucifix. She stopped taking the bus at the end of that year and started getting rides with Ray Boy. He took in her nakedness, all her angles and softnesses, and then put the Polaroid in the fire. The flames slid over her body, lit it up, and then she disappeared.

Conway put everything else in the fire—the notebook of numbers, Mattingly's rookie, the Rolex, the drugstore glasses, the album of stamps—and then he ripped up the shoebox and dropped it in piece by piece.

He sat near the stove and drank his coffee.

He wanted to look through the rooms in the rest of the house. He figured that Ray Boy had other stashes hidden around. But he decided against it. Nothing he found could ever matter. He pulled his knees up to his chest and rested his head against them. He listened to the fire pop and waited for first light.

15

Another bartender came on duty around ten to help out, giving Amy time for a quick smoke break. Alessandra followed her outside. They shared a cig and made out a little. But then some other girl showed up. Looked like a gutter punk with face tats and a pierced lip and clothes that had melted into her skin. She had black dreadlocks and scabies scars on her hands and wore laced-tight combat boots that went almost to her knees and were spray-painted silver. She was dragging around a pit bull with a chewed up ear, using a length of nylon rope for a leash. "You're who?" she said to Alessandra.

Alessandra said her name. "I'm Amy's friend." She put out her hand.

The gutter punk swatted it away. "Amy's friend?" She turned to Amy. "Fuck's this about, Amy?"

Amy said, "Alessandra, this is Merrill."

Merrill got up in Alessandra's face. "Merrill Luckless. I'm Amy's girl-friend."

"Your girlfriend?" Alessandra said.

"Used to be my girlfriend," Amy said.

Merrill exploded. She turned away. She pulled on one of her dreadlocks. She tied her dog to the hydrant on the curb and started pacing back and forth.

"Might be best if you go," Amy said.

"Okay," Alessandra said.

"She gets like this, it can last. I know how to deal with her, but it's probably better if you're not around. I'm really sorry."

"Don't be."

"Another time."

Merrill approached Alessandra again and spit at her. The spit landed on her shoulder. It looked like melted aspirin. Merrill was yelling. Alessandra saw her teeth. Sawed-down yellow stumps. Amy got in the middle of them and pushed Merrill back. Alessandra went inside and gathered her things. Amy followed her in. Hipsters stared at them. Alessandra looked out through the front window and saw that Merrill was pacing around again. Amy took her to the back of the bar, and they walked down a little narrow passage to a door that opened into a piss-fumy alley. Amy said, "I'm sorry again."

Alessandra was shaking. She said nothing and took off down the alley.

On the train back to Brooklyn, Alessandra's nerves were still shot. Men in heavy coats sat slumped all around her. A Chinese woman with a folded shopping cart sat on the edge of her seat across the aisle. Two kids danced around a pole, their pants low, iPod earbuds hanging at their shoulders. A half-full Coke bottle rolled around under the seats, cap off, Coke skittering across the floor. A man hauling grocery bags set them down in front of the doors and started to hand out cards that said he was deaf and needed help. Alessandra refused the card. She'd forgotten the feeling of being on the subway. Everything was a scam. Everyone was out to get you. She felt horrible already and now she felt worse.

The train passed over the Manhattan Bridge. When they went back underground, the lights flashed off and her heart thumped. She saw Merrill's face in the darkness. *Merrill Luckless. Christ.*

By Thirty-Sixth Street, the crowds had mostly filed off. It was just her and some Russian couple snuggled close together in a two-seat wedge with their backs to her. She started to settle down, craved more gin, a cigarette, something to wash Merrill and Amy from her mind. Maybe it'd been a mistake to get with Amy in the first place. It never ended well with the girls she hooked up with. Maybe it was something about her taste. They all had dark histories. Gutter punks with pierced lips and pit bulls. Leslie, that script consultant, had a barista who was into bondage and handguns. Meredith, who used to be a run-of-the-mill housewife with frosted hair and glossy nails, had a loose cannon cokehead ex-hubby who tossed a mocha frap at Alessandra's windshield one Sunday morning. She'd had better luck with guys insofar as there was less drama involved. It never ended well, but no one got spit on.

When the train was back aboveground, Alessandra took out her phone and checked her messages. The first one was from her father. Checking in. Next one was Stephanie. Blubbering. Alessandra skipped it. Another one from her father. Checking in. Stephanie. Blubbering. Then one from Lou Turcotte. More bullshit. Funding. Beau. She wasn't even sure what he was talking about. She deleted the message. Skipped ahead. The next voice she didn't recognize. Heavy breathing. A swampy mouth. Grinding teeth. All business. She said, "Alessandra Biagini, this is Stephanie Dirello's mother." Like they were fourteen. "My Stephanie is," gasping now, "in the hospital. Ever since you showed up, she's changed. I never had problems like this with her." She wailed into the phone and then hung up.

Christ.

Alessandra thought the worst. Stephanie had gotten drunker and washed down pills. She'd cut her wrists in the tub. Walked out in front of a bus. All the Conway shit had been too much.

Poor Stephanie.

The girl was a mess. A fifth grader still in a lot of ways. Dealing with stuff she should've gone through at sixteen, seventeen.

Alessandra dialed information and got the numbers for Maimonides and Lutheran. She wrote them on the back of her hand with eyeliner she found at the bottom of her bag. Where else could Steph be? Victory was closed, she remembered her mom telling her that.

She called Lutheran first. No luck.

Maimonides had her. The nurse she spoke to said Stephanie had been brought in a couple of hours ago. Couldn't really say more.

Alessandra knew Maimonides was in Borough Park, right on the subway line. She was at Twentieth Avenue now and had passed the stop.

She felt like she had to go. Part of her didn't want to. Mrs. Dirello would probably be there, playing the victim, wailing some more. Typical Italian mother shit times ten because Mrs. Dirello was a whackjob. She figured that Stephanie, if she was going to be okay, needed somebody to tell her not to feel bad about anything. Nothing was her fault. If she wasn't going to be okay, that was another story.

At Bay Parkway, Alessandra got off the train and crossed the tracks to the other side of the platform and waited for the D back in the other direction.

Alessandra walked into the hospital room. She'd bought a small stuffed bear in the gift shop downstairs and held it under her arm. Stephanie was hooked up to an IV drip. Her eyes were closed and her skin looked chalky. Her mother was sitting next to her, wearing a black dress and black flats and a mesh net in her hair like a line cook. She was holding Stephanie's hand, hunched over her stomach, praying in Italian. A red rosary was coiled on the sheets. Someone else was on the other side of the drawn curtain, watching *CSI: Miami* at top volume.

"Mrs. Dirello?" Alessandra said.

Mrs. Dirello didn't look up. "They had to pump her stomach."

"Is she going to be okay?"

"Oh, I don't know." She wailed and then started up again with the prayers in Italian.

"What happened?"

"Pills, who knows what else? You should know."

"Me?"

Mrs. Dirello jerked her head up and fixed her beady eyes on Alessandra. She looked like a gypsy from a horror movie. "This all started with you, missy. My Stephanie, with the booze? Never. With the pills? With the wanting to move out? Never. End of story. She was a good daughter. Content to stay at home with us. Now look at her."

"Tell me what happened." Alessandra went over to the bed and held Stephanie's other hand. It was limp. The hair on the back of it looked beautiful.

"What happened? You tell me. She washed down pills with a hundred year old bottle of Sambuca I keep under the sink. Whatever was in the cabinets. My blood pressure pills. The Ultram. Everything." Mrs. Dirello stood up and smoothed Stephanie's hair back.

"The doctors say what?" Alessandra let go of Stephanie's hand.

"Who can get an answer?"

"She's stable?"

"What's stable? Who knows?"

Alessandra put the bear on the edge of the bed and went out into the hallway, wanting to talk to a nurse. Mrs. Dirello was out of her mind.

A lumpy nurse in blue scrubs sat behind a computer at the main desk on the floor. She had bobby pins in her hair and too much rouge on her cheeks. Her lips were chapped. "Help you?" the nurse said.

"I wanted to get some information about Stephanie Dirello," Alessandra said.

"Such as?"

"I want to know what's going on, that's it. Her mother, her mother's not in her right mind. She can't seem to remember anything the doctors said."

"You're family?"

"A friend."

"I can't, I'm sorry. The mother wants to come out and talk to me, that's one thing."

Alessandra didn't push it. She went downstairs and got a coffee in the cafeteria. There was nothing sadder than drinking watery grind-flecked coffee out of a Styrofoam cup in a hospital cafeteria. She looked around. People picked at withered fruit on trays and slurped bottled water or bad coffee. She tried to pick out the people who were upset, who were there to visit relatives who were dying. It wasn't hard. They were slumped in their chairs, the food in front of them for show. One family, well-dressed, the father with a neat mustache, the mother in a pants suit, the kids cow-licked and cooperative, seemed almost joyous. Alessandra wondered what their story was. Maybe they just liked eating in the hospital cafeteria.

She thought about Stephanie. She pictured her washing down pills with a crusty old bottle of Sambuca. Where was she when she did it? In front of the medicine chest in the bathroom? It made Alessandra sick to think about. Poor girl probably looked at herself in the mirror, thought about what Conway did, and figured why not?

Alessandra blew on her coffee. She studied the sneakers of the nurses on the food line.

When she got back upstairs, the doctor was in the room. He was talking. He was a little Indian man with a stethoscope and a packet of Chiclets in his breast pocket. His silver-striped black tie was loosened around his neck. He looked like he'd been up for a thousand days straight. As he spoke, Mrs. Dirello wailed. "Please," the doctor said. "Will you please allow me to finish?"

The person in the next bed still had their TV blaring, too.

The doctor pinched the bridge of his nose.

It was loud in there.

Mrs. Dirello was wailing for no good reason. The doctor wasn't saying anything bad. He was saying that Stephanie was going to be okay. It was going to take a couple of days but studies showed this and test results were that. He got fed up with Mrs. Dirello. He pulled Alessandra out into the hallway and let out a breath. "That woman is a handful," he said.

"I know," Alessandra said.

"Did you hear what I said in there?"

"Most of it."

"You're her friend?"

Alessandra said, "Uh-huh."

"We're going to put her on this." The doctor held out his clipboard and pointed to the medicine Stephanie was going to be prescribed.

"Okay."

"After she comes to, she needs bed rest. We'll keep her here a day or two, but that's it."

"She'll wake up when?"

"Could be now, could be tomorrow. Depends. I'd bet soon."

"Thank you, doctor."

"Good luck with the mother." The doctor walked away. His head was down. Alessandra felt sorry for him. Probably every room had a Mrs. Dirello in it.

Alessandra went back in and sat away from the bed under the TV. "Did you hear what he said?" she said to Mrs. Dirello.

Mrs. Dirello moaned. "What does he know? I want a doctor who speaks English."

"He spoke perfect English."

"Indians. You can't get an Italian doctor anymore. Give me a Jew. Give me a Jew at least."

Alessandra said, "Christ."

"Nice way to talk."

"Did you hear what he said, Mrs. Dirello? Or didn't you? Stephanie's going to be okay. There's no need for the big production."

Mrs. Dirello hissed, such an old Italian lady thing to do. She made claws in the air with her hands. "Who do you think you are? Miss Hollywood Glamour? Who needs you here? *Puttana*, that's it. No good. *Disgraziata*." She fake spit on the floor.

Alessandra shook her head. She decided she wouldn't leave. She'd wait for Stephanie to come out of it. No way she could leave her alone with her nutjob mother.

Alessandra nodded off to sleep when the guy in the next bed finally shut off his TV, leaning her head back uncomfortably on the chair, and she snapped out of it a couple of hours later, maybe more, to see Stephanie's eyes open now and Mrs. Dirello stroking her hair, saying, "My Stephanie. My Stephanie. Thank you, Lord."

Alessandra went over and stood next to the bed. "You okay, Steph?" she said.

Stephanie nodded. Bags were smudged under her eyes. She flexed her hands.

"Why would you do this to me?" Mrs. Dirello said, arranging the red rosary on her daughter's chest and gripping the beads.

Alessandra said, "Not now, lady."

"*Puttana*."

"Save it."

Stephanie closed her eyes again.

"My Stephanie," Mrs. Dirello said.

Stephanie straightened up and pushed her shoulders back and forth, trying to work a kink out of her neck. "Ma, please," she said, her voice raw. It sounded like her throat had been scraped out.

"The scare you gave me."

"I know, I know."

"It was this one, wasn't it?" Mrs. Dirello refused to look at Alessandra now. "She got you started on pills?"

"No, Ma," Stephanie said. "Nothing like that."

"What happened? What was this about?"

"Give her a little time," Alessandra said.

Mrs. Dirello said, "Listen to this one. Like it's her daughter here."

"Ma, I do," Stephanie said, tweaking the IV needle in her arm, "I need a little time."

"Time?"

"Just let me get my head straight a little here."

"I'm your mother."

"I'm just, I don't feel good. Maybe you could go downstairs, get us some coffee, give me just a few minutes."

Mrs. Dirello looked like she'd been hit by a truck. "Downstairs?"

"Yeah, just grab me a coffee and a *Daily News*."

"Send this one downstairs," Mrs. Dirello said, pointing at Alessandra, "and I'll stay."

Stephanie put up a hand. "I can't. Mommy, just please."

Mrs. Dirello trudged out of the room, looking like a fat nun on her way to the gas chamber.

"Christ," Alessandra said when Mrs. Dirello—pausing once to gather her rosary and then again to tie her shoes—was finally gone, "I don't know how you—"

Stephanie said, "Just forget it."

"Steph, what happened?"

"I don't know."

"You don't know?"

"I just, I just saw what I was responsible for."

"You?" Alessandra petted Stephanie's hand. "You weren't, you aren't responsible for anything that's happened."

"I just kept saying to myself, 'What if?'"

"Come on, Steph. Don't do that."

"I'm pathetic. Look at me."

Alessandra stroked the hair on the back of Stephanie's hand. It was above and below her knuckles. It was black and fine. It didn't look beautiful anymore. "You're not, you're not."

"I wish I'd died."

"Don't say that."

"It's what I wish."

"Why would you say that?"

Stephanie closed her eyes. "I'm tired." She opened them and yawned. "Did you hear anything about Conway?"

"No," Alessandra said.

"Are you lying?"

"I'm not lying."

"Where were you after you left the fire? I tried to call you."

Alessandra thought back to her messages. Maybe if she'd picked up, Stephanie wouldn't have taken the pills. "I went to the city."

"I really wish I would've died."

"Please don't."

"How dumb am I? I've always been dumb." Stephanie started to pick at the IV needle in her arm.

"Leave that alone," Alessandra said.

"I can't even kill myself," Stephanie said. She gave a little laugh, but there were tears in her eyes.

Alessandra stroked Stephanie's hand again. "Stop."

"Look at my hand." Stephanie held it up. "The hair." She rolled up the sleeve of her gown. "My arms too. Mary Parente used to call me Teen Wolf back at Kearney."

"Forget that."

"I have a mustache."

"You don't."

"I do."

"Stop saying bad things about yourself."

"Conway—"

"Conway what?"

"I made Conway sick, I bet. I make everyone sick."

"You don't." Alessandra hugged her. "Stop talking down. You're okay, everything's going to be okay. You need some rest, that's it."

The person in the next bed put the TV back on. They sat there and didn't say anything else to each other. Mrs. Dirello came back into the room with two coffees from a machine and two push-up ice pops. Stephanie didn't want anything. Alessandra went out to the waiting room at the end of the hallway and curled up on a vinyl loveseat scattered with magazines. She couldn't sleep.

16

The lady cop didn't even give Eugene or Sweat a second look. Sweat was hunched at the wheel with his right hand at twelve and his left arm out the window as they passed an accident at the on-ramp to the GWB. No tolls this way, thank God, but there were cops in windbreakers scattered around because one fuckhead had rear-ended another fuckhead. The Brooklyn Bridge hadn't been a problem, and the FDR had been a zipping mess of taxis and thumping car service cars—you weren't doing a hundred on the FDR, you were in the clear. Now Eugene wondered if their luck had run out.

But it hadn't. No one noticed them.

Eugene sat up in his seat as they passed over the bridge and tried to look through the dark down to the Hudson. "You ever been over here?" he said. "This side of the bridge?"

"Give me a sec," Sweat said. "I don't want to miss this."

There were signs for the Jersey Turnpike, for the Palisades Parkway, lanes and lanes of headlights and brake lights and silvery glints from the road. Sweat had the GPS on and followed signs for the Palisades, looking nervous behind the wheel for the first time Eugene could ever think of.

"Went up to Westchester that once to visit Uncle Ray Boy in jail but it's my first time this side of the river, first time going upstate," Eugene said. "My mother and grandparents stopped going to Hawk's Nest after he went away."

"Got a cousin in New City."

"Where's Old City?"

Sweat didn't laugh. "Cousin's got a treehouse. It's got like electricity and shit. Got a basketball hoop out front, too. And a movie theater in the basement."

Eugene rolled the window down. "Nice air over here."

"Cold. Shit ton of trees."

They were on the Palisades now—Eugene was following along on the GPS—and Sweat was doing the speed limit, fifty, as cars rocketed by him in the left lane doing seventy, eighty.

"These motherfuckers are crazy," Sweat said. "Deer just jump out at you up here. They're in the trees, waiting."

Eugene had never thought about deer. "No shit?"

"My cousins have hit deer up here about thirty times. Fucked up a Camry. Fucked up an Explorer. Fucked up a Maxima. Deer everywhere. You can see their eyes."

Eugene scanned the treeline for deer eyes. "What color?"

"What color what?"

"What color are their eyes?"

"Green or some shit like green."

Eugene swore he saw eyes everywhere now, little pinpoints of green off in the trees. He wasn't nervous about anything else—Uncle Ray Boy, the card game, being on the lam—but these deer had him almost shitting his pants. What if one of them just jumped out at the car? Fuck would happen? He'd

seen movies. Broken glass and blood. Flipped over cars. "They're all over,"
he said.

"Tell me."

"What if one comes at us?"

"Heard you're supposed to just plow through it, don't hit the brakes."

"Damn."

"These fucking deer."

"Why they got so many?"

"Overpopulation, yo."

"Damn."

Eugene felt tense, on edge. So this was Big Bad Upstate. Deer and trees.
Dark roads. Ticks. Families in minivans. It was probably really just the
suburbs but everything over the GWB was upstate to him. It was pitch
black out now but he tried to imagine trees changing colors, houses on
cliffs, rivers that weren't nasty, towns where people wore fall sweaters and
took their kids trick-or-treating on Halloween. Halloween was coming
up, and he'd loved it as a kid. Dressing up like a ninja or soldier or some
shit. But his mom and grandparents never let him out to hit up houses
for candy because the older kids would be out bombing with eggs and
shaving cream. And once he was ten, it was too late. He wanted to be the
one out bombing. That shit was done by the time he was of age. Dead like
things got dead. Cops crawled the streets, were on the lookout for punks
in hoodies looking to bomb. Up here, though, he bet that little kids got
dressed up and walked through the fall weather with pumpkin buckets and
got good shit at houses where there were pumpkin lanterns on the porch
and that older kids toilet papered trees and threw eggs at gas stations and
cars and front doors.

"You ever get a tick?" Eugene said to Sweat.

"At my cousin's. Just standing in the backyard. My cousin held a lighter
to it and then got the thing out with tweezers."

"Must be so many up here."

"Everywhere. All those eyes, times that by about a million. A billion ticks out there right now."

"Fuck, dude. My skin's itching."

"Ticks are some scary shit. My cousin's good friend's sister caught Lyme's disease and got crippled from it. Can't walk no more. Drools. Eats apple sauce only."

"What?"

"I'm telling you."

Eugene rolled up the window. "Those shits fly?"

Sweat nodded.

The GPS was bright in the car. A little cartoon map. Eugene thought about the names of things. Palisades Parkway. Nanuet. Rockland County. Brake lights blasted the road in front of them. He wrapped his arms around his chest. *Ticks. Shit.* The road got darker and the speed limit went up as they passed Sweat's cousin's town, New City. Eugene wanted to make the joke again about Old City, but he skipped it.

"They got snakes up here too?" Eugene said.

Sweat looked away from the road and nodded. He made this-big hands over the steering wheel. "Rattlers. Copperheads. Cobras probably."

"Cobras? You're bullshitting."

"I'm saying there's cobras."

"I got a one-eyed snake right here for you." Eugene pulled out his waist-band and aimed a thumb down his pants.

"Inchworm's all that is."

Eugene punched Sweat in the arm, and Sweat swerved the Mazda into the left lane. "I got me a seven-inch monster."

Sweat said, "Chill." He got the car back under control.

Eugene looked back at the treeline and saw green eyes piled deep. He thought about the deer and wondered what they were waiting for. "You gonna slam on the brakes if a deer comes out at us?" he asked Sweat.

"Don't know. Gonna try to keep going like they say."

"Must be hard. There's only like a second."

"Less."

"Part of a second. We're fucked we hit a deer. Changes everything."

"Maybe we get lucky."

"Not everybody up here hits them, right?"

"People hit deer *all the time*."

"But not *all the time*. No one's hitting one now."

"Someone's hitting one somewhere."

"Man, you're probably right. Just not in front of us."

"You ever eat deer?"

Eugene said, "Eat it?"

"Venison," Sweat said. "Shit's good. My father comes upstate, hunts, comes back with all this deer meat. Got a freezer at work full of it. Mostly keeps it for us." He quieted down and focused on the road.

Eugene saw signs for Bear Mountain. He pictured a mountain crawling with bears. Bears rising up and growling. Bears killing fish. Bears sniffing out campers. Deer everywhere and snakes probably and now bears. He couldn't imagine being lost in the woods here. He'd have to climb trees and jump from branch to branch to escape the bears and snakes. He was going to ask Sweat about bears, if they jumped out in the road too, if he'd ever eaten bear meat, but he stopped himself. He didn't want to give a fuck about bears.

He curled up against the window and switched his thinking. He thought about Uncle Ray Boy. He wondered what Uncle Ray Boy was doing right that minute. Probably push-ups or sit-ups. Maybe smoking a cigarette. Maybe having a cup of coffee. He got the impression that Uncle Ray Boy didn't sleep much, if at all. He'd wanted to lay down when he first got back to the house but that didn't mean sleep. Probably part of why he was so fucked up was because he never slept anymore. Holding up the card game would bring him back to life, Eugene knew it. Uncle Ray Boy would sleep well at the first motel they stayed at on the road.

Trying to picture the house in Hawk's Nest wasn't easy. Eugene had seen pictures of it in old crumbling albums with black pages but those pictures were thirty or forty years old. The house had a strange history. His great-grandmother, who ran a roominghouse there, sold it to his great-grandfather before his grandfather and grandmother even met. That was in the 1940s and his great-grandmother had already owned the house for twenty years then. So it had been in his family for ninety years. For a long time it was where everyone—the Calabreses and all the cousins—went on weekends. Grandpa Tony drove them up in his old Chevy Caprice and stopped at bars along the way. Great-Grandma Mary, they called her Big Grandma, was in the backseat with Eugene's mom, Uncle Ray Boy, and Aunt Elaine. They'd play board games. At the house everyone played volleyball and they had Sunday dinners around a big oak table in the kitchen. Grandpa Tony burned the garbage in a barrel on the side of the house. Eugene had grown up hearing these stories. In the early Eighties, the house got robbed. Things got stolen that no one expected. The big oak table. A couch. A china closet. Antiques. Trips were cut down to once a month and then twice a year. Uncle Ray Boy got too cool for it and stopped going when he was in fourth grade. If the family went, they'd leave Uncle Ray Boy with Teemo and his mom. When Uncle Ray Boy got in trouble-trouble, no one went to the house anymore period. Eugene imagined that it just got really cold inside with no heat and the paint peeled off and the wood rotted and mice ran wild and bats lived in the attic. He tried to picture it now and he couldn't really. He thought maybe there was an axe leaning up against the wall by the back door. Other horror movie stuff like that. He figured that Uncle Ray Boy probably brought girls up there and they probably took showers and he thought that girls taking showers in the country had to be better than girls taking showers in the city. He pictured flimsy shower curtains, mealy soap, no mold on the walls. He wondered about the woods around the house. He wanted to ask Uncle Ray Boy about deer and bears and snakes. He dealt with them how? That axe? A shotgun?

Eugene knew that Uncle Ray Boy would be happy to see him and Sweat. It was a good thing they'd gone back and staked out Mr. Natale's some more. He didn't want Uncle Ray Boy to think he hadn't prepared. Even if they hadn't learned anything useful, he wanted to be able to say to Uncle Ray Boy that they'd watched the place for hours.

"You did good work, kid," he could imagine Uncle Ray Boy saying.

He'd always wanted to be called *kid* like that.

Eugene fell asleep and woke up as they passed the Monticello Raceway.

"Dead up here," Sweat said. No one else was on the road. They were on Route 17B.

Eugene angled his head out the window, trying to see horses in the stables.

"Look at this place." Sweat pointed at a strip club as they passed it. It was a shitty house with a trailer next to it. The name of the place was Search-lights and a faded sign close to the road said: "Clean girls, topless only, no cover, $3 beer."

"Imagine what that shit's like," Eugene said. Then he settled back into the seat and didn't say anything else. He went back to worrying about deer. This road was the darkest yet.

Uncle Ray Boy's house was frightening. They pulled up the sloping driveway, overgrown with weeds and high grass, and parked next to a Honda Civic. The GPS had gotten them there, but it hadn't been easy. Abandoned-seeming roads with crumbling houses and forgotten mills. Sharp turns. Narrow roads with drop-offs on one side and no guardrail. The sun was coming up now, but it'd been hard to follow directions with no streetlights. They were here, though. And the house was a piece of shit. Paint chipped away. Rotting wood. A limp roof. Dirty shades on the windows. A barrel in the yard for burning stuff. Broken down trucks with tarps over them.

"This is where your Uncle Ray Boy stays?" Sweat said, cutting the lights.

Eugene said, "Guess it is."

"Looks like *The Texas Chainsaw Massacre*. Some shit like that."

"We get in there, I try to convince him about the card game, just let me do the talking. Take that shit outta your ear, too."

Sweat plucked the Bluetooth from his ear and put it in the center console.

"We get the piece from the trunk," Eugene said.

"Why?"

"Show it to him. Prove our level of commitment."

"What if he says no?"

"We convince him."

"How?"

"I don't know. The gun maybe."

Sweat didn't say anything.

They got out of the car, quietly closing the door. Eugene watched his breath in the air. He went over to the Civic and looked in the window. "He must've stolen this shit right here."

"Civics everywhere," Sweat said.

Sweat went back and opened the trunk of his Mazda. Eugene followed behind and then dug around under the spare tire. He took the gun out. "Sweet," he said, laying it out in his palm. He tucked the gun in his waistband the way they did in the movies but he had trouble making it stay. His pants were too baggy and his boxers weren't strong enough to keep the gun from flopping out. He put it in his jacket pocket instead.

They went up the front stoop, careful to avoid a hole that had rotted away a whole section of the second step.

Eugene said, "Remember, let me talk."

The front door was closed. The light above it was on. Eugene knocked. Nothing. The house sounded dead.

"What if he's not here?" Sweat said.

Eugene ignored him. He knocked again. Nothing. Just the sounds of the country. He tried the knob and opened the door in. The house smelled like coffee. There was a small fire going in the wood stove to the right of them. A half-finished cup of coffee was on the floor next to the stove.

"He's here," Eugene said. "Gotta be."

Sweat thumbed through a pile of records on a chair right inside the door.

"Unc!" Eugene said. "Yo, Unc!"

Nothing.

"Maybe he went out," Sweat said.

"Maybe. For a run or something. Dude keeps in shape."

Eugene limped through the hallway into the kitchen. A chair was pulled away from the table and an old-timey percolator was on the stove. Eugene went over and shook it. Still a quarter full.

Sweat came into the kitchen and sat at one end of the table. "We wait?"

"Gonna do what, go home?"

"I don't know."

"We wait."

Sweat went into the room with the stove and Eugene heard him sigh and plop down on the floor. "Gonna sleep," he said.

"Whatever." Eugene sat at the table and put the gun in front of him.

When the back door finally opened, Eugene was surprised to see that it wasn't his Uncle Ray Boy but Duncan D'Innocenzio's loser brother. He was wearing a headlamp that was off and carrying a shovel. "Fuck you doing here?" Eugene said.

"Who are you?" the brother said.

"I'm looking for my uncle."

"Ray Boy?"

"Yeah, yo."

"Your uncle's gone."

Eugene grabbed the gun and stood up. "Fuck you mean, gone?"

"I'm Conway D'Innocenzio. You know me?" Conway leaned the shovel against the wall.

Eugene fixed the gun on Conway. "Your fag brother fucked up my uncle's life by running himself out into traffic."

Conway put his hands up and his head down.

"Where's my uncle?" Eugene said.

"You're just a kid. Don't get involved with this."

"I'm a kid?" Eugene felt fired up. *What was this guy saying? What was he doing here?*

"You aren't a kid," Conway said. "Okay."

"Where's my uncle?"

"I told you. Gone."

"What's that mean? Left? Went where?"

"Means dead."

Eugene moved close to Conway, brought the gun up under his chin. "Dead?"

"He's dead, kid."

"You killed him?"

"I did. I wanted to and I couldn't. He helped me. He wanted to die."

"Wanted?"

Conway nodded.

Eugene wanted to blow the top of his head off. Shoot right up through his teeth so his head exploded like a balloon in one of those Coney water-pistol games. "That's not what he wanted," Eugene said.

"You can shoot me," Conway said. "I don't care."

"Where is he?"

"I told you. Dead."

"Where's his body?"

"Out back."

"Show me."

Conway turned around and Eugene pressed the gun against his back. They went out the back door, leaving Sweat sleeping in the other room. Fat fuck could sleep through a nuclear attack. Eugene's body felt different somehow. He was limping, but he didn't feel like he was limping.

"There's nothing to see," Conway said, as they scaled a craggy hill behind the house.

"Don't talk."

"He's buried."

The hill was difficult to climb. Eugene had to reach down and balance himself with his hands. It was hard to grip the ground with the gun in his hand. He put the gun back in his pocket and focused on making it up the hill without falling. He was afraid Conway was going to run. The fucker kept glancing back at him with these shitty eyes. He didn't look much like his brother. He looked like an old fuck-up.

At the top of the hill there was nothing but trees. Light ribboned down from above. Mist hung close to the ground. Eugene heard noises. He didn't know what they were. Chirping. Hoots. Were they snakes? Did deer make noises? He wondered if there were bears around waiting to jump them. He was in the woods now. He took the gun back out and fixed it on Conway, but he wanted to check his neck and hair for ticks. Were they already all over him, slurping his blood?

They walked on.

"He really did want me to do it," Conway said.

Eugene didn't want to hear it. "Just show me where."

Conway stopped at a place that looked like every other place. The ground was covered with leaves. Trees were all around them.

"This is it," Conway said.

"How you know? There's nothing to mark it."

"I just know. I've been here all night."

Eugene fell to his knees and put the gun down beside him. He touched the ground, sifting up leaves, twigs, and pebbles. "Right under here? How deep?"

"Deep. Like regular grave deep."

Eugene got up and picked up the gun. "Get on your knees. Right where you buried him."

"Kid."

"Do it."

Conway got down on his knees right on the spot where he said he'd buried Uncle Ray Boy. He put his hands behind his head. He wasn't crying. He wasn't shaking. He looked less like an old fuck-up now and more like a dead man.

"How'd you do it?" Eugene asked.

"We dug the hole together. He gave me a shotgun. He—" Conway stopped.

"What?"

"He got down in the hole, and I shot him. Then I buried him. I waited around so I could come out at first light to make sure no one could tell it was a grave."

"You went to that trouble, why'd you tell me?"

"I don't know. I didn't want to lie just then."

"You're gonna die, yo." Eugene held the gun sideways.

"I know."

Eugene closed his eyes and fired at Conway. The gun kicked back. He opened his eyes to see that he had hit Conway in the chest. He fired again as Conway was falling and got him in the neck. He kept his eyes open this time.

Conway was holding his chest with one hand and his neck with the other. He was squirming around on the ground, turning on his hip. Blood was coming out through his fingers.

Eugene fired three more times. He missed twice. He nailed Conway in the forehead on the third one. Conway stopped spinning. His body went limp. Eugene went over and did what he'd seen guys do in mobster movies. He hocked a loogie at Conway. "*Vaffanculo*," he said.

He left him there and walked back to the house, struggling down the hill, slipping a few times and dropping the gun once. He dusted himself off when he was on steady ground.

Sweat was sitting at the table when Eugene walked in with the gun in his hand.

Eugene said, "Check me for ticks, yo."

Sweat said, "Like where?"

"Like my hair and shit. I can't see."

"Where you been?"

"Out in the woods."

"I heard a shot."

"Shit woke you up finally?"

"I was beat."

"You missed everything."

Sweat came over and looked at Eugene's head. Eugene put the gun on the table. Sweat thumbed Eugene's hair. "I don't see nothing."

"I feel like they're all over me. I gotta take a shower."

"Fuck went down?"

"Duncan D'Innocenzio's brother killed Uncle Ray Boy. I killed Duncan D'Innocenzio's brother."

"For real?"

"For real."

"Oh shit. You're a killer?"

"Cold-blooded, motherfucker." Eugene picked up the gun and held it sideways again. He mimed shooting it into Conway. "I went pow pow pow. Bitch didn't even have time to beg."

They slapped hands.

"Yo, your uncle," Sweat said. "Sorry."

"Fuck my uncle. My uncle wasn't my uncle. My uncle was dead already. Fucking pussy." He put the gun back down on the table. "Let me take a shower and then we'll hit it. We'll do this shit on our own."

Eugene went into the musty country bathroom and turned on the shower. No water pressure. Shit compared to what they had in Brooklyn.

He took his clothes off and piled them on the toilet tank. He made the water hot and got in the shower.

The hand that had held and fired the gun tingled. He looked at it and massaged the palm with his other hand.

He checked his hair and under his arms for ticks. He lifted his balls and ran a finger through his ass. Nothing. The possibility of catching Lyme's disease on this trip had him edged up. He didn't want to be any more crippled than he already was. He wished that somehow people could know right now that he'd put Conway D'Innocenzio down like a dog. Then they'd know he was more than a gimp. He looked down and saw a spider between his feet, near the drain. It had long legs and a beady body. He picked up one foot and jumped back. He angled the showerhead down and tried to wash the spider into the drain. The water wasn't strong enough. The spider held on. Eugene opened the door and got out of the shower. He was skeeved out. *Spiders too? Christ.*

Eugene and Sweat walked out of the house and left the lights on and the doors open. Eugene put the gun back in the trunk, and they got in the car. Sweat asked if they should go bury Duncan's brother. Eugene said fuck it, no way. He wanted to think about him rotting out there in the woods. He imagined a bear ripping him apart, vultures swooping down and plucking out his eyes, nuzzling their beaks into his bulletholes.

Sweat burned out of the driveway.

The roads weren't as bad in the light. But it was still dead out. No other cars. The GPS led them back to 17B.

Sweat said, "We gotta rest before we hit that card game. We don't even know what time they start playing."

"Fuck you talking about rest?"

"You ain't tired?"

"You got a nap back there, homes."

"Short one. Maybe we hit up Mickey D's for breakfast, too? Been a lot of driving."

Eugene thought about it. He said, "Here's what we do. Stop. Get food. Gas if you need it. Lean back in the parking lot of the gas station. Catch a couple of hours. Doesn't matter when we get back to the city. Card game's going all the time."

"Twenty-four hours?"

"Not twenty-four hours, but a lot of the time they're playing."

"What happens we get there and there's no game?"

"We feel it out. Money's still there probably. Didn't I say this shit already?"

"Just checking the plan." Sweat paused. "We never got to see the bar run by that Indian."

They found a gas station with a Mickey D's attached to it a few miles up the road. Sweat pumped gas and paid with his credit card. Eugene wondered whether or not that was bad and then figured it wasn't. They'd be gone by the time someone made it here to look for them. By now his mother had to know he was with Sweat.

Sweat ordered three Egg McMuffins and five hash browns and one of those little plastic peel-back cups of orange juice. Eugene got a cup of coffee and a Sausage McMuffin. They sat in the car and ate. Sweat finished all of his food in five minutes. Then he burped and leaned his seat back and closed his eyes. Eugene sat staring out the windows. He wasn't that tired somehow. Part of him wanted to get out and go for a walk. But where would he go? There was nothing but parking lot.

Eugene closed his eyes and tried to get in a nap. He kept opening them to blow on his coffee and take sips. He'd taken two bites of his Sausage McMuffin and thrown it out the window. He didn't see Conway when he closed his eyes. None of that bullshit people made you believe. Which meant one thing probably: he was built for killing.

Uncle Ray Boy, tough as he used to be, wasn't. Fuck, he didn't even really kill Duncan D'Innocenzio and he couldn't get over it.

Eugene wished Uncle Ray Boy had died a long time ago. He would've been better that way. No chance to get ruined. Eugene would have had him to look up to still. Now his hero was dead and the worst thing was that his hero wasn't anything but a pussy who got in his own grave and let Conway D'Innocenzio shoot him.

Let them both rot out there in the woods.

Eugene closed his eyes.

It was hot in the car when Eugene woke up. He'd slept for almost four hours. Sweat was still out, snoring, and it smelled like he'd let a few rip in his sleep. Crumbs from the Egg McMuffins and hash browns were all over his shirt. Eugene opened the door and let some fresh air in. Then he got out of the car and stretched and left the door open. The cold from outside woke Sweat up and he hugged himself and groaned.

Eugene watched people at the gas station. A trucker slugged from a giant Gatorade bottle. A woman who worked there came out and smoked a cigarette, ashing in a coffee cup.

A cop car that looked different from city cop cars rolled in to fill up, and Eugene got back in the car. They didn't need to catch a glance from any cop. Sweat probably looked older than a sophomore, but they still stuck out and he couldn't imagine a cop not wanting to draw a bead on them.

"What's up?" Sweat said.

"Let's hit it," Eugene said.

"My mouth's nasty. I gotta brush."

"Where you gonna brush?"

"Bathroom. I'll buy some shit."

"Fuck it, we gotta roll."

Sweat shrugged and started the car. He pulled back onto the road, swerving to avoid a car in the oncoming lane.

Back on the Palisades, Eugene stared out the window at the trees. He'd stopped being afraid of deer. He was thinking about the card game now. "Here's what's gonna happen when we get there. We're going right by those old guys outside and the Gravy Stirrer."

"Gravy Stirrer?" Sweat said.

"No one'll think nothing of it. Ain't gonna wear masks. None of that. We get in there and I take out the gun, say, 'Gimme the money.' Straight up in Mr. Natale's face."

"There's how many guys around?"

"I don't know. A bunch."

"And none of them have guns?"

Eugene shrugged.

Sweat said, "Us, one gun, against all these old hard-ass gangsters? How you think that ends? They don't want any trouble, so they just let us have the money?"

"They're not gonna shoot us up."

Sweat opened the window and threw his empty orange juice container outside.

Eugene looked back and saw it sputter under the car behind them. In his mind robbing the card game couldn't and wouldn't go wrong. He hadn't readjusted his thinking to account for Uncle Ray Boy not being there, but he knew that things like this went down all the time and that people dumber than him got away with them.

This time they had to stop for a toll at the GWB. Eugene was pissed because the EZ Pass was in Mrs. Scagnetti's Escalade. As they got closer to the tolls, Eugene said to Sweat, "Just go through the EZ Pass."

Sweat said, "I don't have it in here."

"I know. They send you a ticket, that's it."

"They don't chase after you?"

"They're gonna chase after every guy who blows the toll? No way. They shoot your license plate, you get a ticket in the mail."

"You sure?"

"I'm sure. We go through the toll-toll, we're fucked."

Sweat tensed up and gripped the wheel hard. Eugene could smell that he was nervous. They went through an EZ Pass lane at twenty. No alarms sounded. Eugene looked through the back window. He wasn't sure if he was right. Part of him expected to see a cop car bust out behind them.

But nothing happened. No chase over the bridge.

"I told you," Eugene said. "Your mom's gonna get a ticket in the mail, be like, 'Motherfucker!'"

Sweat laughed.

The neighborhood had a glow to it now. Maybe it was just that Eugene was different. He thought about his house. He'd probably never see it again. He thought about lighting candles in his room to get the smell of jerking off out of the air. He thought about playing Suicide in the backyard with Timmy Mumps and Jimmy Schiavo. He thought about Sunday dinners. *Braciole.* Meatballs. Spaghetti with his mother's gravy. Veal cutlets. He thought about peppers-and-eggs on rolls from Villabate for lunch during the week. He thought about his grandmother bringing over warm mozzarella from Bay Ridge. He thought about rainbows and sprinkles and pignoli cookies on big trays covered in colored plastic. He thought about the smell of fresh *basinigole*. Squash flowers frying on the stove. He thought about his grandfather's homemade wine on the table in dark bottles. He'd miss those things.

They were on Cropsey Avenue, not far from Mr. Natale's club. Sweat was gripping the wheel like he was trying to squeeze something out of it again.

Eugene said, "Park up the block. Not too close."

Sweat found a spot across from a hydrant and had trouble parallel parking the car. He went up on the curb and then had to pull out and try again.

He missed it again and bumped the car behind him. It was a Prius and its alarm started to sound. "Fuck," Sweat said, and he pulled out of the spot and raced away up the block, almost clipping a passenger door as it was thrust open by a hunchbacked old man in sweatpants and a Knights of Columbus jacket.

Eugene said, "Just park around the corner."

Sweat blew through a stop sign and turned right. He slowed down, creeping for another spot. A mid-forties lady pushing a shopping cart up the sidewalk gave them a look like she was their mother and what did they think they were doing. And then she thought better of it, not wanting any trouble, and continued walking.

Eugene got out of the car first. He looked around. They were parked in front of the Ulmer Park Library. Nobody was on the sidewalks, except the mid-forties lady with the shopping cart, and she was busting her ass to get away from them. He circled the car and went around to the trunk. "Pop it," he said to Sweat.

Sweat pulled the latch for the trunk.

Eugene took the gun out from under the spare tire and checked it. One bullet left. He ducked his head back into the trunk and rummaged around under the tire and found one of the boxes of bullets. He set the gun down in the trunk. He reloaded it and then he put it in his pocket. He took out the other box of bullets and emptied them into his hand and put them in the front pocket of his shirt.

Sweat got out and made sure the doors were locked and the windows were closed.

Eugene pulled his hood up.

"I wish we had two guns," Sweat said.

"Let's go," Eugene said.

They walked down the block to Mr. Natale's club. The Folding Chair Crew wasn't outside. No boombox blasting WCBS. The place looked deserted, the way it had when they'd staked it out. Eugene tried the front door. Locked. Sweat was close behind him. Eugene tried to push the door in. It didn't budge. He jiggled the handle. "Fuck," he said.

"We don't even know they're in there now," Sweat said.

Then the door opened up. The Gravy Stirrer stood there in a wife-beater with a gravy-stained towel slung over his shoulder. He was sweating. Gravy bubbled on the stove behind him. A bag of semolina bread sat on the counter. He had a cannoli in his hand. "Yeah?" he said.

"I'm the one dropped off that package for Mr. Natale," Eugene said.

"So?"

"I need to see him."

"In regards to what?"

"He said come back."

"He said come back or you need to see him?"

"He said come back."

"Who's this *citrullo*?" He pointed at Sweat.

"My associate."

The Gravy Stirrer laughed. "Your associate? That's good, kid." He motioned for them to come in.

The front room smelled of gravy on a medium heat and sausage frying in olive oil. Eugene looked around. Bottles of Pellegrino and wine were lined up on a foldout table against the wall.

"It's good you're here," the Gravy Stirrer said. "We need a new kid in the neighborhood. And your buddy here, he'll help too?"

"I'll help," Sweat said.

The Gravy Stirrer led them down the long hallway to the no-windows room where Mr. Natale, the Russian in the tracksuit, Hockey Head, and Hyun the Numbers Runner sat around a table with sandwiches in tinfoil—veal cutlets, meatball, mozzarella and tomato, sausage and peppers—on paper plates in front of them. Mr. Natale puffed a cigar. He was wearing a Mantle jersey this time. There was no money on the table.

"Look at this kid," Mr. Natale said. "The gimp. Walks right in."

"Hi," Eugene said.

Mr. Natale peeled the tinfoil away from the bottom of his meatball sandwich and took a bite. "Who's this?" he said, nodding at Sweat.

"Get this," the Gravy Stirrer said. "His associate."

They all laughed, Sweat too.

The Russian said, "Associate. Very good."

"You want more work, that's why you're here?" Mr. Natale said to Eugene.

Eugene said, "I wanted to talk."

"About what?"

"Your card game," he said.

"You want to work my card game? Sweep up, that kind of shit?"

"Maybe, yeah."

"Come on Friday. We play on Friday. Come at four in the afternoon. We start playing at five. You could sweep up, get drinks for the guys."

"That's not what I want," Eugene said.

"What then? You want to rob the game?" Mr. Natale stood up and tousled Eugene's hair. "Gimp's gonna rob my game. Should be good. You wanna sweep up, you could do that. Rob it?—Hell, why not? Give it a shot, kid. I'd be entertained."

Hyun the Numbers Runner said something in Chinese.

"Get a load of this fuck," Mr. Natale said, cocking a thumb at Hyun. Mr. Natale walked back to the table and sat down.

Eugene didn't know what to do. He didn't even know if there was anything to rob. There must have been, though. A safe in the room. A box of cash. A package. Something. He was going to miss his chance. He took out the gun, almost fumbled it out of his grip, and aimed it at Mr. Natale. His hand was shaking. "I want the money."

Mr. Natale doubled over on the table. He was laughing so hard that the room seemed to be rattling. The Russian took out a gun that looked like it did other things too and fixed it on Eugene. So did Hockey Head. "Put your guns down," Mr. Natale said to the Russian and Hockey Head. "This shit's too good. For real he wants to rob my game. The balls on this gimp."

The Russian lowered his gun and held it across his crotch. Hockey Head put his gun on the table.

Eugene was shaking.

Mr. Natale said, "Get the camera. Someone. The instant camera. We need a picture of this kid."

Hockey Head leaned down and went through a cardboard box on the floor. He took out a throwaway camera wrapped in plastic. He ripped open the plastic and took a picture from his knees of Eugene holding the gun. "Flash didn't work," he said.

"Press the button," the Russian said.

Hockey Head pushed a black button on the front of the camera and took another picture. "That one's good, I think."

"I'm being serious," Eugene said.

"You got a list of demands?" Mr. Natale said.

"Helicopter ride over the city?" the Russian said. "New Xbox?"

"I want the money?" Eugene said, turning it into a question.

"You're asking me if you want the money?" Mr. Natale said. "This gimp's too cute. Take another picture."

Hockey Head snapped another one.

Eugene said, "Stop calling me gimp. Stop taking my picture."

"This kid's too much." Mr. Natale stood up and put his arms out. "Come over here, kid. Give me a hug. I got a lot of respect for you. You got balls."

"Give me the money." Eugene turned the gun sideways.

"Look at this. Holds it like a *mulignan* now."

"The money."

"What money, kid?"

"The card game money."

Sweat said, "Yeah, the card game money."

"Look," Mr. Natale said, "the fat one talks." He paused. "There's no money right now. You come back Friday, you try to hold us up then, how about that?"

Eugene knew he couldn't hesitate. He squeezed off a shot and the bullet went in right above the Yankee insignia on Mr. Natale's jersey. Mr. Natale put a hand on his chest and fell back into his seat. Blood started to blossom out around his hand. The Russian and Hockey Head looked at each other like maybe this was a hoax. Hyun had hit the floor at the crack of the gun and covered his head with his hands.

"Holy shit," Sweat said.

The Russian lifted his gun and leveled it at Eugene.

Hockey Head picked his up and fired at Sweat in one motion. Sweat didn't have time. He got hit in the throat and went down, squealing, blood erupting over the collar of his shirt. Hockey Head turned with his gun to Eugene. Sweat was twisting around on the floor, coughing blood-coming-up sounds.

Eugene pissed himself and felt it hot down the side of his leg.

"Very big mistake," the Russian said. He fired, and Eugene dove toward Sweat, managing to hold onto his gun. Hockey Head got a shot off across the table. Eugene tried to use Sweat as a shield. Bullets whizzed by them. One caught Sweat in the knee. He saw Sweat's eyes and they looked empty.

Eugene fired twice over Sweat and missed the Russian but hit Hockey Head in the arm. Then he got up and made a break for the hallway. Shots crackled in the walls around him. He was little enough that they were having trouble hitting him. The Gravy Stirrer was in front of him now, and Eugene busted a shot into his gut. The Gravy Stirrer crumbled to the floor, his hairy shoulders thumping against the linoleum. Eugene skirted him and took off out the front door, dragging his leg.

He got outside and didn't know where to go. He couldn't believe he'd shot Mr. Natale and Hockey Head and the Gravy Stirrer. He couldn't believe he'd gotten no money for it all. He couldn't believe Sweat was dead. He couldn't believe his pants were wet. He couldn't believe the bullets had missed him. He had no more time to think. He headed back in the direction of the car. He was moving as fast as he could. He had no keys. He'd have to keep going and head for the subway.

When he looked back the Russian was behind him. It was strange to see him in the daylight like that, gun across his chest, plodding along. He wasn't running. Eugene guessed he didn't feel the need to exert himself since he was after a kid with a limp. Eugene thought about firing back but he wanted to save his bullets and the Russian wasn't firing yet. He knew he wasn't moving fast enough. He couldn't move faster. He looked up at the El in the distance. A train thundered by. He wished he was on it.

17

Alessandra was on the train home from Maimonides. She didn't know what time it was and she was too lazy to open her phone to check. Afternoon probably. She'd been with Stephanie all night and all morning at least. She needed a shower and an espresso with Sambuca in it and lemon rubbed on the rim of the cup and a long, glorious smoke. She needed to shave her legs. She needed to lose Amy's number. She needed to get Stephanie a gift certificate to a spa. Poor girl. She needed to think about the Lou Turcotte thing. She needed to enjoy her old man a little bit more. He was narrow, defeated and sad, definitely of the neighborhood, but he was so much better than that Mrs. Dirello. Alessandra was blessed in that way. *Blessed*. Funny word. Something her mother would've said. What did it even mean when you didn't believe in anything? She wished she'd been born somewhere other than Brooklyn, other than Gravesend, but she'd been lucky not to wind up like Conway or Stephanie. Had to be something about the way her parents raised her that made her different.

She was the only person on the subway car. She'd chosen the middle conductor's car, an old habit when the train wasn't crowded, and she looked out at the neighborhood below through glass etched with tags. The interior of the car was bright orange and smelled vaguely of honey-roasted peanuts and piss.

As the train turned from New Utrecht Avenue onto Eighty-Sixth Street, she caught a quick glimpse of the building that used to be the Loew's Oriental. She'd seen many movies there. *Goodfellas. Strange Days. Point Break*, four times. Now it was a Marshall's. She thought of folded pants and racks of ugly shirts and it made her wish that the place was still a theater, that she could get dressed and go there alone and order a tall soda and a popcorn and sit with her legs crossed in the tilted mezzanine.

Roofs of apartment buildings and storefronts shot by. She tried to see in windows, attempted to decipher signs written in Chinese and Russian.

She strained to see down to the avenue. Old ladies with shopping carts. Chinese men blowing on hot coffees in doorways. Others with plastic bags, talking on cell phones, texting, looking down. The sidewalks were wet where storeowners had hosed them down. Garbage flitted around, paper bags and rotten fruit, and she swore she could almost smell it all the way up in the train.

The smoke from Conway's house was still ribbony in the air and hung over the neighborhood like a posse of black ghosts.

She wondered what had happened to Conway. She didn't really feel bad for him, not anymore. She felt bad for Duncan, all those years ago, of course she did. And she felt bad for Pop. Ray Boy Calabrese, she wasn't sure what she felt for him. Something like pity mixed with disgust.

She was sick of how she thought about things. She wasn't a very good person, she'd started to understand that. She was self-centered, a bad daughter, and a she had no real friends. She was going to be nice to Stephanie, get her the spa thing, and cook some for her old man from now on even if she was no good at gravy and *braciole*. She could grill salmon and vegetables. He'd appreciate that just as much.

The train slowed down at Bay Parkway, where Alessandra had switched earlier to get back to Maimonides, and she stood up. She wasn't getting off here, but she always liked to stand between Bay Parkway and Twenty-Fifth Avenue, her stop. She clung to the handrail and looked down at the fruit markets, the dollar stores, the new Russian and Chinese bakeries and groceries, the pho and sushi joints, HSBC which used to be—what?—Dime Savings, the Russian video store turned cell phone dive, Sovereign Bank which used to be Independence Bank, the corner Korean restaurant with the bamboo shades that always seemed to have a line out the door, McDonald's, Stephanie and Conway's Rite Aid which used to be Genovese, the salon school with the loopy close-up mural of a woman with Victoria Gotti hair, and the big cement lot with hoops up where she used to watch boys from Most Precious Blood and St. Mary's play basketball or football or kill-the-man-with-the-ball on Wednesday afternoons when school let out early.

When the doors swished open, she walked out onto the platform. One of her favorite things to do on the platform was to look out through the fence at the avenue running off in the direction of Cropsey. She liked the way the blacktop unfolded like a piece of film, the way it cut through the tight little world of cars and houses and trees and sidewalks. She did that now and remembered something she'd long forgotten. In high school, she'd go to the Bay Parkway stop, pay a token—it was tokens then, no stupid cards—just to sit on the bench and look down at the neighborhood. The view was better there. She wouldn't get on the train. Sometimes she'd have cigarettes, sometimes she wouldn't. She'd sit there and look and think about the things you think about when you're a kid and escape seems possible.

She was alone on the platform now, the others who had gotten off at the stop disappearing downstairs and through the turnstiles. She sat on a bench and crossed her legs and faced the north side of Eighty-Sixth Street. The avenue wasn't beautiful. Nothing was beautiful. It was pretty cold, cold enough that her breath leaked out of her mouth like sputtering exhaust. It wasn't beautiful at all, none of it, but it was nice enough.

She wanted to say something out loud, but she didn't know what.

She let go of a long breath and watched it smoke out in front of her. Used to be she thought that meant something, when you could see your breath in front of you, like it was something coming out of you that only had shape on cold days.

It didn't mean anything.

She pretended she was smoking. She closed her eyes and drew a breath in and put her fingers up to her mouth and imagined that she was lipping an American Spirit. And then she exhaled. The fact that her index and middle fingers smelled like tobacco from smoking her father's hand-rolled cigs was almost enough to fool her into thinking it was the real thing.

She heard something then, down the stairs, and looked to her left. The MTA guy in the booth was yelling at some kid for jumping a turnstile. He was on a microphone that echoed through the station. Alessandra watched the stairs, waiting for the kid to come charging up, guessing he was going to get caught since there wasn't a train coming into the station.

He showed up soon enough, limping, holding the railing, not moving very quickly. He was definitely going to get caught, this kid. Alessandra didn't know many things about breaking the law but she guessed it was ill-advised to try to jump a turnstile and skip a fare if you were crippled.

The kid was breathing heavily, looking over his shoulder, and he was palming something she thought was a cell phone. When she realized it was a gun, she stood up and hurried all the way down to the end of the platform.

He got to the top of the stairs and looked at her and then he jerked his head around in every direction. He seemed upset that there wasn't a train and he stomped his bad leg.

Alessandra noticed that his pants were wet. She put her head down.

"Yo," the kid said.

She turned and faced the tracks.

"Lady," the kid said, and she could hear that he was coming over to her. "I know you. I saw you with Stephanie Dirello at the fire yesterday."

"That's not me," Alessandra said. "I don't know you."

"I need help. Bad."

"I've got to go." She turned to him and started to walk, tried to nudge past him, but he put his hand out and grabbed her arm.

"Gimme a sec," he said.

"I've got to go," she said. She pulled her arm away and took a step forward. She tried not to look at the gun, wanting him to think she hadn't seen it.

"Lady," he said, and she saw out of the corner of her eye how he lifted the gun and leveled it at her. "I just need your help a sec."

She stopped. "What?"

He looked back at the stairs. "I've got this guy after me. I need you to help me hide."

She waved her arm in the air. "Where? What can I do?"

He spun his head around. "Fuck. I don't know. Maybe I'll get down on the tracks and when he comes up—"

"Down on the tracks?"

"I'll get down there in that gap." He motioned to the foot-deep space between the rails. It was full of oily puddles and wet garbage matted with pigeon shit. Alessandra had heard of people who had fallen onto the tracks and crawled into that space and gone untouched when a train rolled in, but it seemed like a dumb move. Everything about the kid seemed dumb.

"I can't let you—"

"When he comes, just tell him I'm gone. Tell him I got on a train."

"He's right behind you, he knows there hasn't been a train in a few minutes."

The kid ignored her and limped to the edge of the platform. He put the gun in his pocket and jumped down to the tracks, landing way too close to the third rail.

She shivered at the thought of seeing him zapped. She said, "Watch the third rail—"

"I know," he said, lying down between the running rails. "I saw a show about this."

Her instinct was to take off, but she stuck around for some reason and went back to the bench. She couldn't see the kid from there. He was tucked away. She looked at the tracks in the distance and was glad to see that there wasn't a train coming from Coney yet.

Alessandra heard the guy coming up the stairs before she saw him. He was singing in Russian. His voice was so deep it sounded like he was singing into a barrel. She pictured a fat, bearded man, someone from an opera in a tux, and she was surprised to see a handsome guy with eggshell white skin and Dolph Lundgren hair emerge onto the platform. He was wearing a black tracksuit. He didn't have a gun that she could see, but she figured it could be hidden.

He stopped singing. "You see a little kid with limp?" he said to her. He imitated the kid's walk. "Walks like this. Funny."

"I think he got on a train," she said.

"There has been no train. Not since he came up here. The man downstairs saw him. Said he jumped the turnstile. I told him I'd take care of the kid. There has been no train. Did he go poof?"

"I'm pretty sure he got on a train."

"You protect him. He's just a kid. I understand. But he's a bad kid."

"I don't know." She stood up. "I'm going to go."

"I'll look around. I'll find him. Maybe he's hiding in the garbage?" He went over to the garbage bin and kicked the side of it.

Alessandra started to walk to the stairs.

"He's stupid enough to jump down on the tracks, you think?"

She stopped at the top step.

The Russian limped over to the edge, still imitating the kid, and looked down at the tracks. "There he is!"

The kid stood up, wavering dangerously close to the third rail again.

The Russian took a gun out of his waistband and waved it in the air. "Very stupid to jump down there! What if a train comes? You will be a fucking pancake."

Alessandra couldn't move. The kid took out his gun and fumbled it and it fell through a slat to the side of him. She couldn't hear it hit the street down below, but she imagined it spiraling down in front of a bus or a fruit truck. The kid looked stunned. He turned and started to limp away on the tracks in the direction the train would be coming from.

The Russian laughed. "Pancake," he said. "You will be a pancake!" He fired at the kid and missed wide.

"Don't," Alessandra said. "He's just a kid."

"Not just a kid. A *bad* kid." The Russian fired again and missed behind the kid's shuffling feet. The poor bastard couldn't run. He was blundering along. A moving target but barely. Alessandra got the sense that it'd only be a matter of time before the Russian buried a bullet in his back.

"Tell him to get off the tracks," she said.

"I'll be very happy if he gets off the tracks." He kissed the air and said, "Please, get off the tracks. Come, come."

The kid was almost alongside the spot where the platform ran out. If he continued on the tracks, he might not get shot but he'd have to deal with an oncoming train soon enough. Alessandra wasn't sure if the space between the rails extended that far.

"But he won't get off the tracks," the Russian said. "Now I'll shoot for real."

Alessandra tightened up. She wanted to jump on him, knock the gun out of his hand. But she didn't.

He closed one eye, steadied his aim, pinched his lips, and fired at the kid, hitting him square in the back. The kid made no noise. He just flopped forward, thudding between the rails.

The Russian walked forward and fired twice more into the kid.

Alessandra sat down on the step and put her head in her hands.

The Russian came over and sat down next to her. He put his gun back in his waistband. He took her hand and shook her index finger out of her grip. He made her put the finger up against her mouth. "Shush," he said. "Okay? Shush."

She nodded.

"I don't want to have to hurt you. You've seen nothing, yes?"

She said, "I didn't see anything."

"Good." He stood up and started singing again. Now he was singing "New York, New York," except he was getting all the words wrong. He walked downstairs and through the push-in doors.

Alessandra was shaking. She stood up and turned to the tracks. She couldn't think about the Russian and whether or not he would come after her to keep her quiet. A train was coming. It pulsed the platform, moving closer and closer.

She watched as it went over the space where the kid's body was and cringed. She was going to do what, throw up her hands, try to get the conductor to slam on the brakes?

Doors opened in front of her and closed. The middle car conductor gave her a look: *You getting on or what?*

She stayed where she was.

The train pulled out.

She moved down the platform, hugging herself, and stood across from where the kid was. The crawl space between the rails had kept him from getting mashed. The conductor in the first car hadn't even seen him. Alessandra guessed he'd just looked like more trash.

No way the kid could be alive. She watched his back, and it wasn't moving. She wanted to crawl down to the tracks and haul his body onto the platform. She thought he deserved that. He was just a kid, no matter what he'd done.

But she wasn't capable of it.

She walked downstairs and looked at the MTA guy in the glass booth.

He was reading a book and had headphones on. Acting like he hadn't seen or heard anything. No sirens yet, but there probably would be soon. She went down to the street and moved quickly away from the El, thankful she was wearing flats. She was thinking about going to Villabate later and getting a lobster tail for her father, remembering that it used to be his favorite kind of pastry. She kicked into a run, pulling the flannel up on her shoulder.

BROKEN LAND: AN INTERVIEW WITH WILLIAM BOYLE

Anya Groner interviews William Boyle

William Boyle's debut novel *Gravesend* begins with a lesson at the firing range: "When you shoot, you gotta have confidence. You got no confidence." McKenna, an ex-cop, is coaching his best friend Conway D'Innocenzio. After sixteen years in prison for a hate crime that resulted in the death of Conway's brother, Duncan, Ray Boy Calabrese is back on the streets, and Conway wants revenge.

Though *Gravesend* is about crime, it's not exactly a crime novel. Boyle quickly reveals that neither the would-be avenger, Conway, nor the so-called criminal, Ray Boy, are up for their parts. Conway hasn't the stomach for murder and Ray Boy is so filled with regret that he seeks Conway out and begs to be shot. The plot plays on Boyle's epigraph, three lines by Frank Stanford: "When a man knows another man / is looking for him / he doesn't hide." In this case, it's not courage that motivates characters, but curiosity, soul searching, and plain confusion.

Boyle's characters are far from predictable. Steeped in the gossip of Gravesend, the Italian-American Brooklyn neighborhood where the book takes place, his cast is molded by the streets' complex history. Stephanie Dirello, a virgin who lives with her mother and lusts after Conway, befriends Alessandra, a failed actress who returns to Gravesend after her mother's death. Fifteen-year-old Eugene worships his ex-con uncle, Ray Boy, and goes on a crime spree to impress him. Conway's schoolboy crush on Alessandra returns a decade later and possesses him. Alessandra barely notices.

Boyle's writing is raw, poetic, unflinching, nostalgic, and perverse. Urgency inhabits his pages, and the characters live on weeks after you put the book down. *Gravesend* is a novel read in a day, and then read again, slowly.

————

ANYA GRONER: New Yorkers have the reputation of being worldly, but *Gravesend* operates more like a small town. Everyone knows everyone else, and local gossip thrives. This mentality applies to young residents as much as older ones. Three of your main characters, all in their late twenties, still live with their parents. And when Eugene and Sweat, both teenagers, drive up the Palisades Parkway, Sweat admits he's just crossed the Hudson River for his first time. You grew up in Brooklyn. Was this your experience of your neighborhood? How can such a tight knit community operate within such a cosmopolitan landscape? And to what extent did your own upbringing influence this book?

WILLIAM BOYLE: It was pretty much my experience. I had family in Rockland County and New Jersey and Long Island, so I got around a little more than some of my characters do. And my mom and stepdad took us on road trips to Florida and Maine and Nova Scotia. We even flew to Vegas once. But for me, Brooklyn was just my neighborhood and the neighborhoods close to me, from Bay Ridge to Coney Island. I don't think I even went downtown until I was in college and one of my best friends came from Boerum Hill. I certainly never went to Williamsburg or Greenpoint. And the city seemed so far away, forty-five minutes by subway. I went as a kid to museums and to Radio City and Rockefeller Center, but that was it. It wasn't until I was sixteen or so that I started hanging out in the East Village, seeing shows and going to record stores and to the Angelika for movies.

My neighborhood always felt like a crowded small town and there are neighborhoods like that all across the five boroughs. When I lived in Throggs Neck in the Bronx (where my wife's family is from), it was the same. And Throggs Neck was even more far removed from the city. It was a long walk, forty or fifty minutes, from where I lived to the 6 train on Tremont Avenue and then a long subway ride into the city. We were one of the last stops. In Brooklyn, my neighborhood's one of the last stops on the D before Coney. Maybe it's something about being one of the last stops.

I used to sit out on my grandparents' porch with a cassette recorder and tape them talking. And they were always talking about the people passing by, the people parking their cars. So I had a pretty early obsession with the rhythms of what they were saying but also with the wonderful gossipy content. My grandfather would say things like, "Look at this bastard. He lives around the block and he's gotta park in front of my joint." So there was always that smallness to not only my neighborhood but the block. I could spend the rest of my life writing about the block and not run out of things to say.

I'm also really interested in the narrowness of the neighborhood. When people think about narrowness in terms of race and sexuality, they probably think about the South first, not New York City. But that's not the way it is, certainly not in my experience. I'm always interested in characters who seek work outside those margins, like Alessandra specifically, but also Conway to a certain extent. And even though they're different, even though they've broken from a certain way of thinking, they still belong to the neighborhood. They're chained to it.

I say I'm from Gravesend and I am, technically, but my block is really on the border of two other neighborhoods: Bensonhurst and Bath Beach. Most people on my block, including my family, would say they're from Bensonhurst. And Bensonhurst is where Yusef Hawkins was killed by Joey Fama in 1989. That was an event that opened my eyes to a lot of things I hadn't been aware of. I was eleven and *Do the Right Thing* had come out not long before that—I've always been a movie nut and I saw this other Brooklyn I knew nothing about. I went to a Catholic high school in Bay Ridge, Xaverian (Our Lady of the Narrows in *Gravesend*). I'll never forget being a freshman and seeing *Joey Fama for President* written in Sharpie on a tile over the urinal. That fucked me up. Those sorts of feelings went into making the book.

Your characters both love and hate Gravesend. On the one hand, their homes are vibrant with Italian-American traditions: lemon-rimmed espresso mugs and *braciole*, but this is also a working class neighborhood with limited opportunities. Only Alessandra has dreams of leaving, and all the characters live in the past, idealizing high school troublemakers and resurrecting teenage crushes, while doing little to change their current situation. This is a strange nostalgia, one that memorializes times that weren't all that happy. Is your book an elegy for an older New York City? With the continuing hipsterization of Brooklyn, do neighborhoods like Gravesend still exist?

It is a strange nostalgia. People I've known who haven't left the neighborhood get hung up. They romanticize childhoods that were narrow and oppressive. That's probably true of anyone, anywhere, who doesn't stray far from home, whether they come from Panda Puss, Tennessee, or Blue Fuck Falls, Oregon. Loving and hating the place that you're from is probably true for any sane person. That's how I feel about my neighborhood. I love my grandparents. I love my mother. I love the smells of my grandmother's kitchen, gravy bubbling on the stove. I love the Italian cookies and pastries. I love the pizza, Totonno's in Coney Island and Spumoni Gardens and Lenny's. I love the espresso and the sambuca and the fennel after meals. I love going down to the basement with my grandfather to check the oil, to look for some spare TV tube or wire-cutters or a new sink drain. I love the memory of making struffoli with my grandparents before Christmas. I love how hard my mother's worked her whole life, ten-, eleven-, twelve-hour days at the doctor's office she manages. I love the Russian video store I went to as a kid—I'd rent ten, twelve movies a week; that place was school to me. I love the El. I love walking up my block, Bay Thirty-Fifth Street, and seeing the steeple of St. Mary's rising up over the tracks. I love the little gardens that people have, Mary statues with chipped noses surrounded by weeds and broken cement. I love the divey bodegas where I used to buy Swedish Fish and quarter waters, the memory of playing basketball in the schoolyards all around the neighborhood.

But there's also the stuff that makes me uneasy. There's a feeling I get when I'm back in the neighborhood. I read this great piece in the *New York Times* by Mark Kozelek, where he was talking about the melancholy that's always informed his music, and he used the phrase "unspecific sadness." That's exactly what I feel when I'm home in Brooklyn, especially when I'm alone. I was just back there for a month and both of my grandparents were in the hospital and my mother had to work a lot and my wife and son went up to the Hudson Valley to visit my wife's family, and it hit me all over again at thirty-five. Brooklyn means "Broken Land," and that's what it feels like to me when I'm home, like that Dylan song "Everything is Broken." I think about that song a lot when I'm there. It's funny—on this most recent trip, my three-year-old son, out of nowhere, said, "Everything's broken here." And it was true. My grandmother had broken her hip. The handle on my mother's toilet didn't work. The TV remote was on the fritz. He was playing with my old G.I. Joes, and they were missing legs and arms. He also had a couple of old remote control cars of mine and the batteries had exploded and leaked crust. The heat in my mother's house broke. Her '95 Ford Explorer, used only to block the driveway, wouldn't start and had a flat. A pipe froze in my grandmother's house when it got down to 3 degrees one night. My mother's refrigerator made crazy noises, something between a howl and a thump, like what you'd hear on loop in a Tom Waits song. Her washing machine doesn't drain, so you have to pull the clothes and towels out sopping wet and hang them on the line and let them drip over buckets. I'm not complaining, just pointing to a general brokenness that seems to be amplified to someone prone to melancholy like me. I remember being home to visit last year and a light bulb went out in my mom's house and she said, "Everything goes wrong." That attitude's in my blood.

There's also this terrible dreariness to city living, all city living. There're cracks in the pavement, birdshit, construction, noise, garbage everywhere. Walking around my neighborhood on this recent visit, my son started to call Brooklyn "Rubbish Town." (His favorite TV show, *Fireman Sam*, is Welsh.)

Pretty accurate. A blizzard hit when we were there and the garbage didn't get picked up for over a week and it was piled on the curbs, blowing all around, stuffed into snowbanks. Fucking disgusting. My grandfather's obsessed with garbage. He'll spend hours tearing up boxes and stapling them or tying them with baker's string, breaking his recycling down so it takes up the smallest amount of space possible. Before he got weak and couldn't really go outside anymore, he'd take the garbage out fifty times a day in little bags. He'd always tell me that the world wasn't going to end in fire or anything like that, that it'd end in garbage. I'm pretty sure he's right.

Neighborhoods like Gravesend definitely still exist. Gravesend is still Gravesend, for that matter. And Bensonhurst is Bensonhurst. It's no longer Italian. Now it's predominantly Chinese and Russian. As long as there are ethnic, working-class neighborhoods, there will be places like this, and New York is better for it. Hipsters won't take over certain neighborhoods, I'm sure of that. I thought Coney Island would be a prime candidate and it hasn't happened there. But if you asked me ten years ago, I wouldn't have guessed that Williamsburg would be the fucking theme park it is and I wouldn't have believed you if you told me that St. Mark's Place would be the tourist nightmare it's become. The people who have been chased out of the neighborhoods that have been taken over are settling where the rents are cheaper, where the food's cheaper, and those are going to be the places that are interesting, the homes that people have to escape, the broken and sad places where they fight and strive and fuck and cry. The artists, who used to be able to survive in the Village or downtown Brooklyn on the cheap, no way they're sticking around. If they want a city they'll move somewhere like New Orleans. You can't exist in New York the way you could in the '70s and '80s. When this shit started, I thought a new '70s would be inevitable. Things would be built up, rents would skyrocket, and it would last for a while until the hipsters and yuppies abandoned the city for the suburbs and the neighborhoods would be reclaimed by grime and graffiti and everything would crumble, but I don't see that happening now.

A hate crime lies at the center of *Gravesend*. Sixteen years before the book opens, Ray Boy Calabrese bullied Duncan D'Innocenzio, a gay teenager, so viciously that Duncan ran into oncoming traffic to escape. While it'd be easy to write someone like Ray Boy as expendable—a thug who deserves his suffering—*Gravesend* forces readers to consider Ray Boy's humanity. Defined by poor adolescent decisions, Ray Boy's shame is so great he wants only to die. Though Ray Boy is clearly guilty, the neighborhood is also at fault. His neighbors were the ones who idolized Ray Boy and turned a blind eye to his "pranks." I admire the moral ambiguity here. How does justice operate in *Gravesend*? Is redemption possible? And who do you see as responsible for Duncan's death?

I knew I didn't want anything to be easy. I didn't want Ray Boy to be one-dimensional. And I certainly didn't want redemption to be available to him. He doesn't want it, doesn't think he deserves it, and he doesn't deserve it. I think justice operates in *Gravesend* the way it does in some of my favorite '70s movies. There's no moral center, no lesson. It's pretty representative of my fucked-up view of things. And you're right—the neighborhood is at fault here. The neighborhood is at the center of everything that goes wrong. The neighborhood made Ray Boy. The neighborhood killed Duncan. You see it in the beginning when Alessandra's father says about Duncan, "I don't understand the gay thing, but he didn't deserve this." And he's not, at his core, a hateful person, but that's just the meanness that's seeped into him from the neighborhood and it's indicative of the kind of thinking that made Ray Boy possible in the first place.

The same goes for Conway—it would've been easy to make him this sympathetic avenger, but I didn't want that. He loved and understood Duncan and we feel sad about the loss of his brother, but awfulness comes out in the way he thinks about Alessandra and treats Stephanie. I wanted Conway to be a mess, someone you were torn up about, someone you felt sorry for and hated and wanted to see redeemed and wanted to see dead.

Violence echoes across generations. Seduced by stories he heard about Ray Boy (and by watching *The Sopranos*), Eugene, Ray Boy's nephew, wants to impress his ex-con uncle by taking down Mr. Natale, the neighborhood kingpin. He ends up going on a crime spree that begins with him telling off his high school teacher and ends with murder. I closed the book believing that, like Ray Boy's crimes, Eugene's actions would have unforeseen consequences. There's a tension here between individual accountability and a violent culture. Ray Boy's jail time does nothing to prevent future crimes from taking place. Was Eugene's crime spree inevitable? Is a community subjected to violence condemned to a future of violence? And is there any possibility you'll write a sequel?

Eugene's a doomed character, for sure. Someone recently said to me that they saw the end coming and I was like, "Yeah, it's not a mystery novel. Eugene's fucking doomed from the start. You could sense that because that's the way I made it. There are no options for him."

I don't know if a community subjected to violence is always condemned to a future of violence—I hope it works the other way, but it probably doesn't most of the time. Eugene is fifteen in the book, and that's the most dangerous time, the time when people break one way or the other. I'm speaking generally—obviously, that's not always the case and different things influence different people—but, in my experience, that was true. At fifteen, I looked around and knew I didn't want to be racist or homophobic or sexist. I went from not having words for those things to understanding what I didn't want to be. The lessons came from books, movies, songs, teachers, friends, family. Eugene can't access that knowledge. It's not his mother's fault. A lot of the blame rests with the father who abandoned him—Eugene doesn't dwell on that much but his fatherlessness has certainly shaped him into someone who embraces false masculinity, who learns the wrong lessons from his uncle's incarceration, who's juiced with hate because he doesn't know how else to be. The only model for him is his uncle's former glory.

I don't think I'll write a sequel, but I certainly won't stray too far from the neighborhood and I'd like to return to certain characters in some capacity. I worry a lot about Stephanie. I hope she's okay. I worry for Alessandra too—she has a good heart. I think there's a life out there for her. I hope she finds it. I also think a lot about Amy Falconetti from Flushing. I'd like to see her show up somewhere soon. And McKenna, too. I hope he gets things straightened out with Marylou. I hope he learns how to be a father.

You write about Brooklyn but studied writing in the South, getting your MFA at the University of Mississippi. What influence has southern writing had on your prose?

Wise Blood changed the course of my writing life. All of Flannery O'Connor really, including her letters and now this prayer journal that was just published. Larry Brown has been a hero of mine since I picked up *Big Bad Love* at a bookstore in Austin in 2001. Harry Crews, goddamn, I don't know where I'd be without reading his stuff. And Robert Penn Warren: *All The King's Men, Flood, Brother to Dragons,* his *Collected Poems,* these are books that hit me hard in college and when I was getting my Master's at SUNY New Paltz. Faulkner. Walker Percy. Barry Hannah. Tom Franklin. Mark Richard. Chris Offutt. Jack Pendarvis. John Brandon. Jesmyn Ward. William Gay. Ernest Gaines. Frank Stanford. These are some of the writers who have mattered the most to me. Ask me who my favorite writer is right now, and Mary Miller would be at the top of the list.

So the influence is deep, but I'm also aware of a problem here: Southern writer, like African-American writer or woman writer or Native American writer or crime writer or whatever, shit, I hate labels like that. They're just my favorite writers. I love the way they put words on the page. I love the stories they tell. But I guess there's a reason for it. People don't say they love Northern writing or Midwestern writing or Pacific Northwestern writing. Why not? I guess it's the way place haunts the writing, the way Christ haunts the writing, the way the words are shaped from different clay.

I didn't move here to capture some magic that wasn't available to me in New York, but I did come to learn and I've learned so much. From reading. From studying with some of these writers. From interviewing them. But it's more than that. The place has definitely gotten into my blood. I see Brooklyn in new ways from here.

Women in crime novels are often sidekicks, objects to be fought about, but not characters who fight, but that's not the case in *Gravesend*. Though neither Alessandra nor Stephanie is involved in crime, as the male characters are, both have opportunities to intervene and possibly even prevent murders from taking place, and both fail. How do you see the role of women in *Gravesend*? Are they responsible, as nearly all the men are, for the crimes that surround them?

I think you're right—I think so much crime fiction is full of weak, one-dimensional female characters who are only utilized as objects. They're there to be sexy, to betray, to double-cross, to be slithery. They're, as you say, sidekicks, secretaries, witnesses. That's true of a lot of crime fiction, but it's certainly not the case across the board, not in Megan Abbott's wonderful novels. Or Vicki Hendricks's. Or Elmore Leonard's. Some male writers are fixated on fantasy in all the worst ways. I didn't want Alessandra to be a fantasy. I'm fixated on people's flaws, the things that make them sad and scared. I don't want to write sex scenes that are sexy. There's one in *Gravesend* and it should make you want to kill yourself. Often, in crime fiction, female characters serve as beat-off material—and that's disgusting. If your characters aren't feeling bad about themselves, if they aren't worrying, they're not real. Alessandra is more me than any character in the book. And Stephanie is what I could've been. They're not part of the violence in the way that Conway and Ray Boy and Eugene are but that's situational. Those guys are all marked by violence—Alessandra and Stephanie have lived at the edge of it but haven't been impacted by it directly (until the end anyway).

My view on the role of women in *Gravesend* is dictated by my life. I was raised by a single mom who worked hard. I have a tough wife and her mother and sisters are tough. My grandmother's tough. I love that Joss Whedon thing where someone asks him why he writes such strong female characters and his response is something like, "Because people are still asking that question." It's the dumbest shit. If your characters aren't twisty and complicated, you're doing something wrong. On the same note, it'd be a bad move to make Stephanie something she's not. Here's someone who has lived at home under her mother's thumb her whole life. She's not going to have progressive views about Alessandra's bisexuality. But the thing for me is to make her beautiful in her simple sadness. I will admit this: I'm probably capable of hating the men in my fiction in a way that I'm incapable of hating the women. Maybe that just comes with the feeling of abandonment: my father gone, so many of the fathers I've tried on over the years having let me down. The men I've known have been worse in their failures, the women stronger. I think that general feeling works its way into *Gravesend*.

—Originally published at the *Los Angeles Review of Books*, February 12, 2014

GRAVESEND PLAYLIST FROM WILLIAM BOYLE

Gravesend sort of started with Aesop Rock's *Labor Days*, an album that I listened to on repeat for the first few months I planned and worked on the book. Lou Reed is my favorite New York writer, and none of his albums are ever too far away from being in constant rotation for me—I revisited *New York* a lot during the making of the book, and Velvet Underground's *Loaded*, and I kept Reed's big book of collected lyrics, *Pass Thru Fire*, nearby for inspiration. I also looked to two all-time favorite bands, Sonic Youth and the Ramones, a lot—I wanted to capture some of what they captured about living in the city. Mostly, when I worked, I listened to Dirty Three's *Whatever You Love, You Are* and Nick Cave and Warren Ellis's film scores, especially *The Assassination of Jesse James by the Coward Robert Ford*—it's usually (Aesop Rock aside) difficult for me to work to lyric-driven stuff and those albums run through me like blood.

The characters in the book listen to a lot of music, too. Conway, a washed-up stockboy at Rite-Aid who has never recovered from his brother Duncan's murder, loves Nirvana, the Replacements, the Ramones, and all the stuff he came up with in high school under Duncan's influence. Alessandra, a failed actress who has returned to Brooklyn from Los Angeles, loves X, David Bowie, Roxy Music, the Cramps, Nick Cave and the Bad Seeds, Deer Tick, so much more. Eugene, the nephew of Duncan's killer, Ray Boy, is into hip-hop: Jay-Z, Wu-Tang Clan, Dr. Dre, Ice Cube, Scarface. Songs are played on jukeboxes, stereos, iPods, in cars, and in bars. Songs surround these characters. Despite many of my teachers' best efforts, I'm always writing music into what I'm working on, and I try to be true to the characters. In an earlier draft of the book, for instance, I had Eugene listening to Madlib and that seemed off. And I had Conway listening to Minutemen instead of Nirvana in his car, which seemed too much like me just trying to fit Minutemen in and not getting Conway's taste exactly right.

I also have tons of songs that I think just capture the tone of the book. So, when constructing a playlist, I can't help but think in terms of it being a film soundtrack with certain songs playing over certain scenes for reasons ranging from atmospherics to providing emotional context.

I tried to mix all of these elements together here, picking sixteen songs that I think of as essential companions to *Gravesend* somehow.

"Daylight" by Aesop Rock

I think *Labor Days* is a pretty perfect record, and Aesop Rock sounds more like Brooklyn than anyone to me—raw and rambunctious, part verbal assault and part miracle of rhythm and movement. This is my favorite song of his, and Conway's story was developed around the notion of revisiting the same day over and over again. "All I ever wanted was to pick apart the day / Put the pieces back together my way," Aesop Rock says in the chorus. I think that line speaks to Conway's rage, his fractured spirit, all the things that leave him lost on a dark road.

"Primitive" by The Cramps

The Cramps show up a couple of times in the book. Alessandra and Amy talk about Lux Interior, and Alessandra plays a Cramps song on her iPod while getting ready to go out. The song isn't named but I imagine it to be "Primitive," which also has other resonance with what happens between Conway and Ray Boy. Early in the book, Conway, chomping at the bit for Ray Boy, thinks (perhaps just to brush off how unprepared he is) that he "wants to be primitive" about going after his brother's killer. Conway is a character who, though we occasionally feel sympathy for him, becomes more and more primal over the course of the narrative. When Lux sings, "What you expect, I'll never be," that drives home what I hope is the overall feel of Gravesend. Finally, I can't help but imagine this song playing over scenes of Conway driving up to Hawk's Nest in pursuit of Ray Boy, hands sweaty on the wheel, driven and defeated and damaged all at once.

"Never Really Ever Had It" by The Rock*A*Teens

My friend Jack Pendarvis introduced me to the Rock*A*Teens a few months before I started working on *Gravesend*. I couldn't believe I'd never heard them and pretty quickly counted them up there with the Replacements and X as one of the best bands ever. I had the killer mix that Jack had made me and I bought their five records immediately (and Chris Lopez's Tenement Halls release, too). I didn't often listen to the Rock*A*Teens while I wrote, but I was listening to them almost non-stop otherwise and the tone of the songs is definitely something that influenced the making of the book. This is one of my favorite R*A*T songs (from my favorite album of theirs, *Cry*) and the sound of it really, to me, gets at something about the "sound" of Conway and Alessandra, the way they're screaming on the inside. Lopez has the sort of lonesome howl that I hope comes across in the interiority of these characters.

"Hold On" by Lou Reed

New York isn't my favorite solo Lou Reed record but, goddamn, it really gets the city. It's dated in some ways that albums like *The Blue Mask* and *Magic and Loss* aren't but it's the New York I grew up in and the New York Conway, Alessandra, and Ray Boy grew up in: a city of hate crimes and filth and despair. "There's no such thing as human rights when you walk the New York streets" and "There's the smelly essence of New York down there" were early epigraphs for the book. Reed's also got the ability to lace his dark vision of New York with humor, which is something I hope I do in the book.

"Guess Who's Back" by Scarface, Jay-Z, Beanie Sigel

When we first meet Eugene, he's listening to this song on his headphones in the bodega where he's trying to shoplift. It's his favorite song from when he was a little kid, which means he was listening to it at seven, way too young no matter how good the song is. It introduces Eugene as someone lacking identity, trying to shape himself from what he's heard about his uncle's glory days and from the music that fuels his distaste for everything around him. On a bigger scale, I love the Beanie Sigel line "I hug the block like quarter water." He's talking Philly but it's just such a good growing-up-in-the-city image.

"Guilt" by Smoke

I lucked into discovering Smoke around 2001. A music writer I really like, William Bowers, included *Another Reason to Fast* and *Heaven on a Popsicle Stick* on a Best of the '90s list. I tracked the CDs down, as well as Benjamin Smoke's Opal Foxx Quartet release. I was way removed from the Atlanta scene of the '90s but something about it just struck a chord with me—it felt as unique and important as New York in the '70s. Like his pal Vic Chesnutt, Benjamin Smoke sings pain in a way I've never heard. Songs like "When It Rains," "Friends," and "Chad" just take it out of me. So does this one. When Benjamin sings, "The guilt's so thick in here, I can cut the air," man, I just start to weep. Or when he sings: "The way I see it, God wouldn't fuck you unless you fucked him first." Brutal, beautiful shit. Duncan—Conway's gay older brother, who died as the victim of a hate crime—is a character I love and think about often, even though he's not in the present action of the book. I think of this as his song, as representative of his tragic story.

"End of the Line" by Roxy Music

This song is playing at Seven Bar when Alessandra goes back to visit Amy late in the book. But it's bigger than that—Gravesend is one of the last stops on the D train and there's just generally lots of end-of-the-line imagery throughout the book. I think there's something about being from a last-stop neighborhood in New York City. You're way more isolated and that definitely contributes to the small town feeling that comes through. There's lots of rain/storm imagery in this song (which, obliquely, makes me think of the great, influential chase scene in James Gray's *We Own the Night*), which is true of many of the tracks on my larger Spotify playlist. Storms and crises go hand-in-hand. "End of the Line" is also, I'd say, about defeat in the same way that *Gravesend* is.

"It All Dies Anyway" by The Gits

The Gits are another band I came to through a circuitous route. I'd never heard them until I heard Richmond Fontaine's "The Gits" a few years ago, a song that tells the tragic story of Gits frontwoman Mia Zapata. I went on a Gits kick after that, and I'll often start my writing day off with "Another Shot of Whiskey." But "It All Dies Anyway" is another song that sounds like a screaming from the book's black heart. Zapata, like Chris Lopez, has one of those voices that just burns down to your bones with this honest, heartbroken quality. I don't think Alessandra's ever heard the Gits, but she'd love them. So would Amy Falconetti. If *Gravesend* was a film, I'd want "It All Dies Anyway" to be the tagline on the poster.

"A B-Boy's Alpha" by Cannibal Ox

"My first fight was me against five boroughs . . ." Enough said.

"Not Dark Yet" by Bob Dylan

Daniel Lanois is responsible for several of my all-time favorite records—Emmylou Harris's *Wrecking Ball*, Willie Nelson's *Teatro*, and Dylan's *Oh Mercy* and *Time Out of Mind*—and I want *Gravesend* to sound like his records. It's a noir sound, that echoey, deep-in-a-cathedral loneliness—man, it busts me up. And Dylan's voice on these two records! I picked "Not Dark Yet" because that phrase actually shows up in the book (coincidentally) but it really gets at the atmosphere of doom I was going for. Dylan sings: "I was born here and I'll die here against my will / I know it looks like I'm moving, but I'm standing still / Every nerve in my body is so vacant and numb / I can't even remember what it was I came here to get away from / Don't even hear a murmur of a prayer / It's not dark yet, but it's getting there." Hell, that's pretty much exactly what the book is about. C. P. Cavafy's great poem "The City" is one of the epigraphs and it gets at that same sentiment, that same feeling of brokenness and disillusion.

"The Dark Don't Hide It" by Magnolia Electric Co.

I might get choked up talking about Jason Molina. His death hit me hard. Since I discovered Molina's music in 2001, I've lived with his songs more than anyone else's. So, naturally, I looked to his records as guides when I sat down to write *Gravesend*. (I actually thought about calling the book *The Dark Don't Hide It* before settling so comfortably into the notion that it was actually all about the neighborhood.) Many of Molina's main concerns—darkness and light, the moon and stars, lies and truth, static and silence, leaving and staying, the human heart, history, blood, sickness, change, ghosts, doubt, death, and heaven—make their way into this song, but it's that admiration of the dark for being just what it is, for not trying to be something else, that I love so much. What's that line from *The Princess Bride*? Something like: "Life is pain. Anyone who says differently is selling something." Molina knew that better than anyone.

"You Know You're Right" [demo] by Nirvana

Conway keeps an old Nirvana mix CD in his car and drives home drunk, blasting it. This is the song he's listening to. Originally, I thought it might be "I Hate Myself and Want to Die," but then, in my mind's eye, I saw Conway belting this one out and it felt right. Nirvana means so much to him—they were Duncan's favorite band and they represented everything that made Conway want to be a musician (though, of course, he failed at that too before falling away into nothingness).

"Youth is Wasted on the Young" by Tyler Keith & the Preacher's Kids

This song is so goddamn desperate. It's all about wasted potential and regret. I don't think the narrator has committed the sorts of crimes that Ray Boy and Eugene have but I hear their stories in Tyler Keith's bleeding-edges wail.

"Ride into the Sun" [demo] by Velvet Underground

Loaded was one of my first favorite albums. Of course, I had the *The Fully Loaded Edition* on CD, so the demos and alternate mixes were as important to me as the album tracks. This is Alessandra's song, as she rides the subway back from visiting Stephanie in the hospital. "It's hard to live in the city . . ."

"Shot Away" by Dead Moon

I'd like every book I ever write to be like a Dead Moon album. This song has an end-of-things quality. I won't say too much about the novel's last act, but I imagine this soundtracking one character's demise.

"Stormy Weather" by Reigning Sound

The book closes on Alessandra running away from the El, and I like to picture it as a '70s-style freeze-frame, like the end of *The Outfit* or something, and this is the song that would kick in just then and play over the final credits. It really gets at the spirit and tone of the book. It's dark—"Seems like it's raining all the time"—but also relaxed in a drunken way. I hope *Gravesend*'s more like a punk song than a sad bastard ballad, and I hope that the end, fucked up as it is, feels kind of triumphant the way this song does.

—Originally published at Largehearted Boy

Find these songs—plus twenty-eight more—on William Boyle's Gravesend Spotify playlist: http://spoti.fi/2m2FoZO

THE LONELY WITNESS

A NOVEL

WILLIAM BOYLE

"With echoes of Lehane and Pelecanos, but with a rhythm and poignancy all its own."—Megan Abbott on *Gravesend*

"Boyle launched his gritty vision about this section of Brooklyn in his debut. *The Lonely Witness* offers an excellent sequel with a superb plot, matched by its realistically shaped characters."
—Oline Cogdil, *The Associated Press*

"A knockout combination of in-depth character work, Brooklyn atmosphere, and straight-up gritty noir. The devotion Boyle demonstrates for character, story, and place is perhaps the one unadulterated emotion on display in a story imbued with ambiguous morality and loyalty."
—*Shelf Awareness* (starred)

"What makes William Boyle's work ring with such a strong and true voice is that he realizes for many daily life is a struggle. His writing prays for them." —*MysteryPeople* (Pick of the Month)

"A beautifully nuanced novel that has an unhurried but compelling narrative drive, a central character you are totally invested in, and a locale that does indeed function as a major character."
—*Criminal Element*

When a young woman with a sordid past witnesses a murder, she finds herself fascinated by the killer and decides to track him down herself.

Amy lives a lonely life, helping the house-bound receive communion in the Gravesend neighborhood of Brooklyn. One of her regulars, Mrs. Epifanio, says she hasn't seen her usual caretaker, Diane, in a few days. Supposedly, Diane has the flu—or so Diane's son Vincent said when he first dropped by and vanished into Mrs. E's bedroom to do no-one-knows-what.

Amy's brief interaction with Vincent in the apartment that day sets off warning bells, so she assures Mrs. E that she'll find out what's really going on with both him and his mother. She tails Vincent through Brooklyn, eventually following him and a mysterious man out of a local dive bar. At first, the men are only talking as they walk, but then, almost before Amy can register what has happened, Vincent is dead.

For reasons she can't quite understand, Amy finds herself captivated by both the crime she witnessed and the murderer himself. She doesn't call the cops to report what she's seen. Instead, she collects the murder weapon from the sidewalk and soon finds herself on the trail of a killer.

Character-driven and evocative, *The Lonely Witness* brings Brooklyn to life in a way only a native can, and opens readers' eyes to the harsh realities of crime and punishment on the city streets.

AVAILABLE FROM PEGASUS CRIME IN MARCH 2019

A FRIEND

A NOVEL

IS A GIFT

YOU GIVE

YOURSELF

WILLIAM

BOYLE

"Boyle launched his gritty vision in his debut, *Gravesend. The Lonely Witness* offers an excellent sequel with a superb plot, matched by its realistically shaped characters."
—*The Associated Press*

We hope that you enjoyed this book.

To share your thoughts, feel free to connect with us
on social media:

 Twitter.com/Pegasus_Books

 Facebook.com/PegasusBooks

 Instagram.com/Pegasus_Books

 PegasusBooks.tumblr.com

To receive special offers and news about our latest
titles, sign up for our newsletter at
www.pegasusbooks.com.